THORN

UNCOMMON ENEMIES: PANTHER FORCE (BOOK
FOUR)

FIONA QUINN

THORN

Panther Force

Uncommon Enemies

By

Fiona Quinn

THE WORLD OF INIQUUS

Ubicumque, Quoties. Quidquid

Iniquus - /i'ni/kwus/ our strength is unequalled, our tactics unfair – we stretch the law to its breaking point. We do whatever is necessary to bring the enemy down.

THE LYNX SERIES

Weakest Lynx

Missing Lynx

Chain Lynx

Cuff Lynx

Gulf Lynx

Hyper Lynx

MARRIAGE LYNX

STRIKE FORCE

In Too DEEP

JACK Be Quick

InstiGATOR

UNCOMMON ENEMIES

Wasp

Relic

Deadlock

Thorn

FBI JOINT TASK FORCE

Open Secret

Cold Red

Even Odds

KATE HAMILTON MYSTERIES

Mine

Yours

Ours

CERBERUS TACTICAL K9 TEAM ALPHA

Survival Instinct

Protective Instinct

Defender's Instinct

DELTA FORCE ECHO

Danger Signs

Danger Zone

Danger Close

This list was created in 2021. For an up-to-date list, please visit FionaQuinnBooks.com

If you prefer to read the Iniquus World in chronological order you will find a full list at the end

of this book.

*A hero is no braver than an ordinary
[wo]man, but [s]he is brave five minutes
longer.*

— RALPH WALDO EMERSON

**This book is dedicated to all of you who have survived what life
has thrown your way.**

1

JULIETTE
Toulouse, France
Saturday, 7:30 a.m.

IT WAS EXACTLY like the pictures in her head, but she didn't *remember* any of it.

Juliette stepped forward and laid her hand on the intricate carvings on the ancient wooden doors. They had been here since the late eighteenth century – wide enough and tall enough to admit a carriage into the cobble-stoned courtyard that was protected behind the barrier.

There was a cut out of a smaller door. If she had a key, Juliette could simply step over the threshold, walk in, and stand in the shadowed interior.

The *bijoutier* pressed his shoulder into the door frame of his tiny shop just to the right, watching the comings and goings of the pedestrians. Displays of gold necklaces and colorful earrings filled his plate glass window. To the left, there was a shop that sold leather gloves.

Her gaze traveled across the street to the corner where the bakery bustled with patrons. Juliette breathed in the warm, yeasty scent of baking bread. Every morning, while her mother heated milk on the stove to make their bowls of hot chocolate, Juliette would run down the stairs, across the street, and buy baguettes fresh from the oven for their breakfast. She had a picture in her head of doing just that. Same awning. Same baskets of *boule* and *fougasse,* same glass displays of petit fours, and the jewel-toned, glossy fruit tarts.

Picture after picture flashed in her mind like turning pages in a photo album that belonged to someone else. Juliette didn't have a single memory of actually being there in those pictures. Actually doing the running, and jumping, and climbing the stairs that she knew were just through this door on the right-hand side – wide enough for two ladies in days-gone-by to brush their hoop skirts past each other, the carved stone railing protected them from slips and falls.

It was all so recognizable. And all so eerie.

The doors swung wide, and a car drove out of the complex.

Juliette smiled and nodded at the man in his navy-blue Fiat as she slipped inside. She knew that the style of her clothes, the form-fitting jeans, and high-heeled boots, the quality of her cashmere turtleneck, the Hermes scarf wrapping her neck, would work for her. She didn't look disreputable. There was no need for concern.

She took the stairs, nestled against the inner wall, that matched the picture in her head and walked up the three flights to stand on the landing with its stone mosaic of flowers. There were three identical doors, left, center, and right. The people who had lived in the center and left had not been friends of the

DuBois family. When she was six, and she was supposed to be asleep, Juliette had become frightened and went to the neighbor's for safety. Her mother had gotten in trouble with the police for leaving her child alone to go drink wine with a friend. The neighbors had been angry ever since. At least, that was the story her father told.

Turning toward the door on the right, Juliette tried to recall going in at noon for the lunch recess. Two hours of respite in the middle of the school day. An hour and a half, subtracting the amount of time it took her to walk from school to home, then reversing the pattern. One day, her father said, she had been groggy when she woke up. When she'd come home to meet the family for lunch, he had looked down at her feet and asked if the children had teased her that morning. "No, Papa, why would they tease me?" He'd pointed at her shoes; one was a sneaker and the other her patent leather dress shoe. He'd laughed when he told her that story. How did she walk all the way to school and home again without realizing that there was a difference in her gait or the thickness of the sole?

Someone opened the apartment door, *her* old apartment door. The sudden sound was such a shock to Juliette that she jumped and clutched at her chest.

"May I help you?" Juliette had to watch the woman's lips in order to comprehend all of her words.

"I used to live here as a child." Juliette smiled. "I was just taking a sentimental walk while I was in town."

"Here?" the woman asked, turning to look into her apartment. "You lived here?" She turned back to Juliette with a shake of her head.

"Not recently." Juliette thrust her fingers into the tight front pockets of her jeans. "When I was a child. A long time ago. Twenty years."

The woman shook her head again. "Madame Gigot," she called down the stairs. Her words echoed around Juliette and rang like a gong in her head. She tried not to flinch.

A woman hustled up the stairs. Her gray hair was brushed straight back and pulled into a short ponytail at the nape of her neck. She wore a faded-blue, formless dress and black tennis shoes with bare legs.

"Madame Gigot, do you recognize this woman?" the lady asked, then reached behind her and pulled her door closed.

Madame Gigot came up beside Juliette, but Juliette didn't recognize her. This woman's picture wasn't in her head at all. "I would have been a child," she explained. "I lived here before the fire. My parents' names are Marie and David DuBois."

Madam Gigot canted her head. "What fire is this? David DuBois did live here, but he didn't have a wife or child. He *did* have a boyfriend."

"You know my father?" Juliette pulled a phone from the purse hanging from her shoulder and scrolled to his photograph. Surely, Madame Gigot was just confused. It had been a long time since the family had moved.

"I know David DuBois." She took the phone from Juliette's hand and squinted down. "Yes, that's him. That's DuBois. Scientist. He moved back to the United States if I remember right."

"Yes. That's where he lives now," Juliette said. Madame Gigot obviously remembered him. Why would she think her dad liked men? Why had she forgotten her mother or their child? Yes, Juliette concluded, this woman was simply not remembering clearly.

"And we've never had a fire here, not in over two hundred years, that is." Madame Gigot handed the phone back. "I've been the concierge here since I was a teenager. I would know if there had been a fire. No fire." She waggled her finger back and forth.

Confusion pulled Juliette's brows together. "But...But there are no pictures of my mother or my childhood because they burned. Here." She gestured toward the apartment. "We lost everything. My mother saved me from the flames." And Juliette had the scars to prove it.

The two women scowled at her.

"I lived here," Juliette insisted. Her attention turned to the polished mahogany door. "You don't need a key to get in. You just bump your hip into the door, and it pops open. When I came home from school, I was supposed to pretend to use a key, so no one would know." I moved over toward the door and looked at the woman who had come from the apartment. "May I?"

She lifted her hand to give her permission.

Juliette grasped the door handle and bumped her hip into it. The door popped open, just as she had been told it would. The only way Juliette knew that piece of information was she had been *told*. Juliette had no childhood memories of her own. But, still, she felt victorious and looked up with a laugh. See? She was right. Juliette *had* lived here.

The women started speaking back and forth in very quick French, and Juliette couldn't follow along with their words mashing into each other like that. The range of their agitated voices was too high a pitch, and their mouths moved too fast from pursed lips for Juliette to read them.

Madame Gigot turned and shooed Juliette away. Literally took her two hands and shooed her away. Then Madame Gigot lowered her tone enough that Juliette caught the next sentence. "I don't know what you're up to, but you need to go now before I call the police."

Juliette saw that the woman who had come out of the apartment stood with her hands on either side of the doorframe as if to bodily block Juliette from entering. Juliette hadn't planned on going in, even if invited. She had no pictures of what the inside of the apartment had looked like. And it would be all different anyway, Juliette thought as she scuttled down the stairs. After the fire and all.

The concierge said there hadn't been any fires...

The concierge should know such things. Would she lie? Maybe that hadn't been disclosed when the new owner had bought the apartment.

What if there really hadn't been a fire. What if her father had fabricated that story? Then, what happened to the photos, the souvenirs, the things one accumulated over time? A precious doll. A beloved book. A diary, maybe. Something that would spark a true memory for her?

Juliette felt robbed as she burst through the massive front door, back out on the street. She felt lost. She rubbed her fingers through her hair, feeling the scar that ran along the side of her scalp from the surgery that had saved her life but had stolen her past.

All she had beside her physical scars was a series of flat images that she remembered, like photographs from an album.

Juliette turned left, walking toward *Place Capitole,* begging her brain to remember something. *Anything.*

2

JULIETTE
   Toulouse, France
   Saturday, 9:00 a.m.

THE CAB STOPPED in front of a house. It was small. Neat. And blended in with every other house in this neighborhood.

Juliette looked into the rearview mirror to catch the taxi driver's eye.

"This is it." He pointed at the house with a plaster cat sitting on the steps. He had a deep, resonant tone that Juliette could hear well enough, though his accent was strange to her ears and that presented its own comprehension problems. She held out her credit card and asked him to add a ten percent tip.

There was a woman standing at the picture window, holding back the curtain and peering out at the taxi. She was too young to be Juliette's grandmother.

Juliette pulled up her memory-picture of this house, and yes, it included the same orange plaster cat on the stairs in exactly the same spot. All those many years ago... *It's odd that nothing had changed since I was young. Nothing. It's all exactly as it's always been.*

Those thoughts weren't comforting to Juliette.

As a matter of fact, it set her on edge. It made her feel confused and dizzy. More so than normal. Confusion and dizziness were part of her disability. She'd been in an accident with a traumatic brain injury. But she was lucky. So very lucky. Her father was one of the world's foremost neuroscientists. He had done decades of research into PTSD and brain injuries. Because of her dad, Juliette had gotten cutting edge help.

Her fingers traveled up to the scar hidden by her long, honey-blonde hair. Because of her father's expertise, Juliette had at least recovered some pictures.

And now she'd get to go talk to her grandmother.

Juliette hoped this trip back to her childhood would spark memories for her. Make her feel more whole and less like someone who had plopped, fully formed, into this life.

The taxi driver cleared his throat and waggled her credit card at her.

Juliette sent him a nervous smile as she took it back and tucked it into her wallet. She swallowed as she released her safety belt.

"Hey, do you want me to stick around for a minute?" the driver asked. "Make sure everything's okay?"

Juliette rolled her lips in and considered the offer. "No, thank you. I'll be fine." She pulled the door release, feeling jittery, not quite able to catch her breath.

This should be easy. Juliette was coming home.

She stepped from the car. Along the sidewalk, a young boy peddled on his tricycle. Brown silky curls, rosy red cheeks, a blue, and white striped shirt, he was picturesque. Juliette wanted to save his face in her memory-photos. She glanced up at her grandmother's house, and the woman had moved out of the window. The lace curtain hung straight.

Juliette followed the short walk up to the door, stopping to lay her hand on the plaster cat. Had she petted this cat as she played at her grandmother's house? It must have had some significance to her if this was one of the few picture-memories that she held.

The door opened. "Yes?" the woman asked.

"Hello," Juliette said with a smile. "I came to visit Pascale DuBois."

"Why?" the woman asked, pulling the sides of her cardigan sweater to crisscross them over her chest.

"Oh!" Juliette extended her hand for a shake. "I'm her grand-daughter, David DuBois's daughter, Juliette."

The woman stared at her for a long moment, frowning. She didn't move to accept the handshake. "Stay here."

Juliette looked toward the little boy on his trike. He bustled up and down the sidewalk, peddling as hard as he could, then pulling the handles to the side, trying to get the trike to skid through a one-eighty.

He roared by her again, and the bike flipped when he tugged the handles. The little boy's wail started very low and quickly climbed the scale to where Juliette could no longer hear him.

But she could see him tangled in the wreckage and ran to his aid.

One of the spokes stuck out as she reached to pick the little boy up, and she scratched herself on it as she pulled the little boy free. When Juliette saw blood, bright red against the white stripe on his shirt, she quickly searched him to see where he was bleeding. Scraped palms and holes in his pants' legs, the child had come out bumped and bruised, but it was Juliette who was bleeding.

A man ran down his steps and over to them, accepting the boy from her arms.

"I'm sorry," Juliette said. "I scraped myself. I've gotten a little blood on his shirt. Cold water should get it out."

The man stroked his hand over the little one's curls. "*Pas de problème,*" he said. *Not a problem.* "*Merci beaucoup.*" He propped the boy on his hip, then lifted the broken trike and walked slowly back to his house.

Juliette turned back toward her grandmother's.

"You there." The woman in her cardigan stood at the door, and Juliette walked over to talk to her, adjusting the strap of her purse back onto her shoulder. "I don't know what you're up to," the woman said. "But Madame DuBois says she has no grandchildren. Her son David is a homosexual man and disliked children. There is no way that you are related to her."

Juliette's mouth dropped open.

"I've called the police. They're on their way. Get now! Get!" Then she slammed the door shut.

Juliette was left standing there, blinking.

She didn't know what to think.

She could hardly think.

She was so confused. So disoriented. Maybe when the police came, they could facilitate a talk between her and her grandmother. She could tell her grandmother what her dad was doing. With her phone's album, Juliette could show her grandmother pictures of her and her dad and where they lived in Washington D.C.

Her grandmother was certainly old, Juliette reasoned. Perhaps she had dementia. Alzheimer's would explain this situation. Except the woman Juliette assumed was the caregiver had said her dad was homosexual. That was the second time today that Juliette was told the same thing.

Juliette had always thought her dad's disinterest in dating was because he was still in love with her mother. Still grieved her mother's death. Homosexual? She tried that thought on for size. She'd never considered her father's sexual orientation.

She rested her palm on her forehead. The fever that started yesterday morning, accompanying her from Washington, was getting worse. Juliette wondered how long it would take for the police to get there. She turned to see the little boy was soothed and back to playing in his front yard. His dad was reading a book on the porch steps. She thought maybe he might not mind her sitting on his stairs for a moment while she waited for the police.

Her head swam, and she was afraid the vertigo would make her fall. She had decided to leave her stability dog at home with her caregiver rather than cramp him into the floor space on a plane for hours on end. Toby was a huge Newfoundland dog, a hundred and fifty pounds of black-furry kindness and love. His harness had a handle that she could hold on to as she walked. And if she were to fall, Toby stood by her side until she regained her equilibrium. He helped her feel safe. *I could sure use Toby with me right now.*

Juliette walked across the street to ask if she might sit down. She made it as far as the gate when she staggered forward. As she reached out to grab the post, she heard a car engine roar up the street.

"Ah," she thought, *"an undercover unit."*

The car came to a stop, and two men in plain clothes jumped out, rounding toward her.

Juliette smiled. "Hello, there." And that's when she had her first flash of a memory. A real memory, not a picture-memory. These men she recognized. They were the men who had attacked her at the conference. They had tied her up. The conference? She stepped back. There was more. There was more about the conference. There was more about her past life. It bubbled up along with a giddy laugh that was pure terror.

Each man had a gun in his hand.

Juliette swung her head to make sure the boy was safe.

The father reached out, grabbed his child around his waist, and leaped up his stairs and through his front door.

"Get in," the man growled in Russian.

3

THORN
Brussels, Belgium
Monday, Twelve Twelve Hours

"GENTLEMEN, your plane delay is working in our favor." Commander Titus Kane's voice crackled from the cell phone Thorn was holding out. Three Panther Force operators stood shoulder to shoulder in a tight circle, heads bowed. They huddled around the commander's words, protecting them from intrusive ears.

"I need you in a secure location ASAP to receive orders. Stash your bags. You won't be heading home today."

Panther Force had been in Europe on a protection detail for a group of United States diplomats. Half the negotiation team had moved on to London and were covered by their fellow Strike Force team members.

Thorn, Honey, and Gage drew the short straw. For them, the security mission was over.

They'd already put their principals on the government jet, here at the Brussels International Airport, and were waiting for their own commercial flight home when the call came through from Headquarters.

The three men hefted their duffels to their shoulders and moved in lockstep toward the exit, spooling up for their next assignment.

"I think our best move is to rent a couple of cars. We can store our bags in them and pull up the encryption site on a laptop." Honey lifted his chin toward the car rental signage. "We'll be ready to move if need be." At six-foot-eight, Honey Honig always had the best vantage point for locating things. He was also the most easily located. Six of one, half-dozen of another. It either served them well, or it sucked to be him. There was rarely an in between.

The three brushed past the preoccupied passengers flowing through Brussels International. It was newly renovated from the 2016 dual bomb explosions in the terror attack on the airport. That weighed on Thorn's mind. All that glass. Tons and tons of glass. He imagined, as they jostled toward the car rental booth, what would happen to the people underneath the glass walls if the panes shattered, splintered, stabbed through the air toward those underneath. How would he protect himself and the people around him? Where could he go in an instant to find cover? His head on a swivel, taking it all in, Thorn processed through the options. Those kinds of thoughts were part of Thorn's job. He plotted this kind of information as a habit. Assessed each change in the dynamic. Where was he in the space? Who was near him? What needed to happen?

Thorn worked as an elite operator for Iniquus, a private for-hire protection and operations group, which signed contracts with the US government and, on occasion, with corporations or the hyper-wealthy. Iniquus was an organization populated by the best of the best as they left the US Armed Forces. The Deltas, like Honey, the Marine Raiders, like Gage, and the SEALs, like Thorn. Battle-hardened. Battle ready.

They made their way up the short line to the rental agent, signed contracts for two high-performance cars, and walked away with two sets of BMW keys. They had no idea what they'd be involved with, but rarely was it a good idea to have access to only one vehicle.

The unpredictability of their work always gave Thorn a shot of adrenaline. He liked that about his job. The risk. The challenge. This was his world. There was no such thing as nine to five. He was always in go mode.

The rental cars were parked on opposite sides of the deck. Thorn tossed his duffle in the trunk of one of the cars and jogged through the rows to join up with his teammates.

When Thorn popped open the back door, Gage already had his laptop fired up. His fingers tapped through the encryption protocol to bring up a secure line.

"Gentlemen." Titus's gravelly voice filled the car's interior as Thorn pulled the door closed with a bang that echoed down from the cement ceiling. "We're lucky to have you positioned at exactly the right place at exactly the right time."

"Sir," the men answered in unison.

"We've signed a contract with an alphabet for a new case."

"They need their hands that clean? They're not even giving us their letters?" Honey asked. There was a reason why the US government sometimes preferred hiring a private brand instead of putting their necks out, especially if things went sideways in an allied country.

"Let's just say they'd like to keep a low profile." Two photographs appeared on Gage's screen, a woman and a child.

"Memorize these faces. Chances are you'll never see them, but if you do, you need to intervene by whatever means possible. They were kidnapped this morning in Toulouse, France."

Toulouse was in the south of France and a long distance from Brussels.

The picture on the screen changed to just the woman's face.

Thorn focused on her photograph. It was probably a still frame captured from a video. The woman's long, honey-colored hair was lifted as if she was swinging her head violently toward the camera. Her blue-green eyes filled with fear and what Thorn read as physical pain. Something in his gut squeezed down. His jaw clamped tight. Power surged through his muscles. It was the way his body felt as he threw himself into combat.

"Do you have a larger picture that includes her body?" he asked. "What's happening to her right there?"

"The man who took a video on his cell phone focused in with his zoom at that moment. It's the clearest picture we have of Juliette's face. We're still putting a case file together on the incident. We don't have time to get a complete picture before we put your team on the mark."

The child's image came onto the screen. "This is the boy who was with her."

The child's eyes were wide with surprise. There was the blur of a man's arm, wrapping around him. Thorn didn't see a family resemblance between the woman and the child.

"Her child?" Gage asked.

"We're waiting for answers on the child's connection. Here's what we know," Titus said, putting Juliette's picture back on a split-screen so they could memorize both faces. "The woman is named Juliette DuBois. She is twenty-nine years old. A French citizen living in the United States on a green card. She is the daughter of Dr. David Dubois, who is a Defense Advanced

Research Projects Agency scientist. We all know how important it is to the United States' interests to secure our DARPA scientists. Our reports indicate that Juliette flew to Toulouse, France, yesterday. This morning she went to visit with her grandmother, Pascale DuBois, who lives in the neighborhood where Juliette disappeared, according to our intake report. However, and here's the interesting part, Pascale DuBois denies having a granddaughter. Madame DuBois's caregiver turned Juliette away at the door just before two men pushed Juliette into their car at gunpoint."

A photograph had never pushed Thorn's buttons this way before. This woman, Juliette, was a stranger. But he felt like someone had snuck into *his* home, picked up something precious to *him*, and slid out into the night.

Thorn felt predatory.

On the hunt.

Did he know her?

He searched his memory and came up with nada.

It must be the expression on her face—the look in her eyes that was triggering his protective impulses.

And while he'd depend on his professional ethics to rein himself in, for the first time *ever*, he wanted to find the person who put this woman in danger and make them pay with blood.

Gage sent Thorn a look that told Thorn he wasn't hiding his thoughts.

Honey bent closer to the computer. His face set with concentration. "Have the kidnappers reached out yet?" This was Honey's forte. He was an Iniquus negotiator who made contact with the bad guys and manipulated an opening, then reached in and pulled the hostages out of the line of fire, getting them home as safely as possible.

Thorn knew that the cases Honey hated most were the ones with kids' lives on the line. Honey and his wife Meg had just adopted a young boy of their own. But Honey was in professional mode, and Thorn, yeah, he was fighting something dark inside himself.

Gut check time. Whatever that photo had stirred up needed to calm itself back down. He'd earned his *sang froid* in the freezing cold ocean during his Hell Week for SEALs. He wasn't about to let a picture make him forget his training.

"We have *not* been contracted to deal with the kidnapping. But on background, the tick-tock of the event is interesting. Juliette DuBois showed up at the house and is turned away. The caregiver called the police on Juliette because Madame DuBois said she didn't have any grandchildren, and the caregiver thought Juliette was up to some scheme to hurt Madame DuBois."

Thorn crossed his arms over his chest, his brow pulled in tight as he focused.

"After she was turned away, Juliette walked across the road. A neighbor walking his dog saw two men with guns force Juliette into their car. He filmed it on his phone. He said there was a child and that the child wasn't there anymore once the car had driven away. Just as the kidnappers' car rounded the corner, a taxi pulled up in front of Madam DuBois's house. The video guy was in shock and told Dr. David DuBois, the taxi's fare, what had happened. DuBois responded by jumping back in the waiting cab and left just before the police arrived. The man with the video of the incident walked over and showed it to the officers. Our client believes that the family was targeted in a kidnapping to gain leverage over Dr. DuBois."

"Broad daylight," Thorn said.

"Until the kidnappers make contact," Titus said, "we don't know if the kidnapping time frame, juxtaposed with the father's arriving in front of Pascale DuBois's home, was a coincidence, a mistake, or *the* plan. Our contractor believes it was *the* plan."

"We're in the right place at the right time because Dr. DuBois is heading here to Brussels?" Gage asked.

"Affirmative," Titus said.

"And David DuBois is with DARPA. His research is top secret, then." Gage shifted around in his seat. He was engaged to a DARPA scientist who had developed the BIOMIST system for the military. Someone had come after her full tilt last December. It had been close. But Panther Force was able to pull her out of the net that tried to trap her. They protected her until the bad guys were brought to justice. Panther Force was well aware of how vulnerable the scientists' specialized military research made them to rogue players. "Dr. DuBois, do we know his expertise?" Gage asked. "Do we know why his family might have been targeted?"

"Right now, it's irrelevant to your task," Titus said as he put a new picture up for them. "Dr. DuBois," he said.

David DuBois looked like an ordinary American male: glasses, balding head, paunch belly, with the jowly jawline of a man nearing retirement age.

"Dr. DuBois booked a last-minute ticket for a flight that left Washington D.C. last night. This morning he arrived in Toulouse. He must have gone directly from the airport to Pascale DuBois's home. It was a one-way ticket."

"Just this morning? And now he's flying to Brussels?"

"According to our intake notes," Titus explained, "the Brussels ticket was purchased during the time frame between his leaving Pascale DuBois's house and getting to the airport in his taxi. He booked the first international flight available, which takes him here to Brussels. From Brussels, he has a ticket for a red-eye to Washington – again, it was the first available ticket to the US."

"All right," Thorn said, "the kidnapping is background. We

think that Dr. DuBois is a target. He's trying to get back on US soil. How can we facilitate that?"

"Your assignment is to put eyes on him from the moment he deplanes until he's safely in the air heading toward the States. We're trying to arrange for at least one of you to be on that flight with him. He's not to know you're there. Our client wants to be the one who discusses the kidnapping with him once he's back on U.S. soil. They can better protect him, and they can better interview him from D.C."

"Security watch, yes, sir," Honey said. "Do we expect that someone might be trying to kidnap Dr. DuBois, as well? What are the risk factors here?"

The Panthers didn't have permits to carry guns in Brussels. Conceal carry, silencers, combat knives were all big fat no-goes. If anything sparked, they'd be going at it hand to hand. None of them minded a good fistfight. The problem was bad guys rarely played by the rules. They'd have weapons that Panther Force did not.

"We're all working in the dark," Titus said. "At this point, there's no evidence to believe that Dr. DuBois is a target. There may be a different reasoning behind the disappearance of Juliette DuBois and the child, something that had to do with the woman herself. Or it could have been an opportunity attack."

"Mother and child? Broad daylight in the street? It doesn't read that way to me," Honey said.

"Exactly," their commander responded. "As far as I know, no one has reached out with demands from the bad guy side. After the police watched the video and discovered Dr. DuBois worked for the US government, the police called the American embassy, who contacted the CIA and FBI, and so this very quickly trickled down to you."

"Roger," they said in unison.

Titus gave them DuBois's flight information, and they checked their watches.

"We'd better scramble to case the area before the flight comes in," Thorn said.

"Nutsbe will be your support. Report anything unusual," their commander said. "Remember, foreign soil means foreign laws and foreign prisons."

JULIETTE
Toulouse, France
Saturday, 12:29 p.m.

SHE WAS STRAPPED into the back seat. One man drove. One man sat beside her. Neither man wore a seat belt. Juliette hoped they'd be in an accident. Both men would be tossed from the car. Injured. Maybe even killed. She willed that to happen. Pictured it and prayed for it. But the car just drove farther and farther down the road.

Juliette had her head in her hands. The elevation of her blood pressure had made her head throb. She could feel her pulse beating in her temples. She focused on the tips of her boots to try to still the vertigo that swirled her around.

She wanted to focus on something that would pull her attention away from her current physical distress, so her system could calm, but she kept going back to the memory that came up when she saw the men's faces. It was startling to remember something that happened *before* the accident. *Before* the surgery. Something that was old.

Before these men showed up, all Juliette had was new.

Juliette had been at a conference. Wearing a black pantsuit, she remembered the teal-colored blouse that she thought made her eyes look particularly bright. She had her lecture notes in her hand as she walked through the corridor, nervous but excited.

"Doctor, right this way," the man had said in a thick accent. He was the one driving right now. At the time, he had placed his hand on her elbow to steer her. And because of his accent, she hadn't thought anything of the gesture. Perhaps this man didn't know he shouldn't touch a woman without her permission.

They'd walked back toward the ballroom and then beyond. She'd spun and looked over her shoulder. Ballroom C. That was where she was supposed to speak. When Juliette heard a click and felt something hard at her ribs, she looked down. The man on the other side of her, the one who was guarding her now, had pressed a gun into her ribs. "Keep walking. Don't draw any attention, or I'll be forced to shoot you."

Wait. He'd called her "doctor," and she was going to give a lecture. That wasn't right. It *couldn't* be right. She had been a veterinarian's assistant before her accident. Her father had shown her a diploma and talked about how much she loved animals.

Why would she be seeing these images? Why did they seem so real?

Not just the faces but the voices.

On her grandmother's street, the man had spoken to her in Russian, and she had both known it was Russian and known what he was saying. True, in the past, her father had told her that she'd studied Russian in high school. But that *didn't* explain the thing that she'd call a memory. And it *didn't* explain why this man sat there with a gun dangling between his knees.

In her memory, when she was wearing the black suit, he hadn't spoken Russian. He'd spoken in English. "Doctor, right this way." Maybe she had been with the veterinarian? Was there another person in the memory walking with them, someone else at gunpoint?

Had this man mistaken her at the time for someone she was not, and she was just too startled to respond? But she wasn't startled. Nothing had seemed wrong until they passed the ballroom door.

Why did he point a gun at her then?

Why was he pointing a gun at her now?

How would these men even know she was in the suburbs of Toulouse visiting her grandmother?

Juliette heard a truck pulling up beside them. *Please, tip over.* She sent out her thought waves. *Or don't see us and push us off the side of the road. Hit us. Hit us!* She thought so hard that the rat-a-tat-tat in her head became the booms of a kettle drum. Juliette panted so she wouldn't vomit from the pain.

They kept driving and driving.

Never turning.

The same highway. It had been hours now.

They had stopped for gas, and the men had switched places.

They brought her some ginger ale and salted crackers; she must have looked pretty green to elicit that response. Juliette knew these men didn't care a smidge about her comfort. They probably just didn't want to have to drive in a car full of vomit.

Maybe I should vomit? Juliette discarded that thought. She was fairly sure the men would retaliate, and her body couldn't handle much more. If she'd had her dog with her, would she be here? They'd probably have shot Toby there in the street. Toby would be dead. It was best that she'd left him at home.

Juliette leaned back and closed her eyes. She wondered if

anyone would report that she was kidnapped from the streets of Toulouse.

She wondered if anyone would care.

Her dad? He was far away in America, right now.

He'd moved them when he took a job with DARPA. Something odd was making the U.S. diplomats sick, and he'd been brought home, so he could investigate and come up with a treatment plan.

Her dad was, after all, the foremost researcher in the world when it came to brain trauma. If it wasn't for him, if she'd been just any young woman who'd been in an accident, she wouldn't be able to function this well. She'd be in an institution somewhere. Juliette owed him everything for saving her from that.

Juliette remembered her father introducing himself to her. "Your name is Juliette DuBois. And I am David DuBois. Do you recognize me?" He was sitting by her bed when she came out of surgery. She had one of those flat memory-photos of him that she was able to pull up, but she'd been grateful when he'd labeled himself.

He'd had a photo of a woman. "And this is your mother. She died in the accident. Do you remember her?"

She'd reached for the photo and held it in her fingers. Her hand had moved up to the bandaged dome of her head, her fingers crawling along the seams of tape. She understood the concept of mother. And she wanted one there. Someone who would fold Juliette into her arms and rock her and croon that everything was going to be all right. That she was loved. That she'd get through this.

But when Juliette looked down at the photo, she'd felt nothing. It was like looking at a stranger. She'd learned very little about her mother from talking to her dad, that her mom liked wine and books, and walking at night. But the kinds of things her dad would think to tell Juliette weren't the kinds of things that Juliette had desperately wanted to know.

Was her mother gentle and encouraging?

Did her mom cuddle in bed with her when a thunderstorm blew out the electricity, and would she read to Juliette by flash-light to calm her? That was the kind of picture that Juliette had tried to paint for herself.

But the truth was, Juliette simply didn't know. She'd felt like a usurper. A puppet. A paid actor lying there in her hospital gown, staring at her mother's photo.

She'd thought that she should probably be filled with grief at her mother's passing. She had thought she should probably cry.

Her father.

He knew she was in France. At what point would he wonder why she wasn't in touch with him? They talked at least twice a day, and, surely, he'd want to talk to her about seeing her grand-mother for the first time, post-accident. Juliette's last-minute decision to come, after a price deal popped up in her email, meant she'd only had time to make a hurried call on the way to the airport. When her dad's answering machine picked up, Juli-ette left him a message that she was on her way to France, where she'd start tracing through her past to try to regain some memo-ries. Juliette asked if there was anything he'd like her to say to her grandmother or to send home to him. "Wish me luck! I think this is going to make the difference. I think this trip will change *everything*!"

He hadn't called her back.

Juliette was pulled away from those thoughts when she felt the car start to slow.

Bringing her head up slightly, she peeked through her hair to see what was going on. Brake lights glowed red up and down the highway, and their car came to a crawl as the traffic slowed. She snaked her hand over her lap to unsnap her belt buckle, thinking she could just let it slowly retract, then maybe she could jump from the car. Surely, they wouldn't shoot at her in front of all these eyes.

The man beside her chuckled as he reached out and grabbed her hand, bending her fingers backward. "This idiot thinks I'm going to let her jump out of the car."

The other man laughed in big guffaws.

Juliette pursed her lips, then turned to see what her guard was pulling from his pocket. When she saw it was a syringe, she fought. She kicked and bit and flung her fists, but quickly the vertigo made her world spin too fast.

The stab of a punitive needle.

The tight grip of his fingers...

5

THORN

Brussels, Belgium
Saturday, Twelve Forty-three Hours

"Thorn, check." He directed his voice toward his phone, but that was for show, a reason to be speaking out loud in the airport corridor. He had dropped his magnetic communications devices into his ear canals and could hear both ambient noise and the soft communications from the team members. Thorn's voice carried back over a microphone that wrapped his neck and pressed in on either side of his windpipe. The apparatus was hidden by his turtleneck shirt. He hid the bulk of his muscles under a leather jacket.

"Affirmative, Thorn, I've got you loud and clear." Nutsbe was their mission support leader back in the Panther Force war room at Iniquus Headquarters in Washington D.C., where he had access to the surveillance magic. "I've got the airport schematics up and layered with the team's GPS trackers. I'll be able to watch each of you move through the building. I have Thorn and Honey on CCTV cameras. Gage, you're in a dead zone. Either move or realize I haven't got a way to watch your back."

"Roger. I have a good vantage point from up here," Gage said. "I'm going to sit tight. I'll watch my six."

Thorn swung his head, looking for a spot where he'd have a good line of sight but wouldn't look like he was trying out for a job as a potted plant. He sought out a natural place to lean and play with his phone.

"How'd you get CCTV camera access in Brussels?" Honey asked.

"I know a guy," Nutsbe said, cryptically. "All right then, your target is going to come through the secured area into a long hallway. The half wall with the plants keeps the people debarking separated from the hall traffic. A couple of supply and janitor's closets, a bathroom, and then out into the causeway. Honey, it might be best for you to move to the corner at your one o'clock. You can watch through the windows from your height, and you'll look less lurking down there."

"Less lurking," Honey grumbled, but Thorn could see Honey's head well above the crowd as he moved his position.

"Hey," Honey whispered as he walked toward the sliding doors and his gaze tagged a man in jeans and a ski jacket.

The ski jacketed guy let his head turn smoothly past, and neither of the men gave any further sign of recognition.

"Thorn, heads up," Honey whispered.

"Got him." Thorn stood behind a group posing for a camera and used them to cover his own photography. "Sending."

"That's Hong Wu," Gage said from above them. "What the hell's he doing in this picture?"

"How do you know him?" Nutsbe asked.

"He used to be military. He was a Green Beret I knew

training in Africa. Rumor has it he's working for Omega now. If we rumble, watch his kicks."

"Omega's on location? Things just heated up," Nutsbe said.

Omega did the same kind of contract work that Iniquus did. They tried to fish the highly trained retiring special operators from the same pond as Iniquus did. But Omega was involved in some really dark shit. They were in this business for the money – no holds barred. They were the group you hired when you needed black ops without a conscious or a defining creed.

"Do you think another alphabet hired Omega on? Odd coincidence he'd be walking through the doors at this time, in this spot," Nutsbe said. "Are you sure he's with Omega?"

"Rumor," Gage answered. "I don't know who he's working for now. But I know it's not the U.S. Army anymore. Nutsbe, see if you can get intel on the goons walking toward him."

"I'm putting the images through facial recognition as we speak," Nutsbe said. "Stay the course."

Thorn's gaze scanned the crowd for anyone in the area who was static.

"Heads up, gentleman," Nutsbe said. "DuBois's plane is wheels down, pulling up flush now. They'll be opening their doors here in just a minute."

Thorn pretended to check his phone as he leaned back against a support. Standing kitty-corner to the pathway, which would keep him out of the exiting passenger's line of view, he spread his awareness in a wide circumference. He was depending on Nutsbe's skills assessing the camera feeds to help give him the precious advanced warning he needed before some action flashed. But Thorn also knew that Nutsbe was juggling his time between the three operators, their target, and his detective work on the unsubs—unidentified subjects—who met up with Hong. The three new players had huddled, then they seemed to triangulate on the same stretch of corridor as Panther Force.

The passengers exited their plane and walked forward with the cramped steps of legs packed into confined chairs for too long. Men and women of all shapes and sizes made their way forward, distracted and fatigued, checking their tickets, checking their phones.

There.

That was DuBois.

"Got him," Thorn said. A burst of adrenaline sharpened his senses.

DuBois looked exactly like the photo on the computer screen, with the addition of a day's growth of gray facial hair that made him look scruffy and unkempt. His suit, too, looked rumpled and uncared for as if he'd been traveling in the same clothes for a while.

Behind him, just to the left, was an athletic woman whose body language read nonchalance. *Studied* nonchalance. To an unpracticed eye, she'd look like one of the crowd. To Thorn, she had the look of someone who tried to dim her light.

Her clothes were loose over what must be a killer figure. She wore no makeup to accentuate the soft features of her face. Her black hair was held tightly back in a bun at the nape of her neck. It was military-style if you were a military guy. Someone else might think she looked like a ballerina.

It was her boots that caught Thorn's interest. They weren't the high-heeled shiny leather kind he'd expect a European female traveler to wear. Her boots – just like his – were designed for action.

Thorn called it in as he lifted his phone and took a video. Something clearer and from eye-level, not looking down from the eaves. Something less black and white and grainy than the CCTV cameras.

"Got her. Tagging her on the computer. I'll keep tabs of her whereabouts," Nutsbe said softly. "I'm putting her face into the search engines now. I've got confirmation; Hong Wu is a yes for Omega. He's with Norman Colburn. That's the short guy with black hair. Colburn's an American not welcome on U.S. soil, seems he had a thing for vigilante justice. Now, he takes private contracts, mostly in Eastern Europe."

"Honey here. Are they pursuing Colburn? Do they have extradition papers on him?"

"Negative," Nutsbe said. "He must have some well-positioned friends. He's got no one looking for him unless he tries to cross our borders—no news on the bald guy who's with him. I'm expanding the search to include European and Eastern files. That team is tagged in my map software, and the computer will keep track of them. Right now, they're all looking in the same direction you are. This could get interesting."

DuBois made his way into the men's room located on the corridor just past the janitors' closet.

As DuBois pivoted, the woman rolled in her lips and stared unblinking straight ahead.

A janitor backed his cart out of the closet.

The woman glanced back just in time to see him push the cart into the men's room.

"We've got movement." Thorn broke away from the support column, stretching his long, muscular legs, turning and sidling, shouldering his way through the crowd. He felt like a salmon trying to swim upstream. He turned the corner in time to see DuBois arrive at the last urinal in the overly occupied bathroom.

DuBois unzipped and fished out his dick.

The "janitor" crowded past the men to the back of the room, where he busied himself with a trash bag.

He had smoothly trapped DuBois.

On purpose?

Hard to tell. Thorn couldn't be the first to act. This had to play out.

If this was an attempt on DuBois, the janitor at least had the decency of letting DuBois take a leak, shake it off, and shove himself back in his pants before he made his approach.

The janitor positioned himself, so his back shielded his interaction with DuBois.

Thorn moved up.

A wall and urinal in front of Dubois, a wall to the side, the cart behind him, and a thug. Yup, DuBois was trapped.

The janitor bent his arm, and Thorn knew from his posture that the janitor had a gun shoved under DuBois's rib cage. The janitor bent to whisper into the scientist's ear.

Thorn would normally think the gun was for show. Intimidation. It was meant to get DuBois to act in a specific way. His life shouldn't be in imminent danger here in the men's public bathroom. But the chick with the head swivel seemed to be playing on a different team from Hong Wu. Possibly a third interested taskforce.

Since Thorn was playing on a team with a redacted name hiring them in, Thorn couldn't trust any reasonable scenario. He wasn't quite sure what the hell was going on, but his job was to protect Dr. DuBois.

Sidling up as if he needed to take a piss, Thorn reached for his zipper then let his hand snake around the janitor, gripping the gun barrel and pushing it toward the floor. Thorn turned and wrapped his other arm around the man's neck, catching the guy's chin in the crook of his arm. Thorn grabbed the shoulder of his own leather jacket and used it as a tether as he squeezed down tight.

The sides of the janitor's neck were trapped between his bicep and his forearm, allowing the janitor to breathe, but stopping any blood flow to his brain. Thorn wasn't sure if this was a good guy or a bad guy. If he was a good guy, then Thorn would only be taking the guy out of the game, but the ball would stay in play. If he was a bad guy, coming after Dr. DuBois? Thorn wasn't keen on killing someone here on foreign soil, especially since he wasn't the one being attacked. Thorn had no authority to act here.

The guy dressed in the janitor's uniform struggled. Hard. He was trained and knew what he was doing as he fought back. And worse, Thorn recognized that this guy had the special forces clarity of thought and the determination not to give up. Thorn was exhausting his own energy quickly, not just taking the guy down but doing it as quietly as he could with the bustle of men in and out behind him, taking a dump, washing their hands, and so far, minding their own business.

Thorn shuffled his stance a little wider to stop the janitor from brutalizing his shins and trying to snap Thorn's knee backward.

The janitor was weakening.

Thorn realized he'd only been able to get him in this position by sheer surprise, and Thorn only kept the janitor in the lock because of his *own* training and determination.

Thorn was panting, his heart racing from exertion. He was fighting one-armed. His other hand wrapped the barrel of the gun, pushing the slide forward just enough that the bullet was out of battery. Though, the janitor compulsively twitched his trigger finger, trying to get a round off.

One slip.

One.

And Thorn knew both he and DuBois could be shot.

The thrashing stopped. The janitor's weight slumped on Thorn's arm. Thorn needed to make sure this guy was really lights-out and not playing possum. It had happened to him before – Thorn wasn't likely to fall for that trick twice. Thorn was still counting under his breath as he tossed the gun into the trash bin on the cart. The hell he was going to get caught with that thing on him if they got stopped by the police.

DuBois stood there, eyes wide, mouth wide, frozen with fear.

Thorn needed help stowing the janitor. "I could use backup," Thorn growled under his breath, knowing that the computer would pick up the sounds and amplify them for his team.

"I'm almost to you, rounding the entrance," Honey said.

"Stay still," Thorn told DuBois. "The U.S. government sent us to help you."

DuBois didn't seem to believe Thorn. Plastered against the wall, he raised his hands in front of him like he was getting mugged on the city street.

Honey tapped Thorn's shoulder to signal he was there.

DuBois tilted his head as he looked up to Honey's full height. And then held as if petrified.

"The U.S. government sent us to help you," Honey whispered, a repetition of what Thorn had said, trying to drum the information into DuBois's terror-shocked brain.

Thorn kicked at the janitor's cart to give himself some maneuvering room. He dragged the janitor to the wall and let him drop. Digging his phone from his pocket, Thorn took a few quick photos that he sent on to Nutsbe for identification. He used his foot to slide the guy's limbs in tighter, making the janitor small enough to be hidden as Honey pushed the cart in front of his unconscious form and stepped on the braking mechanism.

"Okay, here we go," Thorn said, turning his attention to DuBois. "Let's go get your luggage and get you out of here."

DuBois's focus slid to the janitor.

"He's not dead. He's just taking a nap," Honey said with a soothing, compelling voice. The kind he used to coax people out into the light when he was on a rescue.

It worked like a charm. Dubois shut his mouth, lowered his eyebrows, and seemed to give himself a shake.

"I need confirmation of your identity. Your name, sir?" Honey asked.

The man nodded his head convulsively.

"You're name?" Honey asked again.

"David. Dr. David DuBois." His words tripped and tangled on each other as they stuttered over his lips.

"I'll take lead. You're right behind me, sir. My partner's got your back." Honey pointed toward Thorn.

Thorn pushed DuBois to get him going. They'd come to the door of the bathroom when DuBois abruptly turned around. "I haven't washed my hands," he said.

It was always funny, Thorn thought, the weird things a brain locked onto in times of crisis.

Honey reached in his pocket and handed DuBois a small bottle of hand sanitizer. "This'll have to do. You'll want to get your shirt tucked in and zip up your fly. Keep moving."

"Nutsbe here. You've got Hong, Colburn, and the unsub still in place, looking unsettled. Heads on a pivot. You've got the gray-lady, who signaled the janitor, positioned, watching from the newsstand. Gage is at the top of the passageway. Ten meters." Nutsbe used the term "gray" not to indicate a color, but to convey that she was operational, whoever she was.

"Copy," Honey said.

Thorn tugged Dubois slightly to the side, so he could get a

shoulder in and block the smaller man from view of the three-man team. Though this move would make him more visible to the woman.

He saw Hong make eye contact with Honey, and the look was not friendly.

"Changing directions," Honey said. "We're heading straight for the cars. We'll deal with the luggage later."

"Copy," Gage responded. "I'm ahead of you. I'll bring the car to the stairwell."

DuBois had been casting his gaze about, searching for cameras, security, or help as they moved down the causeway. Thorn wrapped his hand around DuBois's arm. He wanted to let him know that attention-seeking was a bad idea.

The stairwell was just up ahead.

As Honey pulled the door open, DuBois put his foot up on the wall and struggled away from them. Thorn grabbed both of the man's arms, lifted, and bodily tossed him through the door frame. Honey caught him up by the collar and lowered his head to speak into DuBois's ear. "The US government sent us to protect you. You might want to cooperate a little."

Thorn took the lead as Honey wrangled the guy down the stairs. From above them came the distinctive pop-pop of suppressed gunfire. The blast and ricochet were loud enough here in the echoing stairwell to get security's attention. Post terror attacks, they'd be swarming. And Thorn didn't trust DuBois to say the right things if the Panther Force operators were caught in a police net.

Pop-pop-pop. The bullets made little poofs of smoke where they impacted the cement walls.

"Keep going. Keep moving." Honey hooked a hand into the back of Dubois's belt and used it to maneuver him.

DuBois's feet weren't cooperating. He was stumbling over

himself.

"Nutsbe?" Thorn called.

"I've got nothing. The cameras in the stairwell and part of the garage are down."

Bullets peppered around them from a different direction as Gage's car screamed around the corner then slammed to a stop.

Honey shoved DuBois ahead of him into the back seat.

Thorn dove into the front.

Gage took off with their doors still wide, Thorn and Honey scrambling to get them closed. The passengers flew into the air as Gage powered over the speed bumps and rammed right through the wooden arm that asked them to pay in advance from the machine to the right.

Sure, at this point, they were on everyone's camera. But hopefully, security wouldn't give a rat's ass that they were scurrying away when armed men were shooting in the airport. Albeit with silencers to suppress the noise.

"Bite me," Thorn said, looking at the bullet hole that had sliced into the sleeve of his favorite leather jacket. He slid his arm out to make sure there was no blood. Adrenaline could mask some wicked injuries. Nothing. He shrugged his jacket back in place and pulled his safety belt across his hips.

Gage had melded into the highway traffic and was driving smoothly apace.

"Who had the guns, Nutsbe?" Thorn asked.

"From what cameras were functioning, you had two unidentified, military-aged males entering the stairwell behind you. The gray-lady looked like she was running them. She was talking into her phone and moving in your direction, purposefully, but making it look like she was running for a flight. Whoever she is, she's good at what she does. I don't have her ID'd yet. Which means she may not exist."

"Black ops?" His words were silent, but Thorn knew the computers would pick up the vibrations from his mic and translate them for Nutsbe and the others.

"I'm guessing," Nutsbe confirmed, "or I should have her by now."

"Hong's crew – you've got the third guy?" Thorn could see Gage's mouth move, but the sound came through the earbuds and not from the man beside him. Technology could make their job easier, and technology could also bite them in the ass when used with equal dexterity by the enemy.

"Tibor Yegorovich, Russian national. Because of Wu's involvement, this is a contracted operation. Omega operators can't opt for any side game, so Omega's definitely involved. It looks like there are at least three teams targeting this guy. I'm guessing we're the only ones amongst them that have the doctor's good health in mind."

"Copy," the Panthers said in unison, making DuBois's eyes stretch wide. He couldn't hear the other end of their conversation.

Thorn turned almost backward to catch DuBois's gaze. "Sir, what did the janitor tell you in the bathroom?"

DuBois opened his eyes wide in the way people do when feigning innocence.

"I'm not playing here, sir. I watched it happen. I pulled the gun from under your ribs. I squeezed the blood out of the man's neck. What did he tell you in the bathroom?"

DuBois began trembling, his teeth chattering.

"That quaking's from adrenaline," Honey explained. "It's gonna happen. No need to fight it. But we do need to know what the janitor told you."

"He said there was a kidnapping at my mother's house in Toulouse. I was to go with him quietly, and they'd tell me what they needed from me. Then you came up and wrestled with him. Is it true?" He twisted toward Honey. "Is my family in danger? Who was shooting? Who are you?"

Honey sat silently; they weren't authorized to disseminate that information.

"Sir, what do you do for a living?" Gage asked, repositioning his hands on the steering wheel.

"I'm mostly retired. I give my thoughts now and then on research projects. I teach a few classes for graduate students. I golf, and I fish."

"Sounds like a nice life," Thorn said. "But you didn't mention your affiliation with DARPA."

DuBois flailed about for a moment, sputtering. Finally, he said, "You shouldn't have helped me back there. It's imperative that I get Juliette back." A hangdog look that painted DuBois's face was pitiful. Thorn felt for the guy. In his place, he'd say the same damn thing.

"You want to be kidnapped?" Honey's knee pressed into the back of Thorn's seat.

Thorn reached down and powered his chair forward as much as possible.

"It's my daughter," DuBois said.

"You know that's not how it works." Honey tried to speak reasonably to the scientist. "If they're using a loved one to get to you, they'll keep you tucked tight by leveraging them. You'll be at their beck and call. Let the U.S. intelligence and security communities keep you safe and work to get your daughter back to you."

"No." He reached for the door handle though they were driving at highway speed. "Pull over. You need to let me out of the car. I can't go with you. I have to go back."

"But you have military secrets, *our* military secrets," Gage said. "We can't allow you to go."

"And under what authority will you stop me?" DuBois started to show some spunk.

"Under no authority," Gage said. "We're rogue. We're out doing our best to keep the USA safe, and if you're going to spill some DARPA beans to our enemies? Yeah, that's just not going to happen."

"I don't know who *you* are. You have no right to just force me to go with you. So what if I work for DARPA?" DuBois spat out.

"Doesn't matter if you know us or not. DARPA is DARPA, and secret compartmentalized information is secret compartmentalized information. You are *not* walking into the enemies' hands," Gage said as he checked his rearview mirror. "Incoming,"

Thorn focused out the back window where three motorcycles wove through the traffic at breakneck speed.

A few of the cars were abreast, and the motorcycles moved to the side of the road and flowed around the traffic.

Gage pushed his foot down. He flew down the crowded highway, sliding their car through the small openings like a thread through the eye of a needle.

Thorn pulled out his pocket monocular and worked to get a focus. "Son of a bitch."

"Sitrep. What are you seeing, Thorn?" Nutsbe asked over the comms.

"Well, two of them have guns. The other one…No, I don't know what he's got."

"Do they want to kidnap you?" Honey asked DuBois. "Or do they want you dead?"

6

JULIETTE
France
Saturday 1:40 p.m.

JULIETTE FLOATED on the high-pitched ringing in her head. She used it like a wave, buoying her body. The movement below her was like water in its fluid motion. Above her, she felt brewing storm clouds. The storm. The thunder rumbles of tires against the roadway. Her limbs were so heavy that she couldn't move them; she couldn't open her eyelids.

She had no choice but to float.

She wondered if this was what it was like for the whales. The beautiful, majestic whales, who were assaulted by the US Navy and their sonar sounds. Was it like this for them, the high-pitched whistling in their heads, unable to make it stop? Unable to find relief or escape?

She'd been reading a lot about whales. About sound. When she read the articles, it felt like home to her. Like she'd been lost flailing about the oceans, and there was an island of peace for her to crawl onto and rest.

If only she could rest now.

Fighting this incapacity to fully wake was exhausting.

Air swirled around her face. The fine hairs tickled over her cheek. She had slowly recalled where she was – a car with two Russians, being driven to…somewhere. They'd put the car windows down.

The wind sounds hurt her ears. Made them whistle.

A jet engine, a roaring crowd of sports-goers, whales, elephants, that set of nouns seemed to have little in common, one to the other. Their commonality was that they all produced sound waves that included a frequency too low for a human ear to hear, called subsonic sound waves. Not hearing them didn't mean they weren't dangerous. They weren't innocuous. The sound changed the way the inner ear worked.

It would help Juliette if the Russians would roll up the windows, blocking the low-frequency road sounds. Her head might not hurt as badly.

Since her accident and brain trauma, vibrations had become her enemy. Juliette found it ironic that the word for the sound wave measurements "hertz" sounded *exactly* like "hurts."

Sound could hurt as in physically damaging the ear.

Sounds could hurt as in creating physical pain like she was experiencing now.

Sounds could hurt as in words that no one ever wanted to hear like – *"There was an accident. Your mother is dead. Do you recognize me? Do you know who I am? I'm your father."*

Juliette sometimes thought that her dad was her greatest hero. He was the one who operated on her, who trained, and molded, and worked with her brain.

Sometimes, Juliette was not so grateful.

If she was going to be truly honest, she thought that dying in the accident might have been the kindest thing that could have happened to her and that her dad's efforts to keep her alive were rather a matter of selfishness on his part. She could understand his not wanting a daughter to die, not wanting to mourn two family members at once.

She worked to forgive her father's selfishness.

Her dad, after all, didn't live with her disabilities and could never understand her struggles in anything but an intellectual way.

Maybe these men could just kill her and end this.

Juliette thought that might be too much to hope for.

After all, they didn't just shoot her in the street. They took her away at gunpoint. That was her mistake. She got into their car to protect the little boy from stray bullets. If she'd fought these men, they might have just killed her.

What were they going to do with her?

If she could just remember what happened after she passed by Ballroom C the first time she'd seen these men, then maybe she'd know what was in store for her. What they wanted.

Hot tears made a rivulet along Juliette's nose, followed the swirl of her nostril, and dripped onto her lips.

Salty like the ocean waves was her last thought before she let herself stop struggling, and she was swept back into the darkness.

7

THORN
Brussels, Belgium
Saturday, Thirteen Forty-five Hours

"YEAH, BABY," Thorn hooted as their car bounced over the rail-road tracks and landed on the road on the other side.

DuBois swung his head to look out the back window as the high-speed train zipped along the track behind their bumper. His hand white-knuckle gripped the leather headrest of Gage's front seat.

Gage's knee-jerk decision lit Thorn's system. Thorn rubbed a hand over his face as he laughed, part relief, part astonishment, mostly holy shit!

He couldn't believe Gage had tried that.

Gage had balls of steel, that was damned sure.

They'd come up on the tracks with the safety gate already lowered. Yellow lights flashing. The train in view. There was nowhere to turn off. Deep ditches on either side of the roadway, and the motorcycles hot on their tail.

Boom. Gage accelerated forward. Splintering wood flew. Thorn was sure that the train had just peeled the paint off the car, the engine was moving that fast, and it had been that close.

Honey got out to inspect the car. Reaching down, he pulled a slab of red and white striped wood from the grill. "Broken headlights," he called. "Needs a new bumper and a paint job. Let's get moving. I can't see the end of the train, but I'd like to get some distance between us and the biker gang behind it."

Gage rolled up the windows as Honey got back in and adjusted his safety belt.

After powering down the country roads, they drove more sedately as they hit the suburbs. Nutsbe was reeling them in, using all the technology at his disposal.

It had been one hell of a chase. Those guys on their motorcycles were top notch. Professionals. Thorn wondered whose team they played on…Omega? The gray-lady? Another player? Some intel would go a far piece right now.

After a circuitous route, they'd pulled into a garage, waiting open.

A man stood by the open door, scratching the back of his head.

Thorn powered down the window.

The man looked at each face in the car, then held up his phone and swiped from photo to photo. With a nod, he handed Thorn a set of car keys and flicked his hand toward the car parked to their left.

The team piled out of their broken BMW.

"We've got to get DuBois on to the safe house." Honey tugged DuBois from the back seat, a tight grip on the back of his coat collar. "We left the second rental car back at the airport garage." He lifted a chin toward Thorn. "It's got your computer and duffle. We don't want anyone to get hold of it. Gage and I will move DuBois. You take this wreck back and handle the cars. Head to a hotel for the night in case you pick up a tail. We'll get a plan in play. Obviously, DuBois can't get on that redeye in the morning."

"Nutsbe, do you want me to get DuBois's luggage?" Thorn asked.

"We took care of that already," Nutsbe said over the comms. "We'll get it back to the States. The housekeeper at the safe house is gathering essentials for DuBois. He'll be set enough until we can get him home."

"Roger." Thorn flipped the keys for the new car over to Gage.

While Honey manhandled Dubois to the new vehicle, Gage grabbed up his bag, then slipped Honey's over his shoulder. He clapped Thorn on the back. "Stay frosty."

8

JULIETTE
    France
    Saturday 2:09 p.m.

THIS TIME WHEN **J**ULIETTE TRIED, her eyelids fluttered.

Her butt was numb. Pins and needles burned her feet where they'd fallen asleep.

She desperately wanted to stretch her back, but now that the medication the Russian shot into her bloodstream was fading, she wasn't quite as self-pitying. She actually had a will to live, fight, and survive. And Juliette knew, once she moved, there was the chance that another syringe might pop out of the guy's pocket.

Juliette shifted her eyes to the right at the door. Then left. The men had switched places again. The one with the jeans was sitting next to her now. He had his phone in his hand; the time readout said 2:09.

It had been hours of driving.

Where were they taking her? Surely, they wouldn't be crossing borders with her slumped here in the back seat.

Why would they switch twice?

There must be a strategic reason.

Juliette had read a lot of thriller and suspense novels. They were the English language novels her dad had on his bookshelves. In the months when they were getting ready to move from Lebanon to the United States, Juliette had read them to improve her English. She had lived in Pennsylvania for a few years and in Toulouse for a few years as her dad had moved their little family around for his research. That's why she could speak those languages. Though, Juliette's first language was Arabic. Her mother had insisted on it, according to her dad.

Her English had turned out to be remarkably good. She had no trouble following the plots of the books. Some of the language was strange to her, the military speak and spy jargon. Other than that, she felt quite fluent.

Now, she thought back to those books, trying to think of a character that had been in a place like hers. Awake, pretending, and escaping. She came up with a few, but they had skills she didn't, like coordination, physical strength, and a buddy on their radio.

Okay, let's figure this out. Why would they switch drivers twice in less than four hours?

Juliette thought about water. She often thought about water, but this time it was a pool, not the ocean. She thought she might be having another memory. Long thin brown legs stretched out under the sun—a large striped umbrella overhead. The blazing heat of the sun and children screaming far below her. She blew a whistle, and everyone got out of the pool. Then she climbed down a ladder, and a different girl had smiled and climbed up in her place. "See you in a half-hour," she said. They'd switched to let their eyes rest and to keep their minds sharp.

Juliette would bet that was why the Russians had switched places and thus roles, as well. One would drive, and the other would watch for her to move. Or maybe they expected a tail to roar up behind them as if that were truly possible.

She'd been passed out for a long while. Juliette bet that two things were happening: the jeans guy was getting focus-fatigued and that he'd mostly discounted her since she's been incapacitated.

The car slowed.

She wondered if they were coming to another stop.

If the jeans-guy wasn't watching, she might be able to spring out of the door this time.

"Damned construction," the driver said. "Check the app. How long will we be in this?"

There was a pause, then blue jeans answered, "Twenty minutes delay. It's mostly an orange line. It says about a minute of red."

A minute of red. There were good things and bad things about a minute of red. The car would be going slowly. The car couldn't chase forward. There would be lots of eyes in the area. All good things. She couldn't tell unless blue jeans announced it when they were hitting the red. She had nowhere to go once she was out of the car.

They had guns.

They also had her purse. She could see it there by blue-jeans' foot. Without it, she'd have no phone, no credit cards, no identification, and no money. The strap wasn't visible. If she grabbed at it, the guy would grab back at her, like he did when she reached for her safety belt.

She still had her safety belt in place. That was the first thing that she needed to change.

Juliette's hands dangled on either side of her folded body. As slowly as she could, she slid her fingers toward her boot. When she got them that far, she kept her upper arm still, bending her arm, she slid her hand up her leg under the drape of her hair. When her fingers reached her knee, she stilled to reassess.

She held her breath as she made the micromovements, appreciating the roughness of the road jostling the car and covering the shift of her body as she brought her right elbow in, tight against her thigh, up onto the seat where she could press some of her weight into it. And there she was stuck. Her breasts were resting in her lap. There was no space to slide her hand through to her hip. No joint that would allow her to bend where she needed to.

Perhaps a bump in the road.

Or a swerve of the car.

She waited patiently for either, primed, ready to take advantage of it.

She could hear the sounds of construction trucks with their low rumbles. Men shouted instructions back and forth to each other, but those voices were quite a distance from the car. And Juliette was a little afraid that if all she did was yell and call attention that the men would shoot the someone who might step forward to help her. And once they got away, that she would face their retaliation. In the back recesses of her memory, a glimmer of what retribution felt like snaked out of a dark pit.

The car slowed.

Slowed.

Slowed.

This was it—her minute of opportunity.

If only there was a bump. Or one of the voices sounded closer.

The car slid forward again, picking up speed.

Juliette had missed it.

Now, what was she going to do?

9

THORN

Brussels, Belgium
Saturday, Fourteen Thirty-eight Hours

THORN TOOK a circuitous trip back to the airport in the now battered BMW rental.

With Nutsbe in his ear feeding him directions, Thorn crossed over every bridge, around every traffic circle he could find. He drove through a couple of parking garages for good measure on his way back to the other rental car.

"From the satellite images, you look clean. I'd go ahead and pull in," Nutsbe said.

Thorn tapped on his blinker. "Were you watching the garage?"

"I had the software keep an eye on your car. The computer tagged each person whose been down there. All I can say is none of the known players were picked up by the camera. But remember, most of those cameras are offline. I have a camera feed that has the second rental car in the far corner of the screen, and our software was able to enhance it."

Thorn pulled into the empty space next to the second rental and got out, his head on a swivel.

He got out and retrieved his bags from the rental. "It's been a weird day." He slammed the lid down and strode over to the driver's door of his new car. "What are they saying happened earlier with shots fired in the stairwell? I didn't see police activity on the way in."

"The story is that someone threw fireworks down the stairs. The scene must have been staged by the perps. The shooters probably picked up their casings and threw down the right kind of debris to make that scenario work, then they headed out. That means a lot of pre-planning."

"Team number three, the one run by the gray-lady?" Thorn tossed the fob into the cup holder and reached out to press the button and make the engine purr.

"Looked that way, but as you well know, looks—"

"Can be deceiving. Right." Thorn slid the seat back to make room for his long legs and adjusted his mirrors. "What we do know, or can surmise, is that these were professionals."

"Either that or someone in security was feeling damned complacent because literally, nothing came of it other than a few security guards pushing through the stairwell door. After the terrorist bombs, I would have expected a bigger show of force."

Thorn swiveled his head and backed out of the parking place. "Makes you think there was some kind of collusion with security?"

"My guess is there were no bodies, no blood, no video footage. If they raised too much of a rumpus, they'd have a panic on their hands and a shit ton of flight delays as they shut everything down. All that costs money and puts them on the front page of the newspaper. The security team didn't see anything worth that kind of havoc."

"Okay, where am I going?" Thorn put the car in gear and started toward the exit.

"I made a hotel reservation. Lucky for you, there's a soccer match at the stadium. I had to go upscale to get you anything nearby. You'll be sleeping in the lap of luxury."

"As long as room service can deliver a decent steak."

"I programmed directions into your phone's GPS."

Thorn swiped his cell phone and memorized his route. "Got it. I'm heading for the exit."

"Copy that."

"Shit." Just as Thorn cleared the garage through the battered security arm that Gage had broken off earlier, the woman who had signaled the janitor in the airport – the gray-lady, as Nutsbe labeled her – walked into his path, turned, and stood wide-legged in front of him, blocking the egress.

Her hair was down and flowed about her shoulders in the wind. The sunlight caught in the tangle of her curls, making them a softer brown.

She'd changed her clothes, too. Gone were the loose non-descript clothes. Now, she was wearing skin-tight jeans, heels, and a soft-looking sweater that was light enough for the wind to plaster it around her figure. Big breasts. Tiny waist. She had makeup on now. It enhanced her features rather than painting over and hiding them. Yeah, she'd had to dim her light in the airport earlier, or everyone would have been looking her way. She was both remarkable and memorable. And neither was good for business in the clandestine world.

It was definitely her.

"Yup, got her," Nutsbe said. "She appears to be alone. I can't see any nearby vehicles. No hidden figures that I can make out."

Thorn rolled to a stop, wishing he had a sidearm handy. Thorn watched her hands to make sure she wasn't pulling a gun from somewhere and popping him off. He was ready to stomp on the gas and plow her down if need be. In his experience, the survival part of the brain engaged before impact, and people would jump out of the way. "Nutsbe, we still clear?"

"Brother, that looks like fire you're about to play with. But, I still only see her in the picture. She must have been lying in wait."

"Like the spider and the fly." Curious, Thorn tapped the button to release the locks. They made an audible snap. "Anyway, not much choice. She's blocking the drive."

The gray-lady walked over to the passenger side of the car and climbed in. It seemed like she meant to stay because she locked her door and pulled her seat belt across her lap. She looked straight forward out the front window.

"Okay. Bold move." Nutsbe chuckled. "I'll watch you on satellite to see if anyone's following. But I'm going to use your phone to buzz the car. That'll scramble any radio signals and any tracking devices while you figure out what she wants. I won't be able to hear you while I do that. Clear your throat if that's how you want me to proceed."

Thorn cleared his throat.

"Okay, then. As long as you're in your car, you're offline. Swallow hard to confirm."

Thorn gathered spit in his mouth and swallowed, making the saliva snake down his throat past the mic. He knew Nutsbe would hear the *wallump* on his end.

Adjusting his mirrors, he was able to catch a glimpse of the mystery woman sitting placidly by his side. "Anywhere, in particular, I should go?" He wasn't even sure she knew English.

"Your hotel will be fine." She turned to him. "You're staying at *Le Grand Palais.*" She quirked a brow. "Very *luxe*. Your company takes very good care of you." She turned her head back to look out the front window. "Next exit, you get off." She gestured with a graceful hand.

Yup. That was where Nutsbe had booked him, and that was the route the map had shown. She was connected to an organization with excellent access. She was also checking the side mirrors like a pro.

"Are you expecting someone to be following us?"

"Habit," she said nonchalantly.

"Where'd you develop this habit?" Thorn slid his focus toward her, trying to read her for any information. Just who was he dealing with?

"I developed the habit in the DGSE just as you, Lars Iversen − AKA Thorn, Navy SEAL, retired, now working for Iniquus in Washington DC, under Titus Kane, Panther Force − developed your skill sets through your work."

She had some damned good connections to get all that when he had nada on her.

DGSE − French intelligence. Did he believe her?

She touched a hand to her chest. "Brigitte," she said.

Her accent was not quite the same French accent as Thorn had heard around him during his security detail with the US diplomats. But this was Brussels, and Thorn had learned his French in Africa.

"And when Iniquus is done scrambling the radio waves around your car, you can ask Titus all about me," she was saying.

If she was bluffing, she would be the poker champion of the world. How the hell would she get that information if she wasn't who she said she was? Okay, Thorn was rattled. He much preferred being one step ahead instead of scrambling to keep up, and Brigitte understood that was the case. He'd bet good money that's why she was smiling that secretive-cat smile.

The rest of the drive was in silence.

10

JULIETTE WAS GROWING AGITATED. She was trying to keep herself rational and calm, so she could make the best possible decisions. She tried to listen to her own good counsel from around the tinnitus that obscured her inner dialogue.

She'd have another chance to escape, eventually.

They'd have to slow down again, sooner or later.

If Juliette pulled her eyes to look as far left as they could shift, she could see that blue jeans guy had pushed his gun under his thigh with the muzzle pointing forward toward the driver. Juliette wondered if the car bounced, would the trigger rub against the man's leg and shoot the driver? She willed it. She pulled up the thought and tried with the sheer power of wishful thinking for the gun to go off.

When the bang actually sounded, she froze with surprise.

The driver was yelling and pulling at the wheel. Obviously, he wasn't hurt enough by the gunshot to kill him. Her first thought was disappointment. Her second thought was that his cuss words were vile. And how would she, a student in a Lebanese high school, learn the Russian language well enough that she'd know the meaning of such words?

From out of the barrage of cuss words, Juliette picked out the words, "flat tire."

Not even a gunshot.

Her momentary thrill of power was dashed. Had she been in any other circumstance, she would have laughed at herself and the absurdity of that moment.

Before she landed too solidly on that thought, she felt the car stopping. The driver had straightened them out and moved them to the side of the road. He jumped out of the car, Juliette assumed to check out the damage. He spoke to blue jeans through the window. It seemed that as they'd passed through the construction site, they'd driven over some debris and had a bolt lodged in the tire.

"Is she still out?" the driver asked.

Blue jeans reached over, pinched up the flesh on her thigh, and twisted it viciously.

Juliette's face scrunched tight in agony, but that pain was hidden by her hair. She was able to keep the rest of her body slack.

"Completely out," blue jeans responded. "Let's get to it."

Both doors popped open. Both doors slammed closed.

Juliette waited for the trunk and voices of the men conferring before she dragged her purse over to her. She fished out her phone, her passport, and her wallet. Nothing else in there was important – a brush, her lip gloss, a plastic container of tissues…

She slid the phone in one back pocket, and the wallet and

passport in the other as the car was jacked up, tipping her toward the ditch. The land outside of her window dipped down and then rose quickly into a bank. Juliette thought it would be too steep and too obvious for her to try to scramble up that embankment. The car tipped more, and now she thought that if she opened the door to get out as she'd planned, it would stick in the dirt. She'd only have one way to run, and that was toward her kidnappers.

"Oh shit, look. Here we have a good Samaritan coming up to give us a hand."

"He's shorter than I am. He won't be able to see in the windows with the car angled up."

But he *will* be a distraction, Juliette thought. And she was going to go for it as soon as she heard the man's voice.

She waited. Waited.

"Hello there!"

And that was her cue. With hands on either side of the opened window that had tortured her for most of the drive, Juliette pushed her torso out. She got her hips up on the edge, then reached her hands toward the ground as if she were diving into a pool of water. There was nothing solid there—just a ditch piled with leaves. Juliette reached back to the car and pushed to get the weight of her body to take her the rest of the way through the window. There was a whoosh, and she bit her tongue as she landed, but she was out of the car.

She looked around, and there was nowhere to go to escape except maybe the good Samaritan's car up ahead. Could she hide inside? That seemed dangerous. A trap that would be hard to escape. She could steal it. She hadn't driven a car in so long. Her license had been taken from her because of the vertigo. That's what her dad told her. The truth was, Juliette didn't remember a time when she'd driven a car. Maybe she knew how. Maybe she didn't. When she'd watched her father drive, it didn't seem complicated. Even if she was able to get into the man's car and drive it away, chances were that she'd crash it just down the street, and the Russians would catch up with her and grab her again.

She wrestled herself deeper in the leaf-filled ditch and started snaking away from the Russian's car.

"We've got this. Thanks for your help." One of the Russians was saying in very poor French.

Juliette crawled faster. She needed to get to the other car first.

"You've got a spare tire there, do you?" the good Samaritan asked. "No, look at that. It's dry rotted. Do you have a service who can bring one to you?" The Russians must not have understood him because he simplified. "Look. No good. Danger."

"We're traveling. This is a friend's car. Do you have another? I'd be happy to buy it from you. I can give extra cash for the problems this brings." That was blue jeans voice, and he sounded so polite and friendly.

Juliette stopped crawling when the man said, "Wow, that's an incredibly generous amount. Let me go look at my tire. If it's in good shape, you've got yourself a deal. If it's not, I'll take this money into town and get you a new one."

Now Juliette didn't know what to do. If she stood up and showed herself, the Russians might very well shoot the guy and take his car, and she'd be back under their control.

She decided to lay still. Perfectly still. She wouldn't even breathe. She'd close her eyes and pretend she didn't exist.

After a moment, the man called out, "Good luck. This should work."

There was a thunk as he pulled the tire onto the ground and started rolling it toward the men. She waited until the tire stopped moving so the attention would be down on their task, then she crawled again slowly the way she'd seen in the movies with her weight on her elbows. Her knees were in the muck. But she thought that the color of her clothes would help her stay camouflaged as she moved under the leaves.

Once she came to the car, she tried the back door.

Locked.

She decided that she was down to two options. With minimum distance between her and her captors, she wasn't sure which she should take. She could try to climb undetected into the trunk and hope that the man would shut her in – then she'd have to escape from a locked trunk.

How would the Russians react? They'd do a quick search, probably find her tracks and chase down the car even if it got a good start. The man wouldn't know he was being chased, that the men had guns.

That would be bad.

The other choice again was to steal the car.

They'd shoot at her.

But if she drove away fast enough, they might miss.

She was alongside the car now – the driver had pulled far off on the shoulder of the road. The road curved just up ahead. That was helpful. She lifted up from her squat, her high heels sinking into the moist ground. She could see the keys dangling in the ignition. She could see that the front doors were unlocked.

Without giving it another thought, Juliette's body took over. She pulled the passenger side door open and threw herself in.

She slammed the locks into place, scrambled under the wheel, and started the engine.

That's when the shouting of the three men started up behind her.

The rearview mirror was blocked by the trunk that was still

open. But Juliette knew that all three men were dashing toward her.

Jamming the car into drive, her foot pressed heavily on the gas pedal until she was nearly standing on it. Juliette was terrified as the wheels spun in place, not moving her even an inch forward. Mud spewed out at the men as she watched them race forward where she could see them now in the side mirror.

She lifted her foot a bit to slow the engine, and the tires gripped. She shot off down the road and around the corner.

No bullets flew in her direction.

The man who owned this car would frantically be calling the police. If they stopped her, would that keep her safe or put her in prison?

The road in front of her was swimming in her vision.

Stress always made the vertigo so much worse.

She just needed to get to a town where she could hide. She needed to figure out a plan.

What she *needed* was a miracle.

11

THORN
> **Brussels, Belgium**
> **Saturday, Fifteen Zero Two Hours**

THORN PULLED up to the valet in front of his hotel and popped the trunk. A uniformed man pulled the duffle from the back, another tugged Brigitte's door open. As Thorn crossed to her side, he handed the keys over to the valet and gave his name.

"I need to get signed in," he said as they walked through the heavy glass doors. "Do you want to meet me at the bar?"

"No." She laced her fingers with his and shifted her body as if they'd been a couple for a very long time. "I want to go up to your room with you." She was smiling playfully up at him, running a hand down his arm, and leaving a kiss on his shoulder.

Thorn's dick got a heads up on that one.

He dealt with the desk and reached for his key card. "I'll take it from here," he said, handing a couple euros to the bellhop, who was waiting patiently to the side.

"You're back on comms," Nutsbe said.

Thorn coughed behind his fist to indicate he'd heard. He glanced down to find Brigitte smiling at him, then she winked.

Shit! She either had ESP, or she had someone feeding her the conversation in her ear. Nah, this was an encrypted channel. She'd probably just found his cough amusing because she'd know he'd have comms up.

Thorn pulled out his phone and tapped an icon. No one could hear him now, but Nutsbe could talk. If he had to. Hopefully, he'd get the message and shut the hell up.

When they reached room 527, Thorn swiped the key card and pushed the door open, letting Brigitte go in first.

"Lovely," she said, moving over to the heavy fabric drapes, standing to the side while she took in the view.

Thorn plunked his bag on the lowboy, slid his jacket off and placed it on top, then crossed his arms over his chest. He leaned his shoulder into the wall, watching Brigitte, waiting for some kind of a signal. How was this going to play out?

Brigitte turned and unabashedly let her gaze travel over his body. "I imagine, after all the bustle today, that you'll want to order room service. You have a big appetite, I'm told. Steak, rare. Lots of veggies." Her heavily accented English made her words sound melodic. Maybe Siren-like was a better description. "Good for you. You eat healthfully, and it shows."

"Did you call my mother to ask what I liked for dinner?" Okay, Thorn was getting a little ticked. If she knew things about him, she had leverage. For him, she was a great big question mark.

"Margot and I chat."

"Margot?" That was an interesting connection.

"Your Panther Force teammate." She rested her hand on the table, looking perfectly comfortable. Perfectly at home.

She had the rule book for this game; Thorn was making it up as he went along. "She chatted about me?" Margot wasn't chatty. She was a professional. Thorn didn't trust this conversation.

"Well, you and the people she works with. She's discreet. I'm assuming you were with 'the bear' and 'the brain' today. She calls you 'Thor.'"

"Because…?" *Thor for Thorn?*

"Mmmm." Brigitte licked her top lip and stalked forward. "I think it's because you're built like a Viking. Broad shoulders." She moved her hands to his arms. "Your biceps." She slid her hands over his pecs. "Your chest. Maybe these yummy waves in your blond hair." She reached up and spun her fingers into his hair.

He put his hands on her shoulders and left them there, holding her at a distance. "How well do you know Margot?" Brigitte could have made this up spur of the moment. She did have Margot's name right. Though, Margot's association with Panther Force was less well known.

"She's one of my oldest friends. Margot grew up next door to me in Paris. When we were babies, we would take baths together and played in the same playpen." Again, with that secret smile. "Then she moved to the U.S. when she was ten. Still don't believe me?" She tipped her head and raised an eyebrow. "She's allergic to strawberries, rabbit fur, and the color pink."

True. She hated pink. Thorn didn't know about the other two. "You could get that off Facebook."

"No one at Iniquus is allowed on social media even under a pseudonym."

"Not convinced."

"She has a scar on her palm of her left hand shaped like a C. I was there when she got that scar."

Thorn knew about the scar and knew that Margot decided to

leave the field because of that event, and now she did team support. That was all he knew about it. Margot had gotten that scar when she was with the CIA. So, Brigitte and Margot hadn't just had a childhood connection. They'd been connected out in the field. Okay. Thorn was starting to believe, not because of her words, but because of the tremor that moved through Brigitte's body when she gave up that piece of information. Involuntary. And telling. "And what did Margot say about me, exactly?" he asked.

Brigitte shifted away from that memory and back to seduction mode. Or whatever the hell she thought she was doing. "That you've got a cool head in a hot situation. Keen mind." She opened her mouth then shut it again, yet another cat-with-cream smile. "That you've got stamina in spades. You take your pleasures when and where you can. Sometimes, it's about opening the valve to let the pressure off. 'Blow off some steam,' I believe is the phrase." She stopped for a reaction.

Thorn offered her nothing in return.

She lifted her brow and let it drop, then tilted her head, sliding her hands down to his waist. "Relationships to you aren't a place of comfort. They're stressful. You have enough stress with your job. Some men drink. You prefer more physically exertive ways to release. The gym. Between the sheets." Her gaze shifted to the king-sized bed, then back to him. "Or wherever the mood strikes." Her breath had become shallow. Her eyes dilated almost black. Her face flushed, and her lips parted as that secret smile of hers tickled over her lips.

Cat and cream.

It was provocative, all right. Thorn wanted to strip her bare of her secrets.

His body had picked up on her cues and was responding in kind.

Her hand rested over his heart, and he knew she could feel the beats pumping blood through his body, hard.

"Word has it that a woman can feel safe with you." Her hands swept down to his belt, and she worked to loosen the buckle. "While you have a bad boy reputation, you're a gentleman about your conquests. And, according to Margot, you find these kinds of opportunities rather abundantly."

She was right about that. This situation wasn't unusual for Thorn. Women in this line of work were liberated by the life-or-death calculations of their jobs, and like him, they took what pleasures they could when they could.

He was down for that.

He'd watched enough death and destruction to know life was short. No guarantees. Sweat equity balanced by some sweaty fun helped to even the equation.

"Margot said that a relationship would have you missing out when an unexpected piece of pie was offered up." She yanked his belt, and it slid from the loops like a whip.

Yup. In Iniquus Headquarters — where it would be impossible to plant a bug — Thorn had had the pie conversation with Margot. He'd told her it was a bad idea for him to go out with one of her friends she was trying to set him up with. Margot must have repeated that conversation.

Brigitte tipped her head, let her lashes slowly shut, slowly open again. The move was luxurious somehow. "Savoring" was the word that came to mind, maybe "decadent."

"I could be your unexpected piece of pie if you felt hungry." She unbuttoned the top of his pants. "Today." She slowly slid his zipper down. "Now."

Brigitte stepped back. When she peeled off her sweater, the cami-shirt underneath had an under-arm conceal holster. The butt of her gun was starkly black against the white. Starkly hard against the soft swell of her breast.

"Small world – those who play the ops game," he said.

Her smile changed at the gruffness in his voice. She knew she was going to get what she wanted.

Iniquus had a firm keep-your-pants-zipped policy when it came to clients. Certainly, when it came to dealing with enemies. But there were no rules against engagement when it came to allied operators.

Next off was that little form-fitting cami. She set it down on the low boy. The weight of the gun made a muffled *thunk*. She ran her hands over her breasts and lifted them provocatively. "You like?" she asked.

His mouth found hers as he reached into his turtleneck and pulled off his voice communicator. He reached behind him, feeling for a place to set it down. He was glad Nutsbe couldn't hear any of this.

Voyeurism wasn't Thorn's thing.

Brigitte's brazenness was Thorn's thing.

She turned her back to him, and he brushed her hair to the side as he kissed the nape of her neck.

Brigitte bent over to undo the knots on his laces and loosen them, thrusting her round bottom against him for his appreciation. And he most certainly felt a hefty helping of appreciation as he rubbed his hands over her tight ass.

He yanked his shirt over his head and slid a condom from the tactical pocket of his pants.

When she came back up and saw it, she pressed her body against his. They were kicking at their shoes, yanking and pulling at their clothes, fumbling to shed their encumbrances. After she stepped out of her panties, Thorn wrapped his arms around her and threw himself across the bed, making them bounce, then settle.

She laughed at the move. The merriment and lust in her eyes were a heady cocktail, and he was quickly getting drunk on her.

The pace that had started as carnivorous slowed from crushing lips and jumbled limbs to something much more sensuous as they found pleasure in each other. Her skin under his calloused hands was silk. The stress of the day melted with her smiles and hums.

She was musical in her lovemaking. Her mewling when his tongue found her clit drove him wild. Her long, raven hair tickled across his stomach as she bent low, riding him. He brushed it back over her shoulders so he could watch her face — the concentration lines and tension around her eyes, her mouth open and gasping, tilting her head back with the orgasm that pumped through her body, squeezing his dick in convulsive pulses.

Thorn rearranged their bodies, memorizing the curve of her waist and hips as he took her from behind.

She pushed hard into him.

"Stop now. You're going to make me come," he warned.

"I want you to. Do it," she gasped out her commands. "Come."

God, but that accent worked magic on his dick.

She lay her cheek on the bed and gyrated against him. "I want to feel you coming."

He wrapped his hands around her hips to still her as the tension exploded behind his eyes, through his body, jerking and thundering, leaving him sated. Thorn reached around her waist and pulled her to him as he stretched out a leg and rolled them in to spoon. Her round ass pressed into his hips. His chest heaved while he caught his breath.

THORN
   Brussels, Belgium
   Saturday, Fifteen Fifty Hours

WHEN THE BLOOD stopped thrumming in Thorn's ears, and the sweat had evaporated from their skin, Brigitte turned to him, tangling her legs with his, keeping them pinned together.

He tugged off the condom, knotted the end, and tossed it into the trash can beside the night table.

When he turned back to her, Brigitte brushed the back of her hand over his cheek. "Margot was so right about you," she whispered.

Thorn had never slept with Margot, and even if he had, he couldn't imagine Margot giving a blow-by-blow – so to speak, so he was at a loss. "And what exactly are you agreeing with?"

"A woman could easily find herself taking up the challenge of trying to soften you and bring you under her control. But it would be wasted effort." She slid her hand down his chest, over his stomach, and let it rest on his cock. "You're a hard man."

Thorn's dick stirred awake beneath the warmth — appreciative of the attention.

She sent him a wicked smile, then laughed as she gave his dick, now fully awake and ready to go, a gentle squeeze. "And a hard man is good to find. He knows the *real* rules of the road." She stroked him.

"Maybe we should go over those rules." It was a little late to be gathering this information. But he couldn't turn back time. He wouldn't mind postponing this conversation for another roll, but he'd only brought the one condom. He pulled her hand away reluctantly, kissed her fingers, and held her palm to his chest. "Tell me what your involvement was in the airport today. Is the DGSE working with Omega?"

Brigitte threw her head back and laughed. "Come now. All work and no play makes Thorn a dull boy."

"Play time's over," he said.

"All right." She sat up, pulling the sheet across her lap and crisscrossing her legs in front of her. "Omega? No. We work for ourselves and, in this case, our goals and Omega's are antithetical."

"What are Omega's goals?"

"Omega's client planned a father-daughter reunion on foreign soil. They have been monitoring Juliette DuBois, as have we."

"Juliette DuBois and not David DuBois?"

"Both but for different reasons. Juliette started reaching out to people here in France for information about her family. And then she made a plane reservation just yesterday, a one-way ticket."

"Because?"

"She wants answers."

"Okay. What are her questions? Do you have the answers she's looking for?"

Brigitte shuffled around.

"Do you know who kidnapped her and her child?"

"She doesn't have a child," Brigitte said, sweeping her hair behind her ears and looking him in the eye.

"A witness said there was a child."

She shrugged.

"You said a father-daughter reunion. I saw three sets of players – you and your team, Omega's team, our team." He paused to watch her reaction. Her face didn't change, so he pushed on. "Our team just wanted to watch Dr. DuBois get safely on his plane back to the States. No contact. He wasn't even supposed to know we were there. Obviously, things didn't pan out that way. What did you want with him?"

"Dr. David DuBois and Juliette DuBois both find themselves in difficult situations."

Thorn thought this was an odd statement since it was abundantly apparent in both instances. Juliette was a picture on a computer screen. He was to keep an eye out, intervene if he spotted her. His goal was David Dubois. Brigitte hadn't illuminated her role. *Interesting.* Thorn had assumed that the daughter was taken to use for some goal as it pertained to David Dubois, but Brigitte, through her phrasing, seemed to be insinuating that wasn't the case. Was Juliette a goal in and of herself?

"Do you know the time frame of these circumstances?" Brigitte asked.

Thorn sat still. He didn't want to reveal just how in-the-dark he was here.

"Juliette Dubois got on a plane yesterday in Washington DC, flying to Paris, and then south to Toulouse, where she got a hotel room for the night. She took a taxi to her grandmother's house this morning."

Thorn nodded. He needed to turn on his app so Nutsbe could hear this. That move might break the warm post-coital bubble and might end the information gathering. Thorn started to mind-map the details, so he could recall them clearly later.

"David Dubois got to Toulouse this morning. One-way ticket. When David arrived at his mother's house, the neighbor, who had videotaped Juliette's abduction and called the police, met him outside and told him Juliette was kidnapped. David jumped back into his taxi and left before the police arrived. David made his reservations as he drove to the airport—first flight out of France was Brussels. The first opportunity to get back to America is tomorrow morning."

It sounded like the timeline Titus gave them at their briefing was on target.

What kind of father would act that way? That wasn't what DuBois said to them after they'd yanked him out of the airport. Thorn's focus was razor-sharp.

"You've got physical possession of David. You need to get him home immediately and safely where your intelligence community needs to sit on him. Hard."

"We're working on that." Thorn liked to listen to Brigitte's accent, the way she said David – *Dah-veed*. Though that pronunciation went with a poetic man, not the grizzly old guy in the rumpled suit Honey threw into the back of their car. "Who's got Juliette?"

"We believe it's Omega," she said on an exhale.

"Why?"

"The *why* is classified."

Thorn understood classified. He wouldn't be able to wrangle

that information from Brigitte. But maybe she could tell him…
"Who contracted Omega?"

"The contract comes through a private entity, but if you follow the string, it leads back to Russia."

"Omega is working with Russia?

"*Oui*. Just not directly."

Brigitte had called the information about Omega kidnapping Juliette classified. Maybe she'd share something about papa bear. "Why are you going after David DuBois? Why is Russia interested?"

"You first." She shuffled a pillow into her lap.

"I told you. Our task was to shadow DuBois and provide necessary security from deplaning until he was headed back to the U.S., nothing more. It seems we landed in a minefield." Thorn had been in that position for years – functioning as a small piece of a larger puzzle, necessary to the whole picture but never getting a chance to see that whole picture. He'd learned to put his head down, follow orders, and move on. Speculation only made him nuts.

She canted her head. "David's brain holds many secrets."

"Omega's goal is to get those secrets, so they want to capture him. And you want to…"

"Make sure those secrets don't become a liability."

"Do you know where they took Juliette? Would you help us get her back? She's an American citizen. We won't let that go." That had popped out of Thorn's mouth like some kind of card he was willing to play. The truth was, Thorn didn't have any information on Juliette. He had no idea of her citizenship status.

Brigitte was silent, studying him. She shook her head. "You either know that is the truth, or you're trying to play me." She waggled her pointer finger at him.

Thorn memorized those words. Sure, English was a second

language for her, but still. Thorn thought he'd picked up a clue. He switched to a different tack. "When we got our hands on DuBois at the airport, from my perspective, it looked like your team tried to shoot him while they could. I'm guessing you hadn't identified us yet and didn't know we were the good guys."

"'Good guys' is perspective. Everyone working for their own government thinks they're the good guy."

"Okay, we're the allies, then," Thorn amended. "Omega, working for someone in Russia, was shooting back at your team, trying to save DuBois, so they had another opportunity at the capture, possibly thinking DuBois would cooperate with them because of his daughter." Thorn rubbed his index finger over his chin. "Was that your team that chased us out of the airport on motorcycles?"

"No, it was not. They are unknown subjects, unsubs as you like to call them." She looked at him earnestly. The laughter that had been in her eyes a moment ago had dimmed. "You and your band of merry men have caused us a great big headache."

"Brigitte," Thorn held her chin between his fingers and kissed her, "we're going to get DuBois back to the States, safe from Omega's hands. We can provide him security there."

She sighed as she pulled away from him, rolling onto her back. "We *don't* have the same goals. I can promise you that."

"Sure, we do. We want to secure what this man knows. We can't be going around killing the scientific community because they know science."

She looked him in the eye for a long time as if she were trying to puzzle something through. "Is that what they told you?" she asked softly.

"No – it's what I surmised. Am I reading this wrong? It sounds to me like you want him neutralized."

Her fingers played with the sheet, looking very comfortable with their discussion. "I follow orders."

Thorn scooted up to lean his back against the upholstered headboard. "A good soldier, doing what you're told without a lot of rhyme or reason."

"'Need to know,' isn't that how you Americans phrase it? In most cases, I probably never know. Sometimes, I'm glad. Sometimes, it haunts me. It's part of the territory." She pushed to the edge of the bed. She looked at him over her shoulder. "The answers are above my pay grade. It doesn't matter, I tick this assignment off my list, and then there's another, and another, and another." That thought seemed to fatigue her.

Thorn felt the worry lines deepen across his forehead. "It's a choice. You can stop."

"Isn't that a little hypocritical? You left the battlefield, and your brain, your muscles, your spirit all demand that you serve. Take out the bad guys."

Thorn shook his head a slow no. "I'm not on a battlefield anymore. I don't kill unless I'm being attacked. I only apply the necessary force to accomplish my objective and get out. Iniquus doesn't take contracts that require 'taking someone out' or imprisoning or transferring people to those who do. That's an Omega gig. It's not who I am. I don't think it's who you are either."

She'd climbed from the bed as he spoke. "You don't know anything about me." She stood, arms crossed beneath her naked breasts. Defiant.

"I know you moan when I lick your thighs." His lips quirked into a lascivious smile.

Brigitte narrowed her eyes. She turned and walked, naked and immodest, to the bathroom, throwing a "Fuck you" over her shoulder.

"Okay," he called after her. "But let me drink a glass of juice first."

Water flowed in the shower. He listened to her moving about. He thought about her rubbing soap bubbles over her tight body and wanted to go in and give her a hand, but she'd thrown the bolt when she closed the door. There was a tap of the toilet seat hitting the back of the tank—the flow of water at the sink.

He lay on the bed, his hands laced behind his head, watching the bathroom door and trying to figure out what this scene was all about. There was some "get" from all this activity. Something beyond giving her affiliations so Panther Force wouldn't shoot her by accident. Not that any of them had a weapon. And it wasn't about the orgasm – orgasms. Something else...

The door popped open. Brigitte emerged with a cloud of steam. Her hair hung in a wet ponytail down her back. A towel encircled her waist like a hula skirt. Her breasts were bare, her nipples hard.

Thorn smiled and crooked a finger to encourage her back into his arms.

Brigitte ignored him as she fished up her clothes from the trail they'd left from door to bed. Stepping into the lace and ribbon panties, pulling the tank top over her head, and checking her weapon, Thorn watched the efficiency of her movements. He liked that they were allies but wished they were also playing on the same team with the same end goal. Of course, if that were the case, he wouldn't have gotten to feel her writhing underneath him. It was that whole "keep your dick zipped" policy when it came to teammates and clients. Mess that one up, and it made for a short career.

"You could have shot me in the car, and you chose not to," Thorn said, watching her tug on her sweater and adjust it down.

"It didn't serve my purpose. You're not my target."

Okay. Why not go straight for the intel he needed? "Why are you here with me?"

She raised one perfectly arched brow. The suggestion of a smile twitched the corners of her lips, then she snagged up her pants from beside her foot. "Curiosity."

"Come on, Brigitte, tell me the truth. Why are you here."

The phone in her jeans pocket buzzed; she pulled it out and read the text. "*Merde*," she said under her breath. She slipped the phone back in her pocket, wriggled into the jeans, and slid her feet into her heels. Then she walked out the door. She didn't turn her head. She didn't say good-bye.

Unsettled, Thorn strode over to the door, flipped the lock on the door, and headed to his own shower with his Dopp kit.

Thorn stood on the bathmat staring at the mirror. "Son of a gun."

13

JULIETTE
Exit 2 A71/E9 in France
Saturday 4:15 p.m.

THE SIGN SAID this was Orléans, which was good because she was just about out of gas.

Juliette wanted to look at her phone and find out where Orléans was on the map.

She'd read about cell phones and tracking. She'd used apps herself when she put her phone down in her house, and she couldn't remember where. It was a simple matter of entering the code into the computer. Even if the phone was off, that was overridden, and it would ring loudly.

The men who took her, surely, they found her this way – by her phone's location.

Juliette had pulled her cell phone from her pocket and took out the battery as she powered down the road. She wasn't sure if turning it off or putting it in airplane mode was enough. She'd throw it out the window, but there were some contact numbers on there that she might need.

With no access to the internet, Juliette couldn't look for directions.

There were never any public phones around anymore, so she couldn't make a phone call. Who would she call? Everyone she knew was far away in the United States. Her grandmother, here in France, had denied her existence. And Juliette didn't know anyone else in Europe. She knew very few people in America. Her father was basically her whole world since the accident. The nurses and the audiologists, the physical therapists. She had no close friends. No girlfriends.

Juliette had mourned that. She wanted friends. But she was of such an age that friends didn't come easily. Especially when you had very little to give to a friendship. She had no past to share, nothing that made her interesting. No special hobbies. Toby, her stability dog, gave her an opportunity to talk to strangers. But other than that, Juliette lived in books. She imagined herself to be one of the characters and walked in their shoes. Books gave her freedoms that her body preempted.

No, there was no one, other than her father, that she knew well enough to call and ask them to send her some money.

Her father.

That's whom she *should* call.

But a seed had been planted in her head at her childhood apartment when the concierge had said David DuBois was gay. It had germinated at her grandmother's when even the possibility of Juliette's existing was denied. The flash of the Russian men calling her doctor. Her. Doctor. And not the flat picture memory, an *actual* memory.

The only person she told about going to Toulouse was the voice mail she'd left her dad, and, of course, she told her caregiver who lived with her. How would the Russian men be able to find her in France? Why did they want to find her in France? Where had they been taking her? And to what end?

It seemed that at least some of the stories her father had told her, and that she had believed to be true, simply weren't true. She'd never lived on Rue de Tourneur. She'd never played in her grandmother's yard and eaten her tart tatin.

How staggering a revelation was that?

For the first time, Juliette didn't trust anyone or anything.

She'd have to depend on herself.

What she needed was a plan. And the first step was to get away from the Russian men. They were her imminent threat.

Juliette had exchanged very little money when she'd arrived last night. Her wallet held just enough cash for taxis and a quick bite at a café. The rest she had assumed she'd put on her credit card.

Credit cards could be traced, too. But that was by really bad people.

The Russian men were evil. They'd probably be able to follow her credit card. She'd have to assume they could and that they had use of other kinds of technology, too.

They might even be able to follow this car. It wasn't brand new, but it looked like it was new enough that it would have a computer system that could track it.

The why of all this, that was the confusing part.

There must be a reason.

All right. Okay. She'd assume that one way or another, the kidnappers or the police knew where she was. Someone knew. Should she actually try to go to the police?

Juliette didn't know why, but that seemed like a mistake.

She was going to trust her gut. It was about all she had right now as a way of finding a course of action.

Her gut told her that the kidnappers would know where she was, and they would be right behind her. What she should do is give them a single place to look while she got herself together. They'd pinpoint her there at a single spot, but if she was quick enough, she could get away. And she'd have the supplies she needed to help her succeed.

Cash was a top priority.

Clothes. The books always did that —had their characters change clothing right away. And put on a hat and sunglasses. It was an overcast day and getting late. She shouldn't go the sunglasses route.

The main thing, when trying to escape, was to blend. She'd read the novels where the women had cut off their long hair and dyed it a different color. She could do that, but it seemed to her that those characters were always spotted and recognized. If she'd already cut off her hair and colored it, she wouldn't have any other way to obscure her look.

She pulled up to a shopping area. Staring down the street, she saw the stores where she could go and equip herself. Juliette mapped a path. The electronics shop. The luggage shop for a backpack or such. Her things were still back at her hotel in Toulouse, along with her computer.

She stared down the street, making a mental map and notes of how she'd progress forward without needing to backtrack. A solid plan to stand on. Something that might still her vertigo. After she got a backpack, she'd cross the street for some clothes. Next to that, three doors down, a shoe shop for some tennis shoes, these heels were a stupid mistake. There was a cafe just beyond and a pharmacy for a quick grab of toiletries. All of it put on her debit card.

She scrawled a quick note for the owner.

I'm so sorry to have put you through this. Forgive me. I

was kidnapped and running for my safety. You saved my life. I will always be appreciative and hold you in prayer.

Juliette put that note in the glove compartment with the keys. She left the car unlocked when she climbed out. She didn't bother trying to hide her face. If there was someone watching her on cameras, they'd know where she was going. She thought that was probably a good plan. The car was here; why not get caught on camera? That way, when she decided to disappear, it would be a change in tactic, and it might confuse them. It might give her a little extra precious time.

She shut the car door and walked with faltering steps toward the shop for her phone. If she was only able to do one task, this was the one that was most important.

Juliette decided that she'd get the maximum cash back with each purchase. Then, she'd get out of the area, one way or another. They'd probably expect her to go back to Toulouse to gather her things. Maybe they'd expect her to head straight back to America. Surely if she could get to Paris, she could fly to any place in the world. She just needed to pick a safe place to go.

Juliette pushed through the door into the electronics store. She brushed her hair behind her ears and looked around. The girl behind the counter glanced up from her phone.

"I'm pressed for time. Would you mind helping me?" Juliette asked in French. She reached out to grab hold of the shelving unit. "Whew, excuse me, I'm a little dizzy."

The girl's gaze traveled down to Juliette's boots and back up to her face.

Juliette knew the mud was readily visible on the wet knees of her jeans, though she'd brushed off the leaves and debris from her crawl through the ditch on her way to steal the car. She probably looked drunk...or crazy. The service vest her dog Toby wore announcing her disability was usually enough to take away those judgments. Right now, filthy and disoriented, well, she'd be memorable, that was for sure.

Probably the most expedient way to get out of there was for Juliette to say exactly what she needed to this girl and see if she was helpful. Juliette could always run right back out the door.

"I'm in a big hurry. I'm traveling in France for a short time, and I need a phone I can use while I'm here. A prepaid phone. And a tablet, please."

The girl hesitated for a moment, her gaze sweeping over the storefront window.

"Okay." The girl rounded the counter. She was probably a teenager. She was short and thin with mousy brown hair and an overbite. She wore a pair of ill-fitting jeans and a T-shirt with some game logo. "The tablet needs to be connected to Wi-Fi to work unless you just need it for word processing or plugging in a memory stick."

"Oh." Juliette hadn't thought of that. "I do need to access the Internet."

The girl had moved to the door and was searching the streets, and Juliette didn't know what to make of it.

"Look," she said. "You can get to a Wi-Fi signal privately with a hot spot."

Juliette got the feeling that this girl had some background in working around the system.

"You can buy a thirty-day prepaid on the hotspot that's secure," she said more slowly, enunciating more clearly. Obviously, taking Juliette's confused expression to be a language barrier.

"Secure?" Juliette asked.

"Private. Not traceable."

"Okay. Can I get the phone, the tablet, and the hot spot,

please?" She pulled out her wallet and fished out a credit card while the girl walked around the store, gathering things.

When the girl walked back to the counter to lay the boxes down, she eyed the credit card.

"You know," she said. "There's an ATM two doors down in the *tabac.*" She pointed to the right. "Cash is always good. That and prepaid credit cards." She tapped the display next to her register with plastic cards that read *Joyeux Anniversaire* and *Félicitations*! "When you pay in cash, it's hard to tell which customer bought which thing."

Juliette was torn about what this girl was telling her. Perhaps, she realized Juliette was on the run, and she wanted time to call the police. She could be getting Juliette out of the store, so she could lock the door. She could also realize that Juliette was scared and in trouble and be helping her. Surely, Juliette wasn't the first one to come into the store looking for anonymity. They had a whole wall of prepaid phones available.

Juliette decided that getting to the bank machine was the best route. She hadn't even considered that before. She held up a finger and spun to walk out of the store.

Turning right, walking two storefronts, Juliette pushed through the door of the *tabac* into a dark, cramped space. At the counter, a man was scrolling through his phone and barely looked up when the bells tinkled on the door, announcing her entry. Juliette moved to the ATM. She'd let the bank know before she left the US that she'd be traveling overseas. Hopefully, this would work.

She slipped her card into the slot and waited for the prompts. Here, unlike in the US, there wasn't a list of amounts to choose from increasing in twenty-dollar increments. There was simply a place to type the amount in. Perhaps there wasn't a limit here like there was in the States.

This credit card was connected to her father's account. Juliette didn't have an income; she was completely financially dependent on her dad. An invalid unable to drive, unable to concentrate, unable to do her work as a veterinarian's assistant.

How much money should she take? A lot. Enough to get her out of France. She processed quickly. The machine only held so much money. How much should she try for? She decided on two thousand euro. Just over two thousand American dollars. Her dad would understand. He'd be glad that she did this to stay safe.

Juliette put the amount in, entered her PIN number, and held her breath.

After a moment, there was a whir, and the machine moved the money into the drop.

With a shaking hand, Juliette pulled the pile out. She gave the man a quick glance to make sure he was still engrossed. The man at the cash register was busily tapping a text message; he hadn't noticed what she was up to.

Juliette shoved the wad into her waistband under her turtleneck sweater.

As she hustled out of the door, Juliette decided to use cash for the rest of her purchases, so no one would know the supplies she'd collected. But the prepaid cards were a good idea, too. After all, they said Visa and Master Card on them. There weren't many motels that allowed people to stay just by handing them cash.

With a hand on the wall to help her stay steady, Juliette made her way back to purchase the electronics and the access they'd give her to options. Even if the girl had locked the door to the shop, Juliette had cash.

Money meant choices.

Money was power.

_____

14

THORN
    Brussels, Belgium
    Saturday, Sixteen Twenty-six Hours

    Find Juliette – or your country will suffer. We all will.

THORN STARED at the message written on the mirror. His reflex was to think that Brigitte was trying to split their forces or pull him off the right trail.

That was surely possible.

Thorn had to assume that the conversation he'd had with Brigitte was compromised. He didn't think that the DGSE had time to wire the room, but who knew? His guess was that she'd have comms open on her phone and that she heard directives from her own set of listening devices in her ear canals. That being true, and he had no doubts about it, she had to find another way to communicate with him. Something that wouldn't be seen or heard by her support team.

If she was trying to pull his mission sideways, she'd just say it. Whisper it in his ear at some point. Support would pick it up and high five her on her subterfuge when she got back to her base. But she'd printed it on the mirror in soap. She'd steamed up the bathroom.

Brigitte would have assumed he'd go in and wash up after having sex.

If this was a ploy, she was a master of her craft.

Thorn jumped under the shower, toweled off, and pulled his clothes back on.

Dressed, Thorn went downstairs and found an empty conference room. He snuck in and sat at the table to pull up an encrypted connection with Panther Force war room.

Nutsbe okayed the connection. "You look like a man who's had some stress relief. You were offline for a long time. She must be a happy woman."

"Did my best. I'm about to send you pictures."

"Seriously, Dude? I'd rather not see you getting your rocks off."

"Dream on." Thorn clicked a couple of keys. "What do you think that is?" He sent the images of the bathroom mirror, opaque with fog except for the message.

"Looks like she soaped you a love note on the bathroom mirror. That's very old-school. You wash it off?"

"Yes, Mom. Here's the question. Why go old-school? We were talking fairly freely. Why didn't she just write it down or tell me?" He paused. "When she got in my car, you heard her. She knew my name, my affiliation, my hotel, and the driving instructions. That room has got to be under surveillance."

"I have support directed your way," Nutsbe said. "I was just waiting for you to check in with us, so he didn't come a-knockin' while you had things a-rockin.' They'll sweep the room. And I'm adding it to my to-do list to run a computer search of the amateur porn sites, see if someone tries to make some extra cash on the intel they collected. I hope you were giving it your best effort. I'd hate for you to have embarrassed yourself."

"The quality will depend on the camera angle," Thorn said. "Now, to answer my own question, why would she pass it that way? Answer – surveillance. Another answer would be that she wanted me to think she was giving me a gift, and she was routing me somewhere. She wanted me to go – some kind of smoke and mirrors trick. Well, steam and mirrors, in this case."

"I'll research it and get back to you. You need to go back upstairs. You're about to get a knock on your door. Change into the new clothes support is bringing you. Take the new equipment. I've programmed your route into the texts. I'm taking you offline, and there will be no connection until Honey announces you've arrived at the safe house."

"Affirmative. I'm on it. But can you grab hold of Margot?" Thorn ran through Brigitte's connection with Margot – all the details that Brigitte had shared.

"This is getting interesting," Nutsbe said. "I'll get on that. You need to move."

UPSTAIRS, the sweep team was waiting for Thorn. As they checked the room, Thorn heard their equipment pinging success. He turned to look at the gizmo in the sweeper's fingers. So all that had ended up on a video somewhere, hopefully, Nutsbe would find it if it hit the web – and hopefully, Nutsbe wouldn't use it against him at some future stag party.

Thorn wasn't shy as he stood in the middle of the room — out of the sweepers' way — pulling on his new clothes. He hefted the new duffle onto his shoulder. He took his passport and ID and stuck them in the new wallet with the new cash and credit cards, and secured them into the pocket of his new jacket. The fit wasn't perfect, but it would do. He pulled up the first text directive: **Exit east door.**

They had him following a circuitous route through malls and metros, in cabs, and buses. Now, finally, he was hoofing it up a hill where he saw the car Gage had driven when he'd separated from his fellow Panther Force teammates. It was parked on a corner, ready to jump in and go.

The house number he was looking for was half a block down. He jogged up the stairs to the front door, and Gage let him in. Thorn's head turned as he took in the layout of the small townhouse: living room, dining room, kitchen, a set of stairs to the left. Two doors to the right. He opened the first one, coat closet. He turned the knob on the second; it was locked. "Where's Dr. DuBois?" Thorn asked. A flush of the toilet behind the door answered that for him. "How's that going?"

Gage rolled his eyes.

Ah, so the good doctor was non-cooperative and untrustworthy. They'd need to keep a hand on his shoulder. "He been in their long?"

"International flights can do that to you," Gage said wryly.

Thorn made his way into the kitchen, where Honey was stirring a pot of spaghetti sauce. Thorn still hadn't eaten. Was still famished from earlier. He was clapping Honey on the shoulder when glass breaking in the front of the house had him spinning on his heels.

A brick skittered across the wooden floor in a veil of shards. A black canister flew the same path. "Flashbang!" he yelled as the smoke filled the room. He covered his ears, squeezed his eyes tightly shut, and hunkered down against the wall as the explosive went *BOOM*!

Even with a second to get himself in position, Thorn was off balance from the assault on his senses. His hand on the wall, he moved past where Gage was throwing a shoulder against the bathroom door, trying to break in and grab hold of DuBois.

Thorn was deaf except for the high pitch shrill of his eardrums. Coughing on the smoke that filled his lungs and made his eyes water, at the end of the hall, Thorn dropped to a knee and reflexively reached for his non-existent gun. *Damn it.*

Someone was banging a breacher's ram into the front door. But it was reinforced, giving them the time they needed. Every second counted.

Thorn turned to give Gage a hand as he wrangled Dr. DuBois down the hall toward the kitchen. The two of them forced DuBois out the back door.

DuBois was fighting like a madman, wind-milling his arms and refusing to walk. Gage clocked him in the jaw with his famous right hook, and DuBois crumpled to the ground. Thorn caught the guy around the ankles and pressed forward toward the garden gate with Gage struggling backward, holding the man under the arms.

The sound of sirens, swirling their way from the distance, was no comfort. They were, in fact, kidnapping the scientist. No amount of "By contract…" would help them in court, especially if their contractor refused to step forward and reveal their letters.

They passed out of the gate where Honey was pummeling the Tibor guy. So, it was the Omega crew that had found the safe house, not Brigitte and the DGSE.

Out of the corner of his eye, Thorn saw Honey's lips moving as he yelled. Thorn still wasn't hearing clearly − his senses still had him reeling from the explosives. But something heavy left Honey's hand and came tumbling through the air in his direction. Thorn's hand shot out and snagged the Glock that Honey must have wrestled from Tibor. With another blow from Honey's massive fist, Tibor was out for the count.

Thorn covered the team while Gage dragged DuBois. They made it to the alley. An old-fashioned car sat rusted and tiny but unlocked at the house next door. Gage shoved DuBois in the back while Thorn crouched at the driver's side. There, Thorn quickly hotwired what looked like their only means of escape. Honey piled into the front seat just as the engine caught.

They were crammed in like sardines – no, more like a damned clown car, rolling down the hill. Thorn shoved his foot to the floorboard, almost standing on the pedal, but the car had no oomph. Thorn thought if it weren't for gravity, they'd be going nowhere. "We need a different strategy," Thorn called over the coughs and wheezing of the engine and the tinnitus that made communication a challenge.

"You were followed?" Gage yelled from the backseat. He held DuBois's head in an armlock to keep him still.

"Hell no, I wasn't followed. What the fuck was he doing in the can that long? Did you take his phone away from him?" Thorn yelled over his shoulder.

Gage patted DuBois down and came up with a cell phone.

DuBois's fight kicked up again, and Honey reached his massive paw around and stilled him under his grip.

"Son of a bitch," Gage spat out. "They texted him. He was in there telling them how to find us."

"They're one down – the guy in the garden has a broken kneecap," Honey said. "Anyone see Hong Wu or Colburn?"

"I didn't. If they positioned Tibor out back," Thorn said, "the other two were probably coming in from the front. Surprise, guns, and a willing, participating asshole hiding in a known location, and it should have been an easy snatch and go. The car had to be coming down the hill because I walked up from the bus stop. I didn't see anyone coming."

"So processing the shit show, my guess is they ran through the house, got eyes on our direction of travel, gathered up Tibor and got him to the car and away from the cops, drove down to the next cross street, and around the corner. That takes time."

"Their vehicle probably goes faster than a scooter," Honey pointed out.

Thorn lifted his foot and stomped down again, hoping for a burst of energy from the engine. He got a backfire and a wheeze. "We need to ditch this car."

"And do what with this sack of shit?" Gage asked.

"Hand him over to DGSE," Thorn said. He didn't mean it, but he wanted DuBois to know that was indeed an option.

"Here we go," Gage said as a black car roared down the hillside and rammed them from behind, pushing them out into the intersection and spinning them in place. Horns blared; brakes squealed as those around him tried to make way.

Thorn had his eye on the left road and spun his steering wheel in the direction of their rotation, felt the mechanism align with the tires, and brought them around. Only then did Thorn put his foot back on the pedal and push them forward. They drove down the new hill, all of them leaning forward as if that might give the car some small advantage.

Nutsbe was suddenly in his ear. "Right, then next right, then second left."

They *kathunked* over a pothole, and Thorn did his best to keep them ahead of the black car that was back in his rearview mirror.

He took the next right-hand turn—another right. Then

wheezed down to the second left, wondering how Nutsbe had devised to save their asses.

Thorn came to a sudden stop, jerking the car into a space directly in front of the police station.

The black car skated by with no stopping room.

"That was Hong Wu driving with his middle finger raised," Honey said.

"Sit tight," Nutsbe said, "we have support almost to you."

"Make it fast." Thorn drummed impatient fingers on the steering wheel as the men in uniform eyed their car from across the street.

"Wu is circling the block," Nutsbe said. "Right behind him is our van. White van, man with a red bandana tied around his head. When he pulls flush, you dive in."

"Copy," they said in unison.

Hong Wu made his pass and pulled to a stop just ahead of them in a loading zone. The passenger door popped open. Two policemen headed over to flag them away.

Sure enough, here was the van.

"You give me any trouble, and I'm going to punch you in the jaw again," Gage said, gathering a fist full of DuBois's shirt collar. Dubois's jaw was visibly swollen, and he was holding it shut with his hand. Thorn guessed it was probably broken. Either way, he had to be in a world of hurt because he exited the car meekly and got into the van.

Thorn piled in behind him.

As he left the car, Honey tucked a wad of euros into the car's glove compartment to pay for any repairs and to compensate the owner for the hassle along with the keys.

"In," Honey breathed into his mic as the door slid shut, and they took off driving just as the police hailed them to stop. The driver smiled and waved as if he misunderstood the gesture.

"Where are we heading?" Thorn asked, his words were a breath over his windpipe. The computer would feed the sound to his teammates. They could speak in privacy even within the confines of the van, and the listening ears of that rat DuBois.

"Your driver is going to drop you off at the hotel just ahead," Nutsbe advised. "The guy in a gray hoody and black sweats will hand you a key to room 601. Leave DuBois in the van."

The van pulled flush with the curb.

The man stepped up and handed them the key. The team unloaded. The hoody guy climbed into the back of the van with DuBois and slammed the door shut.

15

Brussels, Belgium
Saturday, Eighteen Forty-four Hours

"GLAD THAT'S OVER," Gage said as the three walked into the hotel and right over to the elevator.

Thorn reached out and pressed the up arrow.

"We have someone meeting you with your duffels and passports that were secured from the safe house. The housekeeper sent it with their courier. Even though that leg of the trip is done, the mission is not over. We're regrouping and reassigning."

They stepped onto the elevator and waited for the door to shut before they all said, "Roger that."

"Anything come of that message I passed you?" Thorn asked, tapping the number-six button.

"Our support team discovered your hotel room was not only under surveillance – it was basically a movie studio, it had so many cameras. I'd say at least one of them caught you at a good angle. I'll let you know if you show up on YouTube in all your glory."

"You do that, brother." Thorn laughed.

They piled out of the elevator car and moved down to their room

"What glory is this?" It was a female voice, Lynx.

"Morning, Lynx," Honey said.

"We just edged past noon here in DC. I was having lunch with Nutsbe and Margot and decided to stick my nose where it doesn't belong."

"I asked her to come along for the ride," Margot said.

"Good that you're there." Thorn followed Honey into the nineteen-eighties-style room, done up in shades French blue and cranberry.

Honey moved to the table and pulled his laptop from his bag. He started working on a video connection with the war room.

"Honey's going to bring you up on a video feed. Two seconds. In the meantime, I have some questions for you."

"Yes," Margot responded. "And I have some answers for you. Let me dive in while we wait. Brigitte is not with the DGSE."

"I figured." Thorn pulled one of the chairs from under the table and sat down. He planted his forearms on widespread knees. His eyes rested on his laced hands, but his focus was strictly on Margot. "I assume Brigitte isn't her name either."

"Her name is Adele Gutterman. She's with the Mossad."

"Crap." Israeli intelligence. Thorn wiped the back of his hand across his nose. "Was she born in Paris?"

"No, she was passing code on to me. First, I don't talk about you. I've never called any of you Bear, Brain, or Thor."

"I kind of liked that. *Thor.*" Thorn chuckled.

"I never talked about your diet, except for the pie. That

discussion we had here at Iniquus was repeated back to my friend in a public sphere. Obviously, the Mossad is interested in Iniquus – especially the Panther Force, but that only makes sense since we've had some of their citizens in our crosshairs since last February when KIA operators came to life as the Rex Deus and attacked Gage's fiancée, Zoe. I apologize for talking about you outside of our campus. It was probably the key to making you feel, uhm…so comfortable with her."

Thorn skipped over that. "She was passing you code? Can you go into that?"

"She said we were neighbors in Paris. That was a reference to a covert op. That I 'left at ten' meant I completed that assignment and moved on after we took down a cell of ten. It was her verifying her identity."

"And you used to take baths with her?" Thorn asked.

"Here we go. You're on video now." Honey said.

The men slid closer to the screen, so the camera could pick up their faces.

"The bath part refers to a classified mission detail," Margot replied from her place in front of the computer in the Panther Force war room. "She told you I was allergic to rabbit fur, strawberries, and the color pink. A rabbit is someone who is on the run, strawberries are for the color red or blood, it tells me that they are injured or ill, the color pink, it's a female."

"She wants me to go after Juliette DuBois. We were told that Juliette was kidnapped. I gave Nutsbe the timeline that Brigitte/Adele told me."

"Just keep calling her Brigitte for now in case you run into her again. You don't want to get mixed up. The police gave our client a copy of the video of Juliette being kidnapped," Nutsbe said. "I'll upload it onto your phones in case you see any of the players as your team moves forward. The police said that the grandmother and the grandmother's caregiver both denied having seen David Dubois or a woman that fits Juliette's description. We *believe* Juliette's still missing. Assuming she's the pink rabbit, she's injured. Keep that in the back of your minds. She may not be ambulatory."

"It sounds like the Mossad know why someone wanted to scoop up Juliette," Margot put in. "It also sounds like what you thought. Brigitte was passing you intel, so you could pursue it. The question now is, why would she want that? We've just started our research. From our end, the DuBois security case came through, and we put you right on it. We thought it would be cut and run. An easy task that would hold you over in Europe for an extra day. Obviously, that's not the case."

"Allergic to pink, huh?" Lynx laughed, brushing her hand over the sleeve of her rose-colored dress. It looked soft and very feminine, and Lynx wore it on purpose, like a uniform. At Iniquus, the workspaces were industrial and efficient. The teams wore gray tactical pants and gunmetal compressions shirts. The support staff wore shades of gray and black. The executives, too, chose their suits in gray and black with subdued ties.

The only flash of color was Lynx.

The only soft spot at headquarters was Lynx.

And time and again, she had been such a soft spot amongst the hard and unyielding that mouths that had been clamped shut opened to spill secrets.

Thorn always liked it when Lynx came along for the ride. She was a good cook. And he wasn't thinking about her skills in the kitchen. He was thinking about her case-solving skill sets. She'd take a pinch of this and a dash of that. Things that had nothing to do, one with the other. She'd add them to the bowl. She'd mix, bake, and there it would be, something completely different than how things had started – an outcome that had been unexpected. Another crime solved. It never ceased to amaze him. And while she was a member of the Strike Force team, Thorn was glad that something about this case had intrigued her enough to walk down the hall to the Panther Force war room and take a look.

Thorn felt in his bones that this wasn't a run of the mill operation. This was bigger, badder, more complicated than anything they'd expected, especially after their assignment was to watch a guy get off one plane, covertly secure him overnight, and see he got on the redeye in the morning.

It was an odd set of feelings that were moving through his system. He'd never even met Juliette. But in the photo... Her eyes... The idea that someone might harm her boiled his blood. That she was the rabbit – hurt or sick?

Yeah, this mission felt different to him.

Dangerously personal.

He focused again on Lynx. She wasn't saying a word. Her eyes had lost their softness. The laughter that was usually part of her joy in solving the case puzzles was gone. Her brows had pulled tight. She was looking through the camera straight into his eyes, reading him like he was a book. She paused for a long moment, completely still. He could see the engine of her mind was humming. "Okay," she said. She nodded her head, pulling her lips in. "Okay. I get that. I understand."

"Get what?" Nutsbe asked.

Lynx turned toward Nutsbe and wagged her hand through the air as if batting away his question. It was the same question that Thorn had. She *got* what?

Understood what?

Lynx was renowned for her ability to read truth on faces, and she had obviously seen something convincing on his.

If she understood that this woman was boiling through his

system, that he was desperate to get to her and help her, well, that was his job.

This was more than his job, and Thorn knew it.

And now, apparently, Lynx knew it, too.

He might even be afraid that she'd talk to Titus about his personal investment and get Thorn replaced on the mission, but instead of answering Nutsbe's question about what she "got," she said, "Juliette isn't the bait the way Iniquus was briefed at the intake. I wonder if they've known all along that she's in play. Rabbit, strawberries, pink. She's hurt. She needs help. We need to check in with the client. Are we authorized to do this?"

16

JULIETTE
   Orléans, France
   Saturday, 7:05 p.m.

JULIETTE DRANK a cup of coffee and popped a pain pill. She'd already paid the check. Looking out the window, she felt relief that the sun was fading. Nightfall would soon give her another layer of safety. Her next moves weren't apparent. Juliette had much preferred it when she had a list of items to accomplish. She was empowered with each checkmark on her mental list. But now she only had two things left – change her clothes and get to Paris. Well, three, stay out of the clutches of the Russian men. Okay, four, try to figure out what was happening to her.

The waiter swung by her table, depositing a white paper bag with her to-go order of dinner, then spun to the four-top of women who began placing their orders.

Juliette picked up the bag and moved to the ladies' room.

There, she braided her hair and tucked the bottom underneath to hide its length. She topped this with a wide black headband, hoping to camouflage the color of her hair a bit. Digging into her backpack, Juliette tugged out the newly purchased pair of ripped jeans and a T-shirt, some socks, and a pair of Converses. She was trying to match the look of the girl in the electronics store. A teen from a middle-class household. She'd even bought a used textbook from the secondhand bookstore next to the pharmacy.

She used the acetone to remove her nail polish then cut her nails short. Her sapphire and diamond earrings went into her wallet along with her rings. After scrubbing her face free of makeup, Juliette searched the mirror. She didn't know if it would be enough. It depended on the training of the men following her and if they had support.

Her last addition was a large zippered black hoody. Juliette figured it could help her disappear once it grew darker.

Rolling her dirty clothes up tightly, she stashed them back in the backpack with her boots. In went the textbook. In went the dinner bag and water bottle. She put a couple hundred euros in her back pocket. The rest of her money stack, her wallet, old cell phone, and passport she stowed in a small purse that she clipped around her waist and hid with the baggy clothing. If she lost these items... Well, she'd be lost.

Zipped into the hoody, Juliette hung the school-sized backpack off one shoulder and exited into the narrow hallway, where a line of females stood looking perturbed at her lengthy hoarding of the bathroom. Juliette avoided their eyes.

Shadowing the kitchen boy as he carried the trash out the back door to the alley, Juliette yanked the hoody up over her head before he could turn around and focus on her. As she sauntered away, on what she hoped looked like a teenager's lope, she could feel his gaze on her back. Would he remember her?

Out on the street.

Now for Paris.

The train, according to the website, left at 22h – 10:00 p.m. She thought it would be stupid to wait that long. Since it was the next train out, the men would assume she'd be on it. And if they caught her on the train itself, she'd be trapped with no chance of escape.

There were no buses available. She didn't have a license to rent a car. She was at a loss for how to move forward.

Even walking down the street was a problem for Juliette. She was swaying and staggering like a drunk as she caught her balance. Though, things *had* improved a bit since she'd changed her high-heeled boots for the tennis shoes.

Juliette had brought the boots, purchased on a whim, as a kind of symbol of her wish to be okay. To be the kind of person who could wear heels and look fashionable. And this morning, she'd pulled them on and pranced around her hotel room to see how she'd do.

Surprisingly, she seemed to do okay despite the fever that warmed her face and the headache that pounded steadily at her temple. She'd decided she'd keep them on to look chic, thinking her style would help her make a good impression, should good impressions be required.

But as the odd experiences mounted, as her anxiety climbed, so did her symptoms.

The headache and vertigo were making her head swim.

Juliette headed back to the pharmacy to buy a pair of crutches. There were pros and cons to every single decision she was making. Each choice felt like it could have life or death implications. When she'd gone into the store earlier to buy her toiletries, she'd considered getting a walker like the one she'd used prior to getting Toby. But talk about a blazing sign, "Ding! Ding! Ding! Here she is." So, she'd rejected it. Juliette had thought about getting a cane, maybe two. But walkers and canes were the things that older people use. If a teenager had them — and Juliette dearly hoped she looked that part — then that teen would be memorable.

While she ate, Juliette had decided the crutches were her best option. They'd help with stability, and they might be helpful in other ways, too. In America, if someone seemed enfeebled by an injury, kind strangers reached out to help. Juliette wasn't sure that would be the case here in France. She couldn't remember the character of the French people from when she lived here as a little girl – or anything else about France for that matter.

Crutches could also be used as a weapon. That was a dilemma. They might help her. But they might also be used against her.

She was going to chance it. She didn't really have a choice.

In the pharmacy, a woman rang up the purchase without looking at her, accepted Juliette's cash with an air of boredom, and handed the crutches over with a receipt.

Juliette took a moment to adjust the crutch height, put her backpack over both shoulders, and hopped her way out of the store, hood up, and wondering where she should go next.

She took out her phone. The girl in the tech store had made sure all of her purchases were user ready. It was nice of her. Juliette was dexterous when it came to technology, but her mind was on other things, obviously.

She thought any hotel or hostel would be found quickly and easily by any bad guy since she'd have to present not only a credit card but her passport as she registered.

Juliette typed "*films*" into the search bar on the browser. Movie theaters were cool and dark. Juliette could hide in there. She could buy tickets for movies that would take her all the way until they closed. Then maybe find a *boite de nuit* close by. After all, it was a Saturday, and the club scene should be in full swing. It would be easy to hide there in the darkness until morning. But the idea of trying to sleep in the corner of a nightclub with its dance floor strobing and the music vibrating low sound waves through the room almost made Juliette vomit.

She tapped the walk icon to bring up a path and turned up the volume before sticking her phone back in her hoody pocket to free up her hands for the crutches. Following the instructions, Juliette made her way toward the movie theater, hoping she could find a film that was low-testosterone and would be as quiet as possible.

She *catchunked* the crutches forward and then walked up to align herself with them before she *catchunked* them out again. The crutches gave her a reason to move slowly. And they did help quite a bit with stability.

Three blocks, then a left turn brought her into a busy square populated with small clusters of friends.

Juliette stood in line to buy a ticket to the next film but still had a while to wait before it started. She moved over to a bench where a group of teens was hanging out. Maybe they wouldn't mind. Maybe she'd look like she belonged with them.

They were a pretty dull group.

There wasn't a lot of conversation as they pecked away on their phones.

She latched on to the part where one of the guys said he had his mother's car and that she was working nightshift. Juliette stored that piece of information away.

Juliette had her phone out and pulled up a YouTube of someone playing a computer game. She thought that was what a teen might do while waiting. It might make her less conspicuous. She couldn't look at the screen though, it made her vertigo worse. Instead, she peeked from under her hood to watch the comings and goings in the square — to see if two burly Russians would barrel in to find her.

Juliette waited until the group gathered up to move to the theater. She pulled the hoody from her head and snagged the guy's arm — the one who had mentioned having a car and no parent waiting for him at home.

He turned his head toward her, and she smiled. "*Ciao.*"

"*Bonsoir,*" he replied, pulling his hands from his pockets and smoothing down the front of his T-shirt.

His pals had stopped and turned back to see what he was doing. Juliette hadn't let go of the guy's arm, hadn't dropped her smile. She worked to get the pain out of her eyes and to look kind.

"I'll catch up with you in a second," he said, waving them on. And once they were out of earshot, he asked, "Do I know you?"

Her crutch slipped from under her arm, and he stooped to pick it up for her.

"*Merci.* I was wondering if you might like to make some money," she said.

"I don't want anything to do with drugs." He put up two hands as if to ward her off.

"Really?" Juliette found that oddly disconcerting. "I look like I'm a dealer?"

"We're in the square, and you're offering me a way to make money."

"I need a ride, that's all." Juliette countered. "I'd pay you for your time and gas." She pulled two hundred euros from her pocket. "I need to get to Paris. My family is facing an emergency. The next train isn't for hours yet."

"That's a lot of money to get to Paris." He searched around

for some cues as to why she would approach him and offer this money.

Juliette decided to play the tourist card. "Is this a lot of money?" She stared down at the bills in her hand. "I just arrived yesterday. I'm not used to the currency. Last time I was here, I used francs. But I need to get to Paris immediately. I need to find a flight home. I'm glad to pay you this if you could take me to the airport."

He nodded as he said, "A foreigner, I can tell from your accent." The young man looked around again, weighed the situation. "You've been sitting next to us for a while…"

"I was trying to figure out what to do next. I was upset to learn there are so few trains to Paris. I don't have anyone here to ask for help, and to be honest, I wanted some time to figure out if you were a nice person. It's frightening for a woman to climb into a strange man's car."

That last piece of information seemed to make sense to the guy. He stuck out his hand. "Jean-Luc," he said. "I can get you to Paris. My car is just over here." He pulled out his phone and sent a group text. **Looks like I'm gonna get lucky**. He showed it to her. "I need a reason to leave my friends."

"As long as you know, I just need an emergency ride to the airport."

"*Compris*," understood, he said. "This way."

Jean-Luc walked slowly beside her as she made her way to the car. Every once in a while, his hand would shoot out, and he'd grab her shoulder to right her.

"I had an accident," she said. "It's not been a very fun trip to your beautiful country." Juliette was having trouble with her eyesight. Things were swimming.

After helping her into the front seat, Jean-Luc rounded the

front of his car, climbed in, and started the engine. "*Charles De Gaulle Airport, oui*?"

"Please."

He started the engine and twisted a knob. Soothing notes filled the car. "My mother." He pointed toward the radio. "This helps after a night at work at the hospital. *Ça va*? This is good for you?"

"*Oui. Ça va. Merci bien.*" Juliette handed him the money. Now, she'd have to hope for the best. She wasn't sure she could stay awake through the drive. She'd have to trust this stranger.

Juliette put her hand to her head and felt the heat. The fever was worse. There was a thermometer in her bag, but she was afraid to check the number. It had started up just as her plane had taken off from D.C. She wasn't sick, per se. It was just another side effect in a long list of side effects. But if this pain took on its normal trajectory, she'd be in bad shape soon.

Being on the run, hiding from boogeymen, Juliette decided, was not an easy thing for anyone without proper training. And here she was, probably one of the least able people to keep herself at a distance.

Here she was scrambling for survival when she couldn't even take care of herself in her normal day-to-day life.

In America, her father had arranged for Roxanne to be her home companion. On days when the world was a dizzy mess, Roxanne would help Juliette get herself to the bathroom, helped her dress, made sure she ate, made sure Juliette had a bucket for when a meal didn't stay down, made sure she was safe.

On good days, when Juliette could get around on her own, Roxanne would spend the day writing. She was a novelist who wrote sweet romances. Roxanne wrote the stories where she could live vicariously through her characters and be beautiful and beloved, swept off her feet, and have great sacrifices made in her name. It was Roxanne's reading her manuscripts out loud and talking about her characters that had inspired Juliette to try on the mantle of thriller-hero – someone who knew what to do to get out of a mess.

As a veterinarian's assistant, Juliette wouldn't have any of the necessary skills in her muscle memory. Juliette had decided to make-believe, gathering her strength from characters who were vital and strong. Characters who survived. Those who ran successfully to the finish at the end of their plot lines.

Juliette thought about Roxanne and Toby back at the house her dad had bought for her on the Virginia-side of Washington D.C. They were probably curled up right now in front of a fire, Roxanne drinking a cup of tea and snuggling up with Toby curled at her feet as she read over her project.

Her dad was probably nursing a glass of scotch as he flipped through the newest medical journals. He lived a few miles away in the city proper. She saw him at least once a week when he picked her up to take her into work with him at his laboratory at Montrim, where he had a DARPA lab.

There, he'd check on her progress.

Since he was the foremost scientist in stress disorders and brain injuries, Juliette knew that if anything could be done to make her better, it would happen. She was the fortunate survivor who got the cutting-edge care not yet available in mainstream medicine.

And that gave her hope.

It helped her in her darkest moments when she simply couldn't stand her brain anymore. The times when she thought that she'd had enough suffering for one lifetime, and she just wanted some peace.

The dark moments when nothing at all mattered.

When all she wanted was for the pain to stop.

17

THORN
Brussels, Belgium
Saturday, Nineteen Fifteen Hours

HONEY FOLLOWED behind Thorn and Gage as they walked through the door of room 601 at the hotel, straight over to the table where Honey, once again, propped his phone after he opened a video link with his encryption capabilities.

"Good, you're back," Nutsbe said by way of greeting. "I hope you had a good dinner because we're about to get you moving again. Time is uber tight, so strap in. Lynx?"

"Thank you." Lynx gave him a nod. "Okay, guys, we have a contract in place. But the suits upstairs want me to remind you all that foreign soil means foreign laws. We can't help you with warrants and such. It is expected that you will conduct yourself in ways that are befitting your positions, will serve the United States, and will not get you into trouble while abroad." She paused. "That said, we certainly do have a mystery on our hands.

Why did our client think that Juliette and her child were kidnapped when Brigitte believes that Juliette doesn't have a child?"

Honey leaned in. "Yes, let's start there. Is there a child in harm's way?"

"That's a question we need boots on the ground to help us figure out," Nutsbe said. "Here's a rundown of what we know right now — I'm creating a timeline and a facts sheet that will go to your cloud files. I'll have it ready as soon as possible and keep it updated — Okay, what we have now is that Dr. David DuBois was born in the United States to parents who held French citizenship. Father deceased. Mother now lives in Toulouse. David DuBois received his master's degree from The University of Toulouse. He received his MD and PhDs in the United States and worked for the US military for a time before settling in Lebanon, where he had research grants and taught graduate classes at the American University. The last time he was in France was almost two years ago. His trip at that time was only for the day, with no overnight stay. He was traveling from Beirut and back."

"That seems odd," Lynx said. "It seemed odd when I read it the first time, and it seems even odder when I hear you say it."

"Agreed, I'll flag it to see if we can't figure out why he was there," Nutsbe said to her, then turned back to look into the camera. "The timeline — DuBois was in the Middle East doing research in a private facility and teaching at the American University in Beirut. When he moved back to the United States, at the government's request to work for DARPA, he brought his adult daughter Juliette with him. Juliette Marie DuBois has a green card that says she holds French citizenship."

"You checked with France to see if there are birth records connected to Juliette?" Thorn asked. "Maybe that was her kid down in Toulouse this morning, and the child is living with someone else. Maybe the reason for Juliette's trip to France was to visit her child?"

"A vital statistics search was conducted, and the reports passed to us by our client. There are no birth records – no records *at all* that include the name Juliette Marie DuBois or any permutation thereof," Nutsbe said.

"Are you serious?" Thorn was hunkered into the tight circle that put all three operators' faces on the camera. "But she must have had French paperwork to apply for her US green card."

"That's true. She presented paperwork, which was apparently counterfeited."

"Could she be…I don't know, an operator working for the Mossad?" Gage asked. "Maybe that's why Brigitte knows her and wants her back. Obviously, that wouldn't be the first time that issues have come up around DARPA scientists and Israeli agendas."

"Whatever the gig is, David DuBois was down with it," Thorn said. "I wonder if that was by choice or by some kind of force."

"We have no clues as to who she is or what she's up to," Nutsbe explained. "But David DuBois emphatically isn't interested in returning to the United States. Whatever is going on, he's married to it. I would also caution that the woman posing as Juliette DuBois could be a highly-skilled, lethal entity. As your team moves forward, stay frosty."

There was a knock at the door.

The room stilled.

Thorn stalked over to look through the peephole. There stood a man with their three duffels slung over his shoulders.

"Got it," Thorn said.

The man laid their bags down and walked away. Only when he was well out of sight did Thorn crack the door, sweep his gaze along the hallway, and drag the bags back into the room.

After he found his seat in front of the phone with his teammates, Thorn told Nutsbe, "The housekeeper delivered the packages."

Nutsbe lifted his head from his focus on the keyboard. "Good. Now that you have your computers. Let's turn off the phone and get a computer booted up so you can see the details better.

Gage dug his computer from his duffle and brought Nutsbe back online.

"I wanted Lynx to take you through the kidnapping tape." Nutsbe tapped a key. "I just uploaded it into your files along with the best still photos we could cull from it, so you'll be able to recognize the players if you see them. I'm working on identifying the assailants by name and country of origin, possibly organization if I can get it. I'll let you know if and when I track down anything concrete."

A shaky video played on the screen. It was short, not even two minutes long.

"Okay." They heard Lynx's voice while the image moved back to the beginning of the video. "We know something odd must have been happening for this man, Gaston Claire, to start taping on his phone while he was out walking his dog. I'll post his address, in case you want to talk to him. But I've read the police report. It basically says he saw something weird, he videotaped it and called the police. He has nothing new to add."

"But you're walking us through it," Honey said, "because you saw something important."

"Interesting, at least. Slowing down the video, watch this part. There are two men, each with an arm bent at an angle as they face Juliette. Juliette's expression shows shock and discovery as she looks at their faces. She knows who these men are. Her focus travels down to what we have to assume are weapons in their hands. And then, as she throws her head around to look back over her shoulder, her expression changes to fear. That's protective fear."

Protective-fear. It was a fear that could turn deadly aggressive. It was a fear that made brains make quickly calculated reactions. Aggression wasn't always the best way to keep everyone safe. Thorn had seen that look in the eyes of families so many times, on so many deployments. And strangely, that was the way he'd describe the adrenaline pumping into his system now as he looked at this woman's image.

He'd do whatever it took.

Her eyes, Thorn could well understand why someone who watched this video would see Juliette's expression and think that she was protecting someone dear to her.

Lynx moved the video forward a few more frames as she said, "She's anxious for the person she's searching out." Lynx stopped the video. "This is who she wanted to protect. Her focus goes to this small child. The child is snatched away by an adult, who is, based on AI calculations, probably five-foot-seven inches in height, and male. That neighbor who was videoing shifts the child and adult out of the frame. The camera swings back to the men pushing Juliette into the car. They're getting in. And taking off."

"So, some random kid was there and saw this," Honey said. "He looks like he's about three years old. That won't help."

"Random isn't a given," Lynx said. "We just know that the child was not placed in this car."

"The child wasn't mentioned in the police reports," Nutsbe said. "I'm guessing...the adult in charge of that child made a grab and ran for safety. That adult probably has some more details about what happened just before the video was shot. The timeline between this event unfolding and our contract being signed is very short. I think our client simply made the call to include both female and child in the description because it was better to be inclusive to cover their bases."

The screen showed Lynx and Nutsbe again.

"All right, so one of us needs to go down there and ask questions," Honey said. "I think that should be me."

"Copy, Honey," Nutsbe agreed.

Lynx stretched out her hand to squeeze Nutsbe's arm. "Thorn has to go."

"I–"

Lynx cut Nutsbe off. "This needs to be assigned to *Thorn*." Her words were emphatic and were met with a shrug and a head nod from Nutsbe.

And Thorn one hundred percent agreed. This needed to be *his* assignment.

"We have the license plate and more information about direction of travel. From this point, our next piece of possible information is that at fifteen-thirty-hours, a man called the police because his car had been stolen by a woman. He has no descriptors other than he knew it was a woman by size and hair length. Nothing else, just female. The victim of the carjacking had stopped by the side of the road to lend a hand after he saw that two men were off on the shoulder, jacking up their car."

"Good Samaritan," Gage said.

"No good deed goes unpunished," Nutsbe replied. "The spare tire in the disabled vehicle was dry rotted, and the two men gave the Samaritan a large sum of money to buy his spare or to go get them a tire."

"What's a large sum of money?" Thorn asked.

"That would be approximately three-hundred dollars."

Honey let out a whistle. "That didn't make him curious?"

"He realized they were foreigners," Nutsbe said. "He thought maybe this was the normal amount that it would cost wherever they'd come from."

"And where did he think they were from?" Thorn asked.

"He said they had Eastern bloc accents. Their French was basic. At any rate, he went to his car and got his spare, took it back, and that's when he heard his car engine roar. Someone was flooring the gas pedal and spraying mud out the back, then the car took off."

"Juliette for the win!" Gage said.

"An interesting detail is that we can't find a driver's license in the United States for a Juliette Dubois," Lynx said.

Gage leaned forward. "She didn't happen to drive to the nearest police station and ask for help, did she?"

"There's no new information about where she went," Nutsbe said. "Certainly not the police. Noteworthy, Juliette might have been chemically restrained. The car's owner indicated that she was swerving over the road as if she were drunk. No accidents have been reported."

"Brigitte said strawberries. That means injured, according to Margot," Thorn pointed out. "Is Margot around?"

"She's in a meeting," Nutsbe said.

Thorn nodded. "Okay. When she's free, can you ask if 'strawberries' could mean medicinally restrained?"

"I'll text her now." Lynx reached for her phone.

"Wait," Gage said. "This good Samaritan is standing by the side of the road with the two kidnappers and calls the police because his car was stolen. The kidnapper's car is on a jack. Did the police get there in time to question these guys? What did they say about the situation?"

"There was construction a couple of kilometers south of

them on the highway that locked up the cops," Nutsbe responded without looking up. "By the time they got there, the kidnappers had replaced their tire and had taken off after Juliette."

"Wait. Do we know this was actually the kidnappers, and we're not following a false lead? They have evidence it was the same car that was used to take Juliette?" Thorn asked.

"The Samaritan described the same car that was in the video and was able to remember three of the license plate's digits. So, it's looking good for a positive ID. All right, here we go. Here are the new assignments…" Nutsbe paused as his fingers flew over his keyboard.

The three operators waited patiently.

"Okay." Nutsbe focused on Thorn. "Tight time schedule."

"Wait. Margot just texted back." Lynx lifted her phone and waggled it, then brought it closer to read. "'Strawberries can be any physical issue that makes the mark vulnerable. Typically, this means they're wounded. We don't have a code between Brigitte and me to specifically indicate someone's been drugged.'"

"Copy," the men said together.

"I have two taxis headed to your location," Nutsbe said. "Thorn, you have a flight to Toulouse. I'm sending your ticketing information to your phone. Let's hope there's a flight delay so you can make it in time. Lynx will be posting files for you to review on your flight, so you can catch up with our intel. Grab your gear and go."

"Roger." Thorn leaped from his chair and moved toward the door, grabbing up his bag. As he left, he heard Nutsbe telling Honey and Gage that they were going to meet the client at the airport and be security as the client flies DuBois home. "Note, he is going home against his wishes."

Before anything else was said, Thorn had shut the door and was jogging toward the elevator.

———

THE FLIGHT ATTENDANT pulled the door closed as Thorn made his way down the aisle. He was the last passenger on board. Belted into his first-class seat, Thorn was alone in his row. He knew that Nutsbe would have purchased both seats, so he could safely read the files that were waiting for him in the secured folder. Thorn downloaded them so he could go over the intel while his phone was set to airplane mode.

The flight attendant stood with her hand on the back of the empty chair on the aisle. "Can I get you anything to drink, monsieur?"

"Just some water, thanks." He offered up a smile.

The flight would take an hour and forty minutes, but the pilot was announcing a tailwind that might get them there twenty minutes ahead of schedule. Thorn hoped that was true. He didn't want to knock on people's doors any later than he had to. He would. He'd drag people out of bed if need be. But it always went better when you showed up at a more mannerly time of day — and this would get him on-site at the hair's edge of polite.

Thorn looked at the address Nutsbe had forwarded. The notes said these were the GPS coordinates for where the child had stood. Plugging it into the mapping app, Thorn thought if he could snag a taxi right away, things might just work out. The house was only a fifteen-minute drive from the terminal.

He tapped his phone to airplane mode as they took off, then closed his eyes for a moment to review all that had gone on that day, to look for small details that might need his focus. What he landed on was the fact that DuBois hadn't mentioned his daughter's well-being, he didn't want to fly back to the United States, and he had not only been fighting against them from the time when Thorn had pulled the janitor's gun out from under the scientist's ribs but had been communicating with the Omega team. And the Omega Team was working, he believed, on a Russian contract.

That could be an individual, or it could be the government.

The Russian government liked to keep an arm's length from any actions, either overt or covert, that took place on foreign soil. Of course, they did. Every country did. That was one of the reasons why Iniquus existed, to do the work that the normal channels couldn't. That's why Iniquus had signed a contract, but the operators remained in the dark as to whose signature was scrawled on the bottom line.

Knowing who had hired them would sure give Thorn a better way to frame up this operation.

It wasn't the lynchpin, though.

Right now, he was on a fact-finding mission. A person-finding mission. He'd probably start to wipe some of the fog off his lenses as he went along. As soon as that metaphor came to mind, he thought again about Brigitte's secretly passed information on the bathroom mirror. Why was the Mossad involved?

With the plane in the air, Thorn lifted his plastic cup of water and took a drink as he scanned the first-class cabin. Sitting in the last row, with the carpet-covered wall behind his chair, everything around him looked copacetic.

He angled his body away from the aisle and opened the file list. Now, he'd get a clearer picture of what was to come.

18

THORN

Air France, French Airspace
Saturday, Twenty Zero Three Hours

THORN TAPPED his finger on the file that Lynx had marked #1. He scanned down the medical journal article about members of the American diplomatic corps who had been stationed in Cuba and had recently returned to the United States with odd symptoms. They called this "The Havana Effect" and referenced the term neuroweaponry.

"Neuroweaponry." Thorn moved his lips as he pronounced the word to himself. That seemed every bit as dangerous and difficult to contain as biological weapons.

There was a mystery that the scientific community was grappling with. More than two dozen officials from the American diplomatic corps were living and working in Havana when they heard a series of strange sounds. They remembered the specific events because they couldn't figure out what could make those particular noises. They also remembered them because soon after those noises occurred, the officials started experiencing some fairly alarming medical issues. They had cognitive issues, including forgetfulness and poor focus, as well as physical issues like dizziness, headaches, and hearing loss.

Here was another word that he hadn't come across before... "neurosensory dysfunction," which the article went on to describe as mostly affecting balance.

And what's more, the article said this experience was not unique to Havana. US diplomats out of Guangzhou, China, were reporting the same symptoms.

At first, the scientists thought that the diplomats were the victims of microwaves. It wouldn't be the first time, Thorn thought. In the 1960s, Russia had shot microwaves toward the US embassy. The US government knew this was transpiring in real-time, but the reaction was simply to monitor the diplomats' blood. Only after their white counts started elevating were any actions taken. The staff hung curtains in the windows that reflected microwaves back out into the atmosphere rather than allowing them to penetrate the interior.

Thorn looked out the oval window at the lights twinkling far below him. *If they knew it was happening, why didn't the government send the curtains right away? Why did they let their diplomats get microwaved?* He shook his head. *Crazy.*

He scanned down the page to find where he'd left off. His eye caught on the name Dr. David DuBois.

Here it was talking about DuBois and peer-reviewed research. David DuBois, after performing his studies on all the affected diplomats and officials, had concluded that they didn't have brain damage. They weren't suffering from a traumatic brain injury (TBI). He thought that what they were seeing could be isolated to the individual's damage in the inner ears. He believed that the balance issues came from the otolith organs in the inner ear, and that would explain the dizziness the officials described.

Thorn took a minute to humanize that information. What would it be like to be one of those officials, going about life in a healthy way and, all of a sudden, have issues with balance, forgetfulness, headaches, and hearing loss. That would be disabling to Thorn. He wouldn't be able to do his job. He wasn't sure what kind of job someone could hold down under those circumstances. How bad were the symptoms, scale of one to ten? Thorn wondered. Could they drive? Could they walk? Could they make safe decisions? Thorn hoped that as he moved through the files, he'd find answers to those questions. It sounded like someone had taken out a large number of diplomats on not one but two diplomatic missions.

Thorn finished the last paragraph, which stated that DuBois's findings stood counter to those found in other medical facilities where the subjects were examined.

Swiping his finger across the screen, Thorn found he'd read to the end of the first article. He wanted to know what the other facilities had concluded.

He opened the next file that Lynx had marked as #2. She must have had a reason for placing them in a specific order. This article was also from a military medical journal. Thorn's finger traced down the page as he read along – twenty-one, American service members from an undisclosed location, were the subjects of the study team headed by David DuBois, M.D. Ph.D.

The article began with the notation that all of the subjects had newly arrived to the theater of operation, and none had a previous blow to the head.

There was a list of symptoms. Most of them were described

in medical vernacular that Thorn didn't have the background to follow. He'd have to research those terms later when he had some downtime. Or get Nutsbe to write a report in lay-speak. Thorn picked back up when it mentioned headaches, sleep abnormalities, and auditory symptoms. He swiped through the pages to find the conclusion. As he took a sip of his water, he read, "While these individuals present with the dysfunctions that are indicative of brain trauma, their symptoms do not fit the military definition of traumatic brain injury, further inquiry is required." The researchers suggested MRIs be taken to see if that offered further information.

Why didn't they do MRIs right away? Thorn wondered.

The third file was a letter filled with redactions, referring to our allies Great Britain, Germany, Canada, and France, all of whom were reporting instances in their Chinese embassies where their diplomatic officials had heard something odd then became symptomatic.

There was David Dubois's name again.

DuBois had asked to be allowed to examine those who heard the sounds and became symptomatic and those who heard the sounds and did *not* become symptomatic.

The allies declined, raising objections over DuBois's past ethical breaches.

Breaches, huh?

The rest of that letter was blacked out with redactions.

Thorn opened the fourth file. This one was about Senator Billings. Thorn had seen Senator Billings in the halls of Iniquus back in DC almost a year ago now.

Gage was just signing on with Iniquus as he finished out his contract with the Marine Corp. Gage sent up a distress signal to Panther Force Commander, Titus Kane, asking for Iniquus's help safeguarding his fiancée Zoe Kealoha. Zoe, a DARPA scientist, was at risk in a kidnapping scheme. Turned out that Gage had arrived at her apartment just in time to hear her screaming bloody murder, and he'd had to neutralize two men later identified as Israeli special forces thought to have been KIA ten years before.

It seemed to Thorn like there might be some parallels here.

Both Dr. Zoe Kealoha and Dr. David DuBois were DARPA scientists.

Both worked in the medical realm of research.

Both had a kidnapping attempt.

And both had a link to Israel. Zoe, through a group of black ops, and DuBois was in the scope of a Mossad operator calling herself Brigitte.

Thorn scratched his cheek. And now, something was going on that threw Senator Billings' name into this mess.

Granted, Senator Billings wasn't directly connected to Zoe Kealoha in any way. It was more that Zoe rented lab space at Montrim industries. Turned out DuBois did too. Okay, that wasn't a big leap; many DARPA scientists did. But in terms of Senator Billings, he wanted to fight Montrim because they were working on an apocalyptic weaponry system. The specifics of which weren't released to the public, but Thorn bet Gage knew.

Thorn decided to ask Gage about the system under development as soon as an encrypted communication was in place.

He made a mental note, then turned back to the file to read more about the senator in the newspaper article:

AT A CONGRESSIONAL HEARING TO discuss the Cuban health issues, Senator Charles Billings, R-Wisconsin, the ranking member of the Senate Committee on Foreign Relations, sought information concerning the decision to put the diplomats and other officials affected during their service in Havana under Dr. David DuBois's care. "After all," the senator is quoted, "it seems problematic that our diplomatic corps, who are suffering from concussion-like symptoms associated with a brain injury, should be assessed by a doctor who does not subscribe to the standard assessments for traumatic brain injuries. I find that odd. Don't you? And he's got some ethical baggage he's toting along."

Gary Hooper, the medical director for the State Department, responded that they had reached out to Dr. DuBois, bringing him back from his teaching position at the American University in Beirut, to do his work here in the United States, in particular, to add his qualifications and unique background to assessing the State employees.

Hooper later asserted that the State Department had come to the conclusion that the injuries were not caused in the acoustic systems but had affected a wider spectrum of the brain process.

Congress has taken issue with the State Department's handling of this mysterious and concerning health anomaly. They noted that it was in the purview of the Centers for Disease Control and Prevention, the CDC, to review and advise.

In December, the CDC began its inquiry. However, a congressional aid, who spoke on background, indicated that immediately upon hearing the reports, the CDC agency representatives had traveled to China but had not done so in Cuba.

Speculation has run from mass hysteria to new weapon systems.

DuBois's task was to identify the mechanism of the symptoms. He and his team indicate that a neuroweapon was used both in Cuba and in China. Possibilities include microwaves, microbes, energy-weapons, and drugs. They also believe that it could have been a combination thereof. Though, DuBois believes that the likelihood is that an ultrasonic weapon was deployed, a means of emitting an electromagnetic pulse.

WAIT A MINUTE; here it is again, they're questioning this guy's ethics.

Thorn read through the article a second time. He'd have to ask Nutsbe and Lynx to look into just what ethical baggage Senator Billings was associating to DuBois.

And there was something just on the edge of his memory. Something from the halls of Iniquus…It seemed to Thorn like it was a story he'd heard about some puzzle that Lynx had solved that had to do with China and sound. *Who was on that case?* Striker and Lynx were brought in when that task force had failed to resolve their mission. He needed to ask Lynx if she could tell him that story or if it was classified.

The focus here seemed to be Cuba, but Thorn had a feeling in his gut that if this new weapon system was being deployed, that Cuba was just a testing ground, and that what was really happening had to do with China. But then why Omega?

He put both things on his mental list, to ask Gage about Billings and Lynx about the Echo Force case once he got them on a secure line.

Closing the folders, Thorn slid his phone back in the thigh pocket on his tactical pants.

He stared out at the night sky.

It was reasonable to say that none of these articles matter at all. Maybe they didn't even edify the situation. They simply talked about what David DuBois had been up to in his body of work.

Right now, what really mattered was finding this woman who

was going by the name Juliette DuBois and figuring out if she was in trouble and needed their help or if she was the enemy who needed to be taken down.

His gut said she was running for her life.

19

JULIETTE
The outskirts of Paris, France
Saturday, 8:00 p.m.

AT THE TOP of the hour, the radio station had shifted to a news show.

Juliette was awake but had kept her eyes shut the whole drive, pretending to be asleep. She didn't want to have a polite conversation. She just wasn't up to it. Wasn't up to any questions. Her list now included − Paris and the airport, some research on her phone for someplace she might stay where they'd be happy to take her money and not ask for an I.D. Then pain pills and sleep.

She still had her dinner in her pack. Back at the café, Juliette had purposefully ordered quite a bit of the kinds of foods that would keep the best over a period of time. If she had a small fridge in her motel room and portioned carefully, Juliette might be able to keep her head low until the fever broke, and she could make a new plan.

One step, then another.

But right now, her vulnerability was inching up.

On the radio, the news castor was advising people of the strange carjacking that had happened earlier in the day. The police had found the car she'd stolen and parked by the shopping area in Orléans.

The news castor said, "The keys had been placed in the glove compartment, and a note read: **I'm so sorry to have put you through this. Forgive me. I was kidnapped and running for my safety. You saved my life. I will always be appreciative and hold you in prayer.** You might note that the grammar and phraseology are non-standard. And reading this, I can tell you there are some slight spelling errors. It is probable that the note was not written by a native French speaker," he concluded.

Juliette tried to tell by the vibrations in the air if Jean-Luc was looking her way. If he were listening and knew that she was the person who wrote that note.

"The police are asking for any information if you saw anything that might help them find the woman. The owner of the car does not wish to press charges against the theft, as the circumstances of the carjacking do align with such a scenario. However, authorities want to ensure that the woman is safe and the kidnappers are brought to justice. Any suspicious activity should be reported."

The radio announcer's update shifted to a mention of something that would come to a vote on Monday. There was information about the football match in Brussels that night and a meteorological prediction of an approaching storm.

The music came back on. Juliette had weathered the announcements.

After a few moments, though, Juliette heard Jean-Luc whispering.

"*Maman,*" Jean-Luc began. "I'm in your car, heading to Paris. I need your advice."

Juliette would willingly jump out of the car going highway speed before she let Jean-Luc take her anywhere other than the airport.

In quiet tones, low enough in range that Juliette could hear almost all of the words, he launched into the story of what had been on the radio and how he came to be in his present situation. After a pause, he said, "She's sleeping."

. . .

"I don't see any blood. No, no obvious wounds. She's on crutches. She was swaying like a drunk as we walked to the car. But I'm pretty sure from the way she spoke to me that she's sober. She fell asleep almost instantly. Maybe she's suffering a head trauma? What should I do?"

Juliette held her breath.

"She's trying to get to Charles De Gaulle to fly home to America, she said."

. . .

"Yes, she was sincere. I think she's in trouble. I just don't know what to do."

. . .

"All right, yes. Will that give her enough time to get away? What if I came home and went to bed, and when I wake up eight hours later, we have this talk again? That would give her more time."

. . .

"You're right. The police could see from my phone records that I called you. But they won't know what we said or that I heard the news. I could, for example, just be telling you that

I'm driving a girl to Paris and will be home before you get there."

…

"No, still asleep. She gave me two-hundred euros. Should I give it back? She might really need it."

…

"I'll stick it in her bag. I don't think she would take it from my hand… Yes… Okay. I will. *Merci, Maman*. I'll see you in the morning."

And that was it. For another twenty minutes, there was the soft music and the rumble of the tires. At one point, Juliette felt a rustle by her feet, and she slit her eyes to see what was happening. Jean-Luc, with his eyes on the road, was leaning toward her with the euros in his hand, trying to shove the bills into the front pocket of her backpack.

She had to stifle a sob.

It wasn't the money. It was the kindness. It was a young man who wasn't willing to profit from a fellow human being in distress.

And at that moment, she remembered elephants.

Juliette didn't know if this was a second real memory where she'd been standing there watching them or if this was something she'd seen on TV. But it seemed very real. A lame elephant cow couldn't get up the bank from the watering hole. One elephant reached out her trunk, and they wrapped together. Another went behind the disabled cow and pushed. Up she went.

However, Juliette had come across that image. She remembered at the time that she'd clutched her hands to her heart, incredibly moved. When she was home again, she'd ask her father if she'd ever been around elephants, maybe something to do with her studies or job as a veterinarian's assistant, Juliette thought as she swallowed down her emotions.

Home. Back to her little house with Toby. And her dad. He would be so surprised and so confused by what had happened to her. But she should tell him right away. He would know what to do and keep her safe. And she'd let him know, somehow along the way, that it didn't matter to her that he was gay. She didn't need to know the "hows" or "whys" of his relationship with her mom. She just wanted him to be happy. In a world where horrible things happened, people really should grab at what joy they could.

Jean-Luc pulled to the curb at the airport and set the gear in park. He reached out and laid a gentle hand on her shoulder, giving her a little shake. "We're here," he said.

Juliette pretended to rouse herself and look around. She smiled at him as she released her seat belt. "Sorry I wasn't good company. It's been a rough day."

He swallowed and nodded.

"*Merci beaucoup.*" Juliette gripped the strap of her backpack with one hand and unlocked the door with her other.

He still had his hand on her shoulder. "Are you okay? Do you need help getting inside? Is there anything I can do?"

She could tell he was doing his best to extend himself for her but protect her anonymity – to not give away that he knew, if not who she was, at least what she was, a woman on the run.

Her lower lip trembled a bit as she looked out at the crowd of people busily getting to where they needed to go. She turned back to him. "No, *ca va*, I think I'll be okay from here." She climbed out.

He reached her crutches out to her.

"*Merci*, Jean-Luc." And she shut the door.

Now what?

Juliette knew from books and movies that there were cameras all over the airport. So as she'd moved out of Jean-Luc's car, she'd pulled her hoody back in place over her hair and had purposefully ducked her head. She stood in place as she watched Jean-Luc's car move out of sight. Squatting on the cement walkway to retie her shoe, she dropped her knees for stability in order to get her backpack over her shoulders. That was a mistake. She couldn't get back up. She floundered there a couple of times before she decided to crawl over to the cement planter and use that for stability. On all fours, she started the crawl, dragging her crutches behind her.

Tsking, followed by an "*oolala-Lalala!*" came before two sets of hands, one on her right and one on her left, lifted her to her feet. An older couple with frowns on their faces looked back at her. "What is the matter here? Are you all right?" the man asked in Arabic.

"Yes, thank you," Juliette replied with a moment of relief for speaking a language that came so much more fluidly to her than French. Her dad had said that her mom had insisted that Juliette's first and most proficient language be Arabic and that she be raised in the Muslim faith. Her dad, an atheist, didn't really care one way or another. After all, he was away at work all day, and it was her mother who had the job of raising their child. Juliette's mother had been Kuwaiti. She and her mother spoke Arabic together and switched to French when her father was in the conversation, which wasn't all that often, he'd admitted to her, somewhat abashedly.

"What are you doing on the ground?" The woman adjusted her hijab.

Juliette attempted to laugh. "I bent to tie my shoe and couldn't get back up on my crutches."

"Are you all right now? Shall I go find a porter with a wheelchair?" She shook a motherly finger at Juliette. "You should not have a heavy backpack when you're on crutches, no wonder you toppled over."

"Yes, this is true, but under the circumstances…" Juliette adjusted the crutches under her arms and hoped she hadn't made a spectacle that would be flagged by security. She didn't want to answer anyone's questions. "Thank you. Have a nice evening," she said. And before the couple could entwine themselves into her misadventure, she started off toward the doors of Charles de Gaulle.

Inside, she went directly to the ladies' room. She hung the pack on the hook and took a moment to relieve herself. From that position of seclusion and relative safety, she started to scroll through student backpacking sites looking for cheap places where she could hunker down.

She found three that might meet her needs. They were all listed as small individual rooms with a sink and bidet. A communal bathroom was available in the hall. All three had pay-as-you-go showers available on-premises. They catered to students and other low-budget travelers. Continental breakfast was included. Pictures showed a plate with a section of a baguette, a hard-boiled egg, a triangle of cheese, and a bowl of coffee. These motels looked clean and reputable enough for safety. But when she read over the criterion for staying, Juliette found that one was fully booked until the end of the month and the next required a passport from those traveling from outside the EU. The third, though, said that identification was not required if a two-hundred-euro returnable deposit was made.

Juliette tapped the phone button and put her finger in her ear.

"*Allô?*" a man answered just as the toilet in the stall next to hers flushed.

"*Bonsoir*," Juliette said. "I've just arrived in town without a reservation. Is it possible that you have a room available?"

"How long will you be staying with us?"

"I believe a week," Juliette answered.

"Name?"

She blinked. A name? Panic made her feet and hands buzz. "Roxanne," she said, borrowing from her caregiver. "Roxanne Olson."

"How many in your party?"

"Just me." Juliette's tongue wanted to weave a story. She wanted to say that she was in Paris to practice painting by the Seine or something. But from her dad's novels, Juliette knew that liars used too many words. They tried to dissemble and hide their lies by throwing out way too many facts. But that was often a tell that was their undoing. Truthful people knew they were being truthful and had no reason to add details.

"Very well, I'm looking. I have a room on the third floor."

"Oh," Juliette breathed out. "I'm on crutches. Is there perhaps anything a little lower?"

"The one on the first floor, but the water pipe is broken. It's possible I could move you down there after the plumber comes to do the repairs. Crutches might be a problem. The stairwells are narrow."

"Well." Juliette laughed. "I can always go up and down on my bottom like a toddler."

"You want to book the room? I'll need a credit card number." Juliette heard the words through the ringing tinnitus. It made her feel unsure, unclear, off-balance as a mental state more than a physical one. She thought she was understanding but wasn't completely sure.

Speaking more than one language was helpful in that no matter the language she was communicating in with a stranger, she could always hide her brain confusion behind "speaking in a foreign language" confusion. That masked the embarrassment that she often felt. But here, she hoped it masked her fear.

Juliette pulled the Visa *Felicitations!* card from her belly bag and read out the number.

"This is a gift card," the man said.

"Yes, I'm a student. That's all I have, gift cards from my family, and some cash."

"In that case, you'll need to leave a deposit. Two hundred euro."

"Yes, of course. That won't be a problem." The woman in the toilet next to hers was moaning with stomach discomfort. Juliette tried to block the sound from the registration guy with her hand. Then came silence and a flush.

"All right, Mademoiselle Olson, your confirmation number is 7852332. You just need to sign in and leave your deposit. Your key will be waiting behind the desk."

Juliette put her phone back in her pocket. She pulled up her jeans. Gave the toilet another flush so it wouldn't seem odd to any woman who might be paying attention. Pulled on her backpack and stumbled her way out of the disability stall.

She moved to wash her hands and looked into the mirror. Her face was red and slick. Her eyes feverish. She felt her head, and the cool pressure of her hand was such a comfort. She splashed her face with cold water then dried her hands on a paper towel. *Come on, Juliette*, she encouraged herself, *one more taxi ride and then a bed.*

A bed sounded like Nirvana.

20

THORN
   Toulouse, France
   Saturday, Twenty Thirty-five Hours

THORN HAD PAID the taxi double to get him there by twenty-hundred thirty hours. And promised another generous payment if the driver would wait at the curb for him as he had a brief conversation.

The light was on in the downstairs area of the little house and off on the second level. Thorn hoped that meant that someone was still awake to answer as he rapped his knuckles softly against the door.

"I'm calling the police," a man's voice called.

"United States official, sir." Thorn's French accent had a decided African timbre as he'd learned the language on assignment in Niger. "I'm holding my credentials beside my face." Thorn lifted his Iniquus identification up with its official stamps and his photograph. A badge with the Iniquus logo on the left of the wallet. It usually got him in when people thought he was the law.

"I see that. What do you want?"

"I would be grateful if you'd answer a few brief questions for me about the event that happened earlier in the day. One of our citizens was kidnapped." All right, she held a green card, but he was willing to stretch the truth.

Thorn was dressed for the part. He wore his Iniquus uniform of gunmetal-gray tactical pants and a compression shirt under his black jacket with a silver Iniquus crest over his heart. His body was fit and strong. He'd been told many a time that he looked like he'd been cast by Hollywood for a role in a spy movie. When it worked for him, he used it. That thought brought a flash of Brigitte to mind. Dimming her light to blend when she was on the flight with Dubois, then turning up the volume to spark his interest as he headed to the hotel. Same thing. Just another tool in the toolbox.

When Thorn had been over doing a tour as a SEAL, their base had housed a French unit for a short time. One of their soldiers sent him a Paris magazine article later that described the Frenchmen's experience living with the Americans. The lines that Thorn remembered the best was that no two soldiers had the same accent, and as far as the Frenchmen were concerned, none of the Americans actually spoke English. They ended up having to write notes back and forth to save time. Standing head and shoulders above the French soldiers more diminutive size, the Americans were teased about having protein shakes, and creatine served to them in their baby bottles.

They said the Americans were successful because they rallied to the fight. They could go from shorts and flip flops to full battle rattle in less than three minutes. They saw the enemy, and they pounced on them. Ran straight at them, guns a-blazing.

But most importantly, the article said, the Americans always came to the rescue. Not individualists. They were all about the team.

Thorn, standing there identifying himself as an Iniquus operator, knew he had a team behind him.

He wondered what Juliette was thinking right now. She probably had no idea that they were coming after her full tilt. To help her or to stop her was yet to be determined.

The door swung open, but a safety chain hung in place.

A safety chain had absolutely no stopping power. It served as a pacifier to help a home feel like a safe place. But, hey, if it made this guy feel better, fine, he'd talk to him past the chain. "Sir, have you spoken to the police about the events that you witnessed this morning concerning a young woman?" Thorn held up his phone with her picture.

"No," he said. "I've been away all day. I wasn't here to talk with them."

Thorn flipped to the next photo he'd queued up and turned his phone. "This is your child?"

"My son, yes." He puffed up a bit, showing Thorn that he felt protective if not combative when it came to the boy. Bold move since he came up to Thorn's shoulder and weighed about as much as Thorn's leg.

Thorn kept his tone neutral and non-threatening. "Do you or your son have a relationship with the young woman?"

"No, none. Nothing. No. I have never seen her before this day. She certainly has nothing to do with my son."

Thorn scrolled and brought up the film of the kidnapping and turned it, so they could watch at the same time.

The man shifted his weight back and forth between his feet. Obviously, seeing this triggered him. His emotions rippled across his face.

Thorn could use that. He scrolled back. "She's in trouble. Look at the fear on her face. Do you see what she does at that moment?" And it struck Thorn, again, that this was a very telling frame. It spoke deeply of who this woman was. "She didn't spin toward you, looking for help. She spun around to check on your child. Her instinct was to protect your son."

The man closed his eyes for a moment, then nodded and shut the door. A scrape of metal against metal sounded as he removed the chain. He opened it again and waved Thorn inside.

Thorn stepped into a living room strewn with toys. The television was set to the news channel.

"Did she introduce herself to you? Do you know this woman's name?"

"No." He reached out to scoop up a pile of half-folded laundry at the end of the couch and pointed his chin to the cleared space.

Thorn took a seat with a nod of thanks. "Again, she doesn't have *any* connection to you? Your family? This little boy?"

The man perched on the edge of the coffee table. "I don't know her. I've never seen her before. She was across the street at my neighbor's house. The house with the statue of the cat on the steps." He flicked his finger to show that he meant across the street. "My son was riding his tricycle on the sidewalk and had a fall." He tapped Thorn's phone. "This woman lifted him up and made sure he was not hurt. She was comforting him as he cried. I walked across and took him from her arms, then I brought him back to my yard where he played. That's when the car came. Two men. You can see in your video what happened."

"She didn't say anything to you?"

"She said that cold water would take the blood out."

Thorn stared down at the man. "Blood?"

"Yes. She cut her hand as she pulled my son from the tangle of the tricycle. When it turned over, one of the spokes broke. She apologized that her blood got onto his shirt."

Thorn's gaze traveled to the laundry that the guy had moved to the end of the couch. "Did you do that? Did you soak the shirt in cold water?"

The man ran his hand over his head. "I just got home. I thought it safest to go visit a friend until whatever was happening was done. I don't want any trouble. No. Soak it in water? No, I haven't done that yet."

"May I have the shirt with the blood?" Thorn asked.

The man stared at him for a moment and then moved out of the room toward the back of the house. He came back with a tiny navy blue and white striped shirt. He unfurled it and turned it to the side to show the blood to Thorn. "She wasn't bleeding a lot. After I took my son, he calmed, and I let him continue to play in our front yard. I saw that she spoke to the woman who is my neighbor's caregiver. Then she was waiting on the road. I assumed she was waiting for another taxi. When she was walking toward me, I thought maybe she needed a bandage. I got up to go in and fetch one for her when the car pulled up. That's all I know. I *don't* want any trouble. I don't want my family to be in danger."

Thorn held out his hand for the shirt, careful to take it by the hem and not touch the bloodstain. "Thank you for your help," he said and walked out the door.

Thorn stood beside the cab, considering the house with the cat outside. The lights were off. If it was an old woman and a caregiver, the chances were that if he knocked on their door, they wouldn't answer, and they'd call the police. The police would have their own questions about him, and honestly, it was just better to be humming below the radar for the sake of speed.

Speed, when it came to someone trying to disappear, was paramount.

21

JULIETTE
Paris, France
Saturday 9:46 p.m.

JULIETTE EMERGED from the taxi after paying the woman. Her hand rested on the hood, and the opened door as the scene swam in her eyes. She was so close to crawling into a bed. So close. As she gripped at the car and her body swayed, she heard the woman say, "I'm coming, just a moment."

The driver had tapped on her emergency flasher and rounded toward Juliette. Reaching into the back seat, the driver retrieved the crutches and handed them off, then grabbed up the backpack. "I'll help you in," she said, pulling the backpack over a shoulder.

Juliette was both grateful and worried. She thought that if she looked too sick − or drunk, or drugged − that the motel wouldn't let her stay. But her crutches might be the cover she needed.

The woman walked over to the door and held it wide as Juliette *katchunked* forward. She stumbled as she crossed from the darkness outside to the illumination inside the tiny lobby area. She laughed it off, saying in French, "My first day on crutches. I'll figure it out sooner or later."

The driver set the bag by the desk, wished everyone a good evening, then left.

Juliette moved toward the clerk, plastering her game face in place. First, she covered for her red, sweaty face. "Whew, who knew it was so much work to use these things?" Then she smiled and spoke to the man beside the computer screen. "*Bonsoir, monsieur.* I'm Roxanne Olsen. I called and made a reservation a short time ago."

The man looked her over. "Yes, a two-hundred-euro deposit. And I need to see some I.D."

It had specifically said that they didn't need I.D. on their website, but obviously, she was lifting red flags for this guy. She had thought this might happen and had come up with a plan. She opened her new phone case and pulled out the money and one of Roxanne's business cards. "Deposit. And I'm sorry, but my purse was stolen earlier this morning on the train. Luckily, I had my money and gift cards tucked in my phone, and that was in my hand. I have my card, other than that…"

He picked up the card and looked it over. "You are American?"

"Yes."

"You are a writer?"

"Yes, I'm here in Paris working on a new story." She reached out and tapped the card. "I do romance, and what city is more romantic than Paris?"

He nodded and moved to tuck the card into the register.

"Oh," Juliette said. "I need that. It's the only thing I have with my name on it."

He stared at Juliette, then at the card. He set it in front of his keyboard and typed the information in. It included Juliette's actual home address and Roxanne's home office number. Juliette wasn't sure if that was dangerous or not.

Her immediate danger was fainting.

She needed to eat, take more pain pills, and sleep. She wasn't sure that would fix her. This wasn't an abnormal occurrence. About every couple of weeks, but nothing like clockwork, this happened to her. Her father would take her to his Montrim lab and hook up an IV. He said it was, for the most part, electrolytes and hydration. Since she didn't know the cocktail, Juliette couldn't tell a doctor or hospital what she needed. Of course, she could just call her dad and ask.

Juliette didn't know why, but that's where that thought ended. She knew she wouldn't be calling her dad. Something had shifted for her when she visited her childhood apartment in Toulouse, and that something had solidified when she was soundly dismissed at her grandmother's house. Her memory pictures lined up with both places, but living breathing people contradicted those pictures. *That was strange, right?* she asked herself.

"*Mademoiselle?*" The man held up an old-fashioned room key on a plastic keychain. He'd canted his head and was scowling.

"What? Oh, sorry. I was running a character conversation through my head." That was a typical sentence that Roxanne used when Juliette was trying to talk to her, and she got that far-away look in her eyes.

"Since you're on crutches, I'll carry your backpack for you. I don't normally do that." His tone seemed strange to Juliette. Did it put him out that badly? She hadn't asked for help, but Juliette guessed that the taxi driver had made that a precedent and he'd look like a cad for not offering. Juliette wished she could say, "No, that's okay. I'm fine." But she wasn't fine. The picture of her crawling toward the planter at the airport came back to her. "*Merci.* I would appreciate that."

He locked the front door and put up a sign that said, "Back at" and had a clock with moveable hands beneath. He checked his watch, then set the clock for five minutes in the future and stuck it in the window.

Juliette was dismayed when she saw the steep, narrow steps. This was all but impossible. "I think perhaps if you'll take my crutches as well, I'll just crawl up the stairs on my hands and knees."

He reached over, took them from her hands, and moved up the stairs.

Juliette did her best to follow him.

Her room was tiny. A slender bed was set against the wall; beyond that, an armoire took up the rest of the space on the left. A narrow walkway allowed her to move through the room. On the right, the bidet was, disturbingly, directly across from the head of her bed. Beyond that were a sink and a narrow desk with a stool. The wall opposite the door had a long window that opened out to a balcony, just wide enough for a single person to stand.

The toilet was at the end of the hall. Next to that, the man explained, she'd find shower stalls. She'd need coins to access them. The hot water was purchased in five-minute increments. He had change downstairs if she needed it.

"*Merci bien,*" she said, waiting for him to leave the room. There wasn't enough space to cross paths inside.

When she heard him on the staircase, she locked the door and slid the chain into place.

Juliette's face swayed in the mirror as she dragged the head-band from her hair. After pulling off her clothes, laying them across the open armoire door to air, she got the soap from her bag and gave herself a sink bath. Her hand brushed over the burn mark on her thigh. Unlike the silver ones on her feet that she'd gotten in the accident that killed her mother, this burn was pink. It looked like she'd painted herself with a brush. The larger beginning that tapered and feathered as it wrapped her thigh. This burn, her dad had said, was from the fire at the apartment in Toulouse. Her mother had saved her, he'd said, but everything they owned had been lost. She was their most precious treasure, so who cared about the rest?

But the concierge had said there hadn't been a fire in the last hundred years, Juliette reminded herself as she used the rough hand towel to dry herself off.

She used the bidet to relieve herself and wash.

She was clean enough.

This was good enough, she cajoled herself as she pulled the newly purchased nightgown over her head, letting it fall over her body, the hem resting on the orange and green patterned carpeting. It was a cheap polyester material. But it felt silky, and it was a pretty shade of pink. Juliette felt like she needed a little pink − a little softness against her right then.

Her food was tasteless as she swallowed down a few bites. She put the rest of the food in the tiny dorm-sized fridge inside the armoire. After refilling her water bottle, Juliette dragged the desk stool over beside her bed to function as a table. She tipped two acetaminophens into her hand, setting the bottle next to her new cellphone and water. When she pressed the button on her light switch, the room became a dark background with dancing shadows cast from the streetlight through the curtains.

She lay down. And snuggled beneath the sheets. Her heated cheek rested on the cool cotton pillow.

Hopefully, sleep would bring her some relief. Hopefully, her brain would function better in the morning.

22

THORN

Toulouse, France.
Saturday, Twenty-two Hundred Hours

THORN CLIMBED into the cab that had patiently waited for his return from interviewing the eyewitness. "The airport, *s'il vous plait.*"

Without a word, the driver put the taxi in gear and started them down the road.

Opening his duffle, Thorn pulled out a brown paper envelope used for evidence collection. He slid the toddler's shirt in, careful to keep his fingers away from the bloodstain. He sealed it, labeled it, and tucked it away.

His comms in his ears, his microphone around his throat under the turtleneck of his compression shirt, Thorn dug a set of earbuds from his pocket and stuck them into his phone. He would use them as a cover. While he spoke with his team, it might look to the driver like he was mouthing along to a song. He then dialed through to Panther Force war room.

"Sitrep?" Nutsbe asked for Thorn's situation report as they spoke over an encrypted system, allowing them to speak freely.

Thorn ran through the information about the boy being unharmed and merely a bystander in the event and the fact that he'd been able to collect the shirt with the bloodstain.

"What are your thoughts concerning the blood?" Nutsbe asked. "We can get it tested for DNA – see if there's anything in the FBI CODIS system that would be a match. But that'll take time, brother, and I think our leash is too short for that."

"Granted, but I had another thought. When Zoe Kealoha was targeted for kidnapping, we learned that she had developed a means to check bio-markers in the blood. That system is almost instantaneous. But the device she described uses strips that uptake fresh blood. I'm not sure if it could work on dried blood."

Nutsbe paused. "It would have to. Remember she said that one of the ways her system had made her feel proud was its use to help resolve the Paris terrorist attacks. The French authorities had blood samples from the terrorist at the scene of his suicide bombing. They put it through the BIOMIST collection, hoping to find his family. It brought up Salah, and that led to them naming Brahim Abdeslam. The CIA stayed off the radar, but it was dried blood they collected and put into BIOMIST that did the job. The problem I see is that Juliette is ostensibly French, and the database is made up almost uniquely of those from the Middle East and some asylum seekers from Africa."

"All right, but what if she was testing Juliette's blood with DuBois's? Couldn't Zoe's machine tell us if they were actually genetically related?"

"As long as it was a close family relationship, yes."

"DuBois claims this is his daughter for green card purposes.

With a father as an American citizen, she should have naturalization rights." Thorn was angled away from the driver, looking out the window as they drove along the Garonne River. "But she may not want to become a US citizen. At any rate, she's traveling on French vital records that don't exist. If nothing else, this will tell us if they're father and daughter. Whether that's helpful in the end or not, I don't know."

"There's also the possibility that your sample was compromised if anyone touched the blood. But I think it's worth a try. We can do a blood draw on DuBois en route."

Thorn was watching the driver's body language to see if he was paying any attention to his passenger in the back seat. He seemed too busy tapping at his computer screen looking for ways to dodge traffic to care what Thorn was talking about. "Where is DuBois now?

"The team's still in Brussels. I'm going to contact our client since they're providing the plane for transport. I'll make a plan. Are you heading toward the airport?"

"Affirmative."

"So, you'll be in place if we decide to fly you to them. It seems the quickest way of getting the blood to one place unless we could fly one of Zoe's machines to you instead. The reason I don't think that will work is that your sample is dry, and she may need to manipulate it in the lab."

"Copy," Thorn said. "Is Lynx there?"

"Yeah – hang on. I'm going to let you talk to her while I call Zoe and double-check that this is even doable."

Lynx came over his comms. "Hey, there. How can I help?"

"I'm not sure." Thorn scratched a hand over his head. He wished that France had some drive-through restaurants. A cup of coffee would be appreciated right about now. He was looking forward to finding some grub. He'd eaten an MRE earlier, and frankly, he could use something that required less Tabasco to make it palatable. "About a year ago, when you were coming back to work at Iniquus, there was a case. I'm not sure about the specifics. I wasn't read into the program, but there was a hum about it."

"Okay…"

"We had planted an operator at Montrim. Montrim was our contractor, I believe. Do you know what I'm talking about?"

"I think so. Command asked me to take a look at the video they'd shot where they were trying to light a fire and see where the guy ran. The concern was that they were tracking the wrong mark. I confirmed they had the right guy in their scope. Striker was there in case that wasn't true so that we could come up with a different strategy to find the right guy. What makes you think of that now?"

"It just pinged when I was reading the files from DuBois," Thorn said. "Is that classified? Can we talk about it?"

"I don't have much on it. But it pinged for me, too. The mark was a researcher for Montrim industries, Dr. George Matthews. He wasn't a DARPA scientist. But he had contracted with the Pentagon to develop a weapon that used energy waves to take out anything warm-blooded in an urban environment while leaving the structure in place."

"Was this considered a neuroweapon? Was it approaching completion?"

"When I was helping to pinpoint Dr. Matthews as having a relationship with China, the research hadn't gotten very far. It was still in the conceptual stage: Paper and pencil. The concern was about ongoing connections as the technology was developed. Absolutely, this was a concept for a neuroweapon. Montrim and the Pentagon decided not to fire or arrest Dr.

Matthews. They wanted to catch everyone that might belong in that net."

"Okay. Second question. I was thinking about when Zoe was being chased down — I don't know if you had any of this information. As I remember it, you stuck your toe in to help out, but you were on your way out of town to Miami — Senator Billings…"

"I did an interview with Senator Billings. My goal was to discover the name of the private investigator that he had hired to follow his mistress, to see if she was some kind of spy or "swallow" as he described the concern. Is that what you have a question about?"

"You don't know the story where Gage was at Colonel Guthrie's house when Senator Billings showed up drunk, begging Colonel Guthrie to help him stop Montrim and their apocalyptic weapon of war?"

"No." Lynx paused. "No, I don't know about this. What kind of apocalyptic weapon is this?"

"I'm not sure. If you don't know, I'd ask Gage. It wasn't fully on my screen at the time. But your articles are about sound and ensuing health issues. They mention China and Billings. There seems to be a pattern here. And then there's Israel."

"Thorn, Nutsbe here, I'm back on the line. As to Israel, that's an iffy connection. I mean, the Rex Deus were Israeli citizens, but I really think they dissociated from the government. They're a rogue group. But in this case, Margot identified Brigitte as Mossad."

"I can see that you might want to put that all together," Lynx said. "I wouldn't get lost in the pattern. I'd focus on clues that you come across as we're looking for our pink rabbit."

"Just putting a pin on the corkboard," Thorn said.

"I hear you," she said. "You holding up okay? It's been a long day."

"Interesting day, to say the least. We're coming up on the airport now."

"Nutsbe here. Zoe says she can use a dry blood sample. It just needs a couple of extra steps in processing. She can't compare the two blood samples for familial blood markers, but what she can do is enter both samples into the BIOMIST catalog. Then she can tag them. The computer system will make a comparison of information against all samples in its database and will list out those that match up. If David DuBois and Juliette DuBois are related, then that will come out in the report."

"How long will that take?" Lynx asked.

"Zoe said that she'll prioritize this for us," Nutsbe said. "From the point of getting the samples into her lab until we have a printout, less than thirty minutes. Knowing if David is Juliette's biological dad could be an important piece of information. Too bad you're in Toulouse, and DuBois is in Brussels. Right now, our client is rerouting to Paris. And I'm trying to get you booked on the next flight. We're working with the airline to boot someone off the plane and get you on."

"They do that?" Thorn asked.

"We grease their palms pretty well. It's a win-win. They give a couple hundred bucks to the person willing to wait for the next flight, they get our support when they have something weird going down, and we get where we want to be when we want to be there."

"Roger. I'll grab some grub and wait for your directions. I have one more question. There's information in the DuBois files that mentions his ethics breaches. I'm wondering if there's any connection there that might give us a clue as to who Juliette DuBois might be and what's going on with this case."

"Yes," Lynx said. "I've been culling through that information. So far, I've found something filed with the U.S. Navy per Dr. DuBois, and his use of treatments that aren't FDA approved, basically experimenting on the sailors after they survived the Al-Qaeda attack October 2000."

"Can you put that info in the file? I'll read up while I'm in flight."

"Yeah, you'll have to wait to get to a secure place for that," Nutsbe said. "If I can't wiggle you into a seat on this next flight out, you might end up in the holding area with the dog crates."

Lynx chuckled, but Thorn didn't think Nutsbe was joking.

"I'll get that file up for you," she said. "So, the newest information, are you ready for this?"

"We just pulled up to the curb. Let me pay the guy and move away from the crowd. I'll call you back. Okay?"

23

Thorn
Toulouse, France
Saturday, Twenty-two Forty Hours

"It's surprising how busy the airport is for this hour." Thorn had taken a seat on a bench in a green area that would allow him to see any lurkers who might be trying to listen in on his conversation. Still, he kept his tone low. He had a ham and cheese sandwich on a baguette, unwrapped, and resting on his knees. He'd placed his duffel between his feet.

"Are you clear to speak? We have information about Juliette's escape from the kidnapping attempt."

"It's confirmed that was her in the stolen car?" Thorn asked, taking a bite of his sandwich.

"Yes, and there's some interesting information for you in that vein." Lynx's voice shifted away from the phone. "Nutsbe, are you ready with that?"

"Yeah." Thorn heard him call from a distance.

"Nutsbe here. Okay. Here we go. Lynx and I tried to figure out her possible direction of travel along the highway. We thought she'd take the highway north to Orléans, and we sent that information to the local police. Following this, our computer picked up police comms. They located the stolen car there at the top of a pedestrian-only shopping area. The keys were left in the glove box."

Thorn swallowed his bite of food. "That's exactly what Honey did earlier when we stole the car. He threw in a wad of cash to cover repairs and inconvenience."

"No money, but there was a note."

"Yeah?" His heart rate ramping up, Thorn modulated his tone to professional. "Any clues there? What did it say?" He reached for his water bottle.

"Hand that to me Lynx…Okay, it said, 'I'm so sorry to have put you through this. Forgive me. I was kidnapped and running for my safety. You saved my life. I will always be appreciative and hold you in prayer.'"

A prickle slid over his scalp, and Thorn ran his hand through his hair to make the distraction stop. Only a tender-hearted person would wait to write that and leave it behind instead of wiping the steering wheel and tossing the keys in the trash.

The same could hold true if it were someone coldly calculating that was leaving a trail of a fake story that would serve them if they were caught.

Thorn couldn't believe that last one was true.

And therein lay the danger. He had made up a narrative based on his reactions to her images. That narrative could very well make him miss or discount something that was imperative. He had no reason to believe anything one way or another about Juliette. All of her choices could be coldly calculated or just as easily be genuine.

Thorn was on a fact-finding mission.

He needed to screw the feelings to the wall. Emotions had zero place on a mission.

They were dangerous.

"OKAY, THEN." After he took a swig, Thorn screwed the top back in place. "She didn't leave money like Honey did, but chances are that she has no cash, or she wanted to preserve what cash she has. But, as Lynx would say, extra good karma points were given."

"It's true, though," Lynx said. "There are no coincidences. She needed help, and an angel pulled over and let her steal his car. He deserves an extra boost of good karma points. Don't you think?"

"I'd never deprive a guy of his karma," Thorn replied.

Lynx laughed. "Okay, here's the great news. The DGSE gave our client CCTV footage, and it's very interesting, to say the least."

"I haven't worked European cases very much. Is French intelligence usually this helpful?" Thorn asked.

Lynx said, "I don't know. I can ask around. Echo Force is normally in Europe. I'm writing that down for a follow-up. But in this case, I think they're concerned about someone claiming French citizenship and traveling on a fake French passport when they don't have her information in their system."

"Hey, man," Nutsbe cut in. "I loaded the edited video onto your cloud, so you could look while Lynx takes you through it."

"Do we have time for this?" Thorn asked, wrapping his sandwich up and shoving it into the side pocket of his duffle. He looked down and saw a polished red stone near the instep of his boot. "When does my plane leave?" He gave it a quick wipe on a napkin and looked it over. He thought it might be a piece of red jade that someone had carried as a worry stone. He shoved that into his coat pocket as he retrieved his phone.

"I'm watching for progress," Nutsbe replied. "They're still trying to force some passenger to give up their seat for you. I'll give you the heads up when you need to go in."

Thorn tapped at his phone to bring up the video file. "All right, I've got the footage queued up."

"Press play," Lynx said. "We'll start. Here we see Juliette. That's an electronics store. Fast forward and stop when you see her get to the next point."

Thorn tapped and scrolled. "Got it."

"That's a *tabac*. We got a ping on Juliette's bank account. At the time when she was inside this store, she withdrew a wad of cash. It converted after fees to two-thousand dollars in cash."

Thorn let out a whistle. "Smart move. Now she has an invisibility cloak."

"Scroll forward. You'll see that she goes back to the electronics store."

"To buy a burner phone?" he asked.

"Our team hacked the store computer, and during the time she was in there, a cash transaction was registered for a tablet, a pre-paid phone, and a prepaid hotspot," Lynx said.

"Interesting. She seems to know what she's doing. But it looks like she was having a hard time walking a straight line. Let me play that again." Thorn scrolled back and watched frame by frame. "She's not clutching any one body part. She's not limping. We talked about the possibility of a medicinal restraint. It could be they drugged her."

"Yeah, Nutsbe and I have watched it a couple dozen times now. And I'm hard-pressed to find an explanation. I'll show you why," Lynx replied. "If you move the video forward, you'll see we edited out sections when she's not in the frame. She goes to the clothing store. She goes to the pharmacy. She goes to the used bookstore."

Thorn watched as Lynx labeled the stores that were too grainy for him to figure out on the small screen of his phone. "She's gathering pocket litter, making an alias for herself." He spread his fingers on the screen to focus on what type of clothing store she'd chosen. "That clothing store looks like it had a teen vibe to it."

"Exactly," Lynx said. "Then she goes into this café and never comes out."

"She changed her clothes? The camera didn't catch it?"

"It means she didn't come out of the front door," Nutsbe said.

The video blipped, and it was on to another section of the footage. "Yup." Thorn nodded toward the screen, pressed stop, scanned his own surroundings to make sure no one was approaching, then focused back in. "She's this girl in jeans and tennis shoes, stumbling out of the alley. Hood up."

"That's her," Lynx confirmed. "This next part shows her progress back to the pharmacy and then walking to the square where she buys a movie ticket."

"Which is a great place to disappear, especially if you need to nurse your wounds. She's too practical and strategic to be doped up. Do you know what she bought at the pharmacy the first time around?"

"Hard to say." Nutsbe's voice was in his ear. "We hacked in, but there were a lot of transactions at that time period and multiple cash registers. Tech tried to get internal CCTV footage, but their cameras are on the fritz."

"Too bad," Thorn said. "Buying bandages and alcohol would tell us a lot." He watched the small woman hidden under an over-sized black hoody walk back out the door. "So this is her second trip to the pharmacy, and she buys crutches. Why didn't she buy them the first time?" Thorn asked. "If it were me, I'd guess that she wanted the crutches to be associated with hoody-teen, not high-heeled chic woman."

"That makes sense. She must know there are cameras all over the public spaces. If she'd bought those crutches when she was dressed chicly, we'd see her come out with the crutches in her hand. If she waited until she changed her clothes, we might not have identified her."

"I haven't seen her face on camera since she went into the restaurant. You're sure this is the right woman?" Thorn asked with another scan of his area. He couldn't see anyone, but he felt eyes on him, and they felt predatory.

"We have her face farther into the footage," Nutsbe said.

"Got it. Someone trained her well," Thorn said under his breath. He wondered if she had a connection to the Mossad herself? It was possible that one of them fell off the grid, and they needed help getting her back. Or perhaps the Mossad simply wanted to let America know that they were on the same trail, so they wouldn't step on each other's toes. Thorn thought that then rejected it. If that were the case, Brigitte wouldn't have needed code words for Margot to interpret about strawberries and pink rabbits, and he wouldn't have found the soaped message on the bathroom mirror. For a flash, Thorn thought that perhaps Brigitte had sex with him for the sole purpose of having an excuse to shower and for him to shower as well. There was almost no other scenario that would have given her the chance to pass by surveillance. And she seemed to know exactly where that surveillance had been placed. The sweepers didn't find anything in the bathroom. *Clever*, he thought.

"Juliette never goes to the movie," Lynx was saying, "she

just buys the ticket and goes to hang out near this group of young adults – late teens."

"Solidifying her cover. She's acting like a pro—hood up, I see. And the crutches seem to be helping with stability. She was wobbly coming out of the alleyway. Whatever's going on for her, they seem to be helping."

"Watch carefully here," Nutsbe said. "She grabs that guy's arm. Drops the hood and smiles. Guy looks to his friends who are walking toward the theater. Back to her. Texts his friends to head-on and he walks with Juliette to his car."

"Were you able to capture the license?"

"We have it. Lynx has got a field trip to take. But I'll keep working on a destination point."

"All right." Thorn rubbed his palm over his five o'clock shadow. "What's your take? She seems to be working protocol. She's acting like a professional. There's probably not anything that I would have done differently if I were in her shoes. Is she friend or foe?"

"Shit if I know, man," Nutsbe said. "But I just got pinged by the airlines. We'll keep working it from our end. It's time for you to hang up and start running. I got a green light on your flight, and they've already started boarding passengers."

Thorn was already in motion as he said, "Roger. Wilco. Catch you on the flip side."

24

JULIETTE
Paris, France
Sunday, 12:01 a.m.

JULIETTE DRAGGED herself away from the monster that was holding her down in her dream. The streetlight filtered through the long window, past the heavy curtains. Her sheets were damp with perspiration, and she shivered beneath them. As she pushed herself up to sitting and let her feet find the floor, Juliette realized her vision was worse instead of better. The ringing in her ears was louder.

With a lunge, Juliette caught herself on the back of the bidet and yanked at the hem of her nightgown. Turning, she plopped onto the seat and struggled to get the gown over her head. She thrust her hand out, taking three tries before she could loop her gown over the towel rack to dry.

Juliette was thankful to have made it as far as the bidet, thankful that it was here in her room, directly across from her bed. While it wasn't supposed to be used as a toilet, Juliette didn't think that even crawling, she could make it all the way down the hall to the communal bathroom. She'd read about a character who was doing surveillance, and he'd peed into a bottle. Easier for men to do than women.

Without getting up, Juliette turned and rested her forehead on the sink until the heat from her fever warmed the porcelain, and it was no longer comforting. She ran the cold water and dangled her hands underneath, gathering strength. If this was how an addict felt as they were detoxing, Juliette could understand the struggle to get clean. Right now, Juliette thought she would stab anything into her arm to make this torment of sensations stop.

In some ways, Juliette wished drugs were her problem. She'd know that sooner or later this would abate.

For a moment, she thought about calling her dad. He knew the concoction that made her feel better. He could probably tell a hospital here. But that thought drifted away on the ringing of her tinnitus.

From her seat on the bidet, Juliette pulled the wash glove to her. She dipped it in the stream of water and did her best to wipe off the oily sweat of her fever. With trembling hands, she dragged a brush through her damp hair, braiding it and securing it with a hair tie. Her body shook convulsively, and Juliette thought that she should get away from the hard surfaces in case she had a seizure. She'd never had one before. But she had little control over her body right now and could certainly imagine that it might happen.

Another set of lights must have come on outside because the room seemed to brighten, all of a sudden. She needed to get that curtain closed. Juliette made a plan. She'd crawl to the window to shut out the light, then get herself over to the armoire and take two bites of food. She thought she could keep two bites down.

And while she was there, she'd see if there was an extra blanket. On her crawl back to the bed, she'd fill her water bottle, drink it down, and fill it again, take two pain pills, and then get back in bed and try to sleep.

Yes. That was her plan.

It was a good plan.

But that's as far as she got with that plan. Instead, Juliette sat there naked on the bidet, with her hands draped into the sink under the cold running water.

25

THORN
Paris, France
Sunday, Zero Forty Hours.

THORN HAD HOPED to nap on the plane. The woman sitting next to him had a baby in her arms, and as soon as they took off, the baby had started to cry. The woman was jostling and crooning to her little one. Every few seconds, she would send Thorn a frown to tell him she was sorry.

Honestly? It wasn't a problem. Thorn found the sound of a healthy baby crying to be wholesome. He'd been to enough countries where the babies were too malnourished to have the strength to cry. Their rounded tummies and stick-thin arms and legs, the flies swarming their faces looking for moisture around the babies' mouths and eyes...not a peep. Thorn could sleep through a baby's hearty wails. What kept him up was when the infants were silent.

He'd tucked into the corner, resting his head against the side of the plane, and told himself to sleep. Shoot, if he could sleep on a battlefield with explosions going off and a rock as a pillow under his head, this plane was as close to a five-star as he needed to grab some shut-eye.

But sleep hadn't come to him.

With his eyes closed, he saw Juliette's face. The fear. The determination. He thought through her choices, and he had to admit it, she had him confused. It was an odd kind of push-me pull-me of emotions. Emotions had no place in the field. You did what was necessary to complete your mission, and you washed your hands of it to move on to the next, and the next, and the next. It was exactly the way Brigitte had described it in his hotel room.

Something about Juliette made this different.

It was probably the fact that he couldn't put her in a neat category. The cryptic message Brigitte had left on the bathroom mirror did nothing to clarify the role Juliette played. She was staggering about, obviously impeded, but with the tenacity of a woman, every bit as dedicated to her survival as the janitor had been back in the bathroom when Thorn had wrapped his arm around the guy's throat to save Dr. DuBois.

Obviously, she was brave.

Obviously, she was intelligent.

Brigitte had said, "'Good guys' is perspective. Everyone working for their government thinks they're the good guy."

No matter what was happening from his own perspective, Thorn felt certain that Juliette believed herself to be a good guy here. That was something that a soldier should always remember. Evil wasn't fighting for evil. Evil fought for what they thought should be right.

Right also fought for what they thought was right. And sometimes had to do evil to achieve it.

The question wasn't really if Juliette was a good guy or a bad guy.

Her eyes told him that she believed herself to be doing something that was right.

Nope, he didn't get a single vibe from her that she was a criminal. Now, what they needed to figure out was, did Iniquus's creed and obligations align with this woman's? Were they fighting for the same vision of good?

Thorn chuckled to himself as he scratched a hand through his hair. That was much too damn philosophical for this time of night.

The plane landed with a jolt. It woke the baby who the mother had just cajoled into sleeping. Thorn thought that she was about to cry. She looked exhausted. He helped her get her bag down and offered her a smile when she thanked him for not being angry with her. The way she said it bothered Thorn like she had specifically been afraid that she'd disturbed him because men shouldn't be disturbed. It wasn't her words as much as her inflection.

Now that she was standing in the aisle, Thorn could see the last of a fading bruise on her cheekbone. Anger brewed in his gut. But he forced it down. Survivors often developed a sixth sense when dangerous emotions swirled near them, and Thorn didn't want her to become anxious because of him.

He hoped that this flight was taking this woman and her baby to safety.

He'd never know.

Walking down the gangway and into the terminal, the woman turned toward baggage collection, and Thorn turned toward the exit. He used his thumb to swipe his phone, taking it off airplane mode. He read his text instructions and headed toward the rally point.

Now that he was in Paris, Nutsbe had sent him to one of the hangars for private jets. Two members of Lynx's Strike Force team – Blaze and Gator – were coming in from London with two of the primaries that they'd been securing. They'd be taking the same jet back to the United States as DuBois. Blaze and Gator would sit on DuBois and make sure he behaved until the FBI grabbed him at Dulles to ask him some pointed questions. And they'd wait until they were over international waters before they did the blood draw for Zoe.

The plan was for them to contact Zoe upon landing and meet her at her lab.

Thorn had been ushered into a conference room to wait for both of the teams to come in. Gage, Honey, and Thorn would be heading to a hotel just down the road to hit the rack while Nutsbe and Lynx did what they could from stateside to track Juliette down.

With any luck, by the time his team had themselves fed and underway, Zoe would be done with her science experiment, and they'd have at least some of their questions answered.

Thorn patted his thigh pocket where he'd stored his phone, then pulled at the hook and loop closure.

He opened up the file that Lynx and Nutsbe had loaded up for him.

Ethical issues, Navy sailors, following ship attack 2000. The file title read. These issues were almost two decades old. That seemed kind of irrelevant to Thorn. After all, DARPA had hired the guy in, which required an FBI background check to get credentialed, so the guy would have access to sensitive compartmentalized intelligence. The FBI must have concluded that this ethics breach was water under the bridge.

Thorn glanced up to check the door, swept the room, then put his back to the wall as he swiped to open the file.

There were some notes at the beginning:

- Dr. Dubois was contracted with the Navy to work with sailors with PTSD following the ship attack in 2000.
- Sailors complained about the process of treatments that were *not* FDA approved.
- Dr. DuBois admitted to using laboratory techniques he was developing in his research, effectively using the sailors for human research without the necessary scientific protections, including the subjects' knowledge or consent.
- The techniques Dr. DuBois used included targeted use of memory implantations.
- Based on Dr. DuBois's laboratory notes that were seized by investigators, Dr. DuBois's experiments were unsuccessful.

Thorn,

Most of that file was redacted. Below you can find the only portion that was left readable, Lynx.

Researchers in the field of thought processes have long sought out an explanation for memory. A physical basis for memory has been elusive to our scientific understanding of brain function. Dr. David DuBois believes that it is possible to transplant memories, much like a computer download, from one sentient being to another.

. . .

IN HIS INITIAL STUDIES, Dr. DuBois studied sea snails. Sea snails, like many marine organisms, transmit nerve impulses similarly to the way other mammals, including humans, do. In his experiments, DuBois trained a snail in a simple performance of self-protection when being shocked. RNA (genetic information) was extracted and implanted into a snail, which had not received any training. This snail changed its behaviors to include the performance of self-protection.

THORN READ IT AGAIN.

Well, DuBois was supposed to be the foremost thinker on the subject of PTSD and traumatic brain injuries. It would make sense that if he was working with folks with traumatic events that he might want to find a way to manipulate memory. Experimenting on humans without consent, though, should probably have gotten his medical license revoked. It seemed to Thorn that a man who would do that felt that his theories took precedence over the sailor's free-will, and that was about as anti-American as you can get. It was narcissistic to think that you had the answers. That your needs and goals and desires were more important than someone else's.

Thorn read through the material a third time.

Then he thought about DuBois being Juliette's dad. And he thought about the woman with the bruise on her cheek. Maybe Juliette was on the run because she knew her dad wielded a great deal of power. And she was in an untenable situation as a subject of that power.

There was that anger boiling in his gut, again. Thorn had quashed it down earlier to protect the woman as they disembarked the plane. But there was no reason for him to do so now that he was alone in this room.

Any person of power who wielded control to cause pain was low life scum in Thorn's book.

He rubbed a hand over his face to get his thoughts back in line. Sure, it was probably a normal reaction to find out his fellow sailors had been mistreated. But this emotion seemed bigger than that. This emotion expanded when he thought DuBois had been abusive to his daughter – well, to Juliette. That relationship hadn't been confirmed yet.

He pictured the flash of her face on the video when she was kidnapped – her eyes, the fear.

When Nutsbe was handing out assignments, Honey had said he should go down to track Juliette. That was Honey's specialization. Lynx knew that. But Lynx had been staring Thorn in the eye, then she'd intervened, insisting that Thorn be handed the assignment.

Thorn had never known Lynx to be wrong in the way she read people. She'd seen something playing out on his face.

He wondered what it was.

26

THORN
Paris, France
Sunday, Zero Eight Hundred Hours

THE ALARM on his phone beeped beside Thorn's head. He stretched out to swipe it silent. Relieved to have been jarred awake, Thorn rolled over and stared up at the shadows cast across his ceiling.

The last picture he'd seen in his dream was of Lynx, her hand on his shoulder, nodding. For most of the dream, he saw himself with the world beneath his feet, shifting and spinning as he tried to catch his balance. It reminded him of the Greek pictures of the Titan Atlas. But in this dream, Thorn wasn't trying to support the world. He was simply trying to find his place to stand on it. He'd been working to catch his balance all night.

And like a veil over all of this were Juliette's blue-green eyes.

Juliette's eyes were an astonishing color. She reminded him

of the National Geographic cover of the iconic Afghan girl from the mid-eighties. Juliette's hair was honey blonde, and her skin was a lighter shade than that girl's, but their eyes were almost the same color and held that same haunted expression. Maybe that was what got its hook into him.

He threw back his covers and climbed from the bed. Before Thorn hit the shower, he moved through his exercise routine of planks and squats, pushups, and some stretches that kept him flexible. He showered and decided to just let his beard grow for the time being.

Today, he wore civilian clothes. He thought if they were going to be going on a Juliette hunt, that blending in would serve him better than looking official. When Gage and Honey knocked on his door, he saw that they'd thought the same.

"What happened with DuBois?" Thorn asked after they'd ordered room service.

"He was uncooperative," Gage said dryly. "We offered him a couple of diazepines, which he refused. We handed that assignment off to Strike Force. Maybe they had a better time of him."

"Is that a bite mark on your hand?" Thorn asked Gage.

"Yeah, when they do his blood draw, they'll check for rabies and let me know."

By the time room service brought up their steak and eggs, Thorn had caught his team up with what he'd been up to. They'd read the same files he had.

The case was intriguing, that was for sure.

Gage's computer pinged right on time, and he booted up on his encrypted video conference into Panther Force war room.

Lynx was in the view. "Hey, guys!"

"Good morning," they said.

"For you, well, I guess for me too. The cock hasn't crowed

yet, so I still think of it as night. Nutsbe's going to be here in a minute. He's just looking into something for you."

Thorn swallowed down his bite of food as he wiped his mouth on the overly-starched linen napkin. "While we wait, I'm interested to hear you said you were heading out on a field trip?"

"Right. So the only information Nutsbe or I could find about Juliette Marie DuBois was her green card and her stamp entering the United States. After that, she became a ghost. No car insurance, or driver's license, no residence, no residential phone number under her name. She has a bank card that's tied to Dr. DuBois. It looks like he's paying her bills."

"But you tracked something down," Thorn said as he cut into his steak.

"I tracked David DuBois down. He has a lovely home in D.C. proper. It's in a chichi area where the houses cost mega. It could mean something nefarious, but it's not completely telling because people often have income streams that aren't connected to their professions. But on a DARPA contract, he'd never be able to afford it. He also has another house. This one is in a suburban neighborhood in Alexandria, Virginia. A pleasant neighborhood with a lot of older people."

"Does he rent it out?" Gage asked.

"Interesting question," Lynx said. "I stopped by to find out. When I drove over, there were two packages on the front porch. One was for Roxanne Olson, and the other was for J.M. Dubois."

"Bingo," Honey said.

"In spades. A woman and her dog were walking up the street as I was standing at the door. I introduced myself and asked her if she was Roxanne. Roxanne, very thankfully, is a very friendly person, and I gathered some information about the strawberry part of our pink rabbit mystery."

"What was your excuse for prying?" Honey asked.

"I told her that Juliette was having some medical issues in France. Then I explained how when someone is overseas with such problems that the Red Cross can sometimes step in and help the situation."

"From that," Gage asked, "she assumed you were with the Red Cross?"

"I have a friendly face and a helpful attitude." Lynx smiled.

"I want to hear this now, but will you also send me a report for reference?" Thorn asked.

"Yes, I've typed it up. I just need to upload it for your team."

"Who is this Roxanne Olson?" Honey asked between bites.

"Roxanne is an author who is living with Juliette as her care-giver. The dog she was walking was Toby, Juliette's stability dog."

"Stability dog, huh?" Thorn said. "That might explain the video in Orléans."

"Almost guaranteed," Lynx said. "My understanding is that Juliette and her mother were in an accident. The elements of the accident were never described to Roxanne, but Juliette's mother was killed, and Juliette sustained significant disability. One way that you can identify Juliette is that on her feet, there are white marks from burns."

"Do we have photographs of that?" Honey asked.

Lynx pulled a hairband from her wrist and stuck it between her teeth. "No, I don't, sorry." She reached up and gathered her hair back in a ponytail and was winding the elastic around it as she explained, "Juliette sustained a head injury that affected her memory. She has issues with stability, tinnitus, confusion, some-times she is hard of hearing — more specifically, there are certain ranges that she can't hear. These hearing deficits cannot be corrected with hearing aids."

The men were hard focused on these details. They'd be important during a rescue attempt should one be called for.

"Juliette also has unexplained fevers," Lynx said. "That can exacerbate these effects, with accompanying headaches and confusion. So, all in all, I would say your pink rabbit is severely affected by her medical condition. And the fact that she was able to get to France on her own in high heeled boots, no less, is quite remarkable."

Honey asked, "Does she wear glasses or contacts? Are there any medications that she takes on a regular basis, something we need on hand if we were to scoop her up?"

"No, there are no medications that can help her. Roxanne said that when Juliette starts to become feverish, her father takes her to his lab and gives her an IV drip of electrolytes. And that seems to help. Her vision is fine. That is to say, she has twenty/twenty eyesight on her good days, but when she's experiencing what Roxanne refers to as a 'bad spell,' she has difficulty focusing. This is why she can't have a driver's license and depends on Roxanne to drive her around and care for her. Juliette also has good days where her symptoms are less aggressive, and she can take care of herself."

"Except for the driving," Thorn said. "Which explains the weaving of the car that she stole from the good Samaritan."

"One would assume." Lynx nodded. "Another weird one, I got David DuBois's health insurance information. Juliette is assigned to his policy. There's never been a claim declared for Juliette. And nothing in the credit cards going back to their arrival in the United States paying for Juliette's medical needs."

"What does that mean?"

"I don't know. Perhaps, for some reason, she's paying cash out of pocket, or that she's not seen a doctor in the time, she's lived here."

"With her level of disability?" Thorn asked. "That's curious."

"My thoughts exactly. Why hasn't she even gone for a flu shot?"

Suddenly, the monitor shifted to a split-screen of Lynx's face and Nutsbe's torso.

"Good morning, lads," Nutsbe called as he set his cup of coffee in front of him and maneuvered himself into his chair. "I hope you all went straight to bed and had a good night's rest."

"Yes, Mom," they said.

"Good. I have a feeling you're going to need it. Was Lynx telling you about Roxanne?"

"Affirmative," Thorn said, and while Lynx had provided them with important information, he wished they could just cut to the chase. Where was Juliette, and was she okay? "Did you find Juliette? Were you able to get CCTV of the airport from French Intelligence?"

"No, not from the DGSE, but I know a guy. What I had available wasn't helpful. There's something on the lens of the camera by the taxi queue. Bird crap, I'm guessing." He squinted at his monitor and tapped at the keyboard. After a moment, Nutsbe focused back on the field operator. "Let me back up. I just want to hammer this piece home. It strikes me how odd and out of character it would be for Juliette to travel to Toulouse on her own and be able to − with her level of disability − escape the two Russian guys and get secretively to Paris."

Honey pushed his plate away and scooted closer to the table. "Did Roxanne say anything about what Juliette did in her life prior to the accident?"

"Yes," Lynx answered. "She was a veterinarian's assistant."

Honey, Gage, and Thorn chuckled.

"No, she wasn't," Gage scoffed.

Lynx shrugged. "I'd have to agree, but that's the story

Roxanne was told. Juliette had brain surgery, and most everything prior to the surgery is gone from her memory bank. So Roxanne got that information—"

"From DuBois," Thorn cut in.

Lynx nodded. "Exactly."

"Apparently, our rabbit doesn't like to make too much contact with those around her either. When Lynx and Roxanne were chatting, Roxanne described how narrow Juliette's life is in Northern Virginia. She's home with Roxanne. She often goes out with Toby for walks – that's her dog."

"Roger," Thorn replied.

"She just goes up to a nearby park," Lynx said. "She goes with her father to his work with him about once a week. Roxanne said it was just a way for her dad to get her out of the house. Juliette's being new here in America. She hasn't made any friends. She was very isolated by her disability."

Thorn leaned in. "Something changed to bring her to France."

"Agreed." Lynx paused. "Yeah, what that something is, I have no clue. Roxanne said it came out of the blue. Apparently, Roxanne was out doing the grocery shopping for the week when she got a text. Of course, Roxanne immediately called her employer, Dr. DuBois. I followed that timeline. The text came in, the call went out, DuBois was on the next flight to Toulouse."

"Getting there the morning after Juliette did and missing her by minutes. Good thing or bad thing?" Honey asked.

Gage turned to him. "Do you think her being kidnapped might have been a good thing?"

"Yeah, I think Honey's right to ask that question," Thorn said. "Look what happened. DuBois didn't go in and talk to his mother. He didn't wait to talk to the police. He jumped in his cab and took off for the airport. Strange set of actions for a loving father."

"Beyond that," Honey said, "he fought us in the airport. He had the phone number for the Omega crew and called them for an extraction. He fought us out to the car and fuckin' bit Gage trying to get away."

"Now, see?" Nutsbe chuckled. "I thought the poor man was just hungry because you guys forgot to feed him."

Gage pursed his lips as he shook his head. "He was still fighting when we handed him over to Strike Force."

Lynx nodded. "Yeah, I can see the confusion. Not knowing what's going on in DuBois's mind means we don't know if he knew who had taken Juliette and how to get her back. He might have had a connection to Omega, and they were there to assist him in getting to his daughter. He could have been fighting you in an attempt to get back with the team he thought would be of the most use in the situation."

"And he was chasing her to France, why?" Gage asked.

"Again, the obvious reason would be that she is disabled and could get herself into a life-threatening situation. Roxanne said that normally Juliette wears a tracker at home."

"Like for someone with dementia?" Gage asked.

"It was on a bracelet that also had her contact information and medical records. She wore it so that if Juliette went somewhere on her own with Toby and didn't get home in a certain amount of time, Roxanne could go out and find her. Juliette can become cognitively and visually disoriented. And she can lose her hearing – not all the way – but so that conversations aren't possible."

"Right. No hearing aids. Does she know sign language?" Honey asked.

"She does. So lucky you that you're required to have some basic skills in that. When you find her, that might be helpful."

God, that sounds like a difficult life, Thorn thought. *Especially without much of a support system – old friends, a larger family...*

Thorn came from a big family. Five boys. Tons of cousins. They leaned on each other. Sometimes, he just took it for granted that everyone had that kind of support. Family behind them. A team like the Panthers behind them. Juliette had DuBois and this Roxanne person.

Thorn shifted in his seat. He was done gabbing. He wanted to be out prowling the streets, finding Juliette, making sure she was okay, not just from the kidnappers who might still be on her trail, but from anyone who might want to take advantage of a woman in a physical crisis.

When he looked up, he found Lynx's eyes hard on him. There was a trace of worry between her brow. A slow nod of her head. Thorn wished she'd share that thought. There was conviction behind it, whatever it was. He thought if they were alone, she might just tell him; instead, he said, "All right, let's get on it. Any crumbs to lead us toward her?"

"We didn't have a license plate, but I tracked cab destinations from the taxi queue at the time we saw her in line. I called each of the hotels where they took their fares—no Juliette DuBois. But Lynx had suggested that I also ask for Roxanne Olsen, probably the safest name for someone with Juliette's brain injuries to use. And she was right. We have Juliette registered as Roxanne at *Petit Coin*, a hotel in the ninth *arrondissment*. I put a satellite on the place with a computer watch, and I haven't mapped her coming or going. We have to assume that Juliette went to bed and hasn't gotten up and mobile yet today."

"She took Roxanne's ID?" Honey asked.

"Her caregiver is African-American," Lynx told him. "I'd say that was a no. She's just using her caregiver's name. Taking Roxanne's I.D. would be significant though, it would show premeditation for going to ground. I really don't think that's the case here. Based on her behaviors, I'd think she would have been better prepared."

"We hacked the *Petit Coin* computer system," Nutsbe said. "Juliette paid for a week in-full using a gift card and left a two-hundred-euro cash deposit. I'm assuming that's because she didn't have a credit card to give them."

Thorn pulled that name up on his map app. After giving it a look, he shoved his phone back in his pocket and reached out to tap his teammates. "Okay, Lynx and Nutsbe – if there's nothing else, we should move."

27

THORN
Paris, France
Sunday, Zero Nine Forty-five Hours

GAGE DREW their car into the alley behind the hotel.

They dropped their comms into their ears, wrapped their microphones around their necks, and did a soundcheck.

"No comings or goings of anyone who might be Juliette?" Thorn would normally call her their "mark," but that felt like putting her into his crosshairs and seemed impossibly wrong. "Lynx said that Juliette had good days, so she might not be on crutches or staggering."

"Nothing to report," Nutsbe said. "I loaded up the schematics. She's on the third floor in a front bedroom. You shouldn't have much in the way of foot traffic getting in your way."

The team opened the file on their phones. "Those halls and rooms look mighty narrow," Honey pointed out.

"You may have to duck and walk sideways, Honey," Nutsbe said. "But the other guys should fit just fine."

"It sounds like he's joking," Gage said. "But looking at this, he's *not* kidding."

Thorn held his phone in the flat of his hand, so the team was all looking at the same view. "I'll walk around, go in the front door, and make my way up this stairway. Gage and Honey, it looks like someone propped open the back door." He lifted his chin toward the building. "Why don't you take the back stairs?"

"Roger that," Honey said. "Just give us a heads up as you get in there."

Thorn climbed out of their rental car. He snagged his day bag, a lower profile backpack. Between them, they'd chosen the equipment most likely to be of help on a mission like this. Their duffels were in the trunk, their computers hidden beneath the seats, trackers on, and just in case, Nutsbe had placed a computer lock on the car from his satellite image.

Thorn sauntered down the alley, around the corner, and up to the hotel's front door. The awning cast a shadow across the building where a sign hung on the window indicating they'd be back at ten hundred hours.

He wasn't willing to wait. After a quick canvas for cameras, Thorn hid his actions behind the bulk of his body.

Pulling his lock drill, fashioned from an electric toothbrush, from the side pocket of his bag, Thorn plucked the tooth-cleaning head from the top and pressed the lock-picking drill into the opening. After inserting a shunt to hold the pins open, it was a quick one, two, three with the drill, and the lock was tumbled. Thorn cast his gaze down the street both ways before he pushed through the door, flipped the lock back in place, and whistling, took the stairs two at a time.

"I'm in and heading up. No one was in the lobby. Hide nor

hair of anyone. The place looks dead." As soon as the words passed his lips, Thorn immediately regretted them.

"In," Honey said over the comms.

Thorn had arrived at the room. He put his ear to the door and could hear the water running. Okay, now they were getting somewhere. He rapped his knuckle gently against the door.

No answer.

He rapped again. In French, he said, "Repairman." He put his thumb over the peephole.

No answer.

He thought, perhaps, Juliette might not be able to hear him. But when he rapped a third time, and much louder, he listened with his head to the door. There was no change in the sound of the water, which meant that she wasn't reaching into the flow as she washed or filled a cup. He watched as Gage and Honey strode up the hallway.

He mouthed the situation to them, their comms shifting his whispers into an audible feed.

With them blocking the view. Gage put his finger over the peephole, and Thorn pulled out his lock picks. This time he chose to do the work by hand rather than have the whir of the electronics bring any attention their way or make them memorable.

It was a cheap lock, and he had easy access.

The chain kept the door from opening. Thorn could take it down with one swift kick.

Knocking again, he called out, "Repairman." When no one answered, Thorn reached his hand through the door, he felt the wall until he came across a light button and pushed it in. Thorn pulled out his phone, tapping to start videotaping, and thread his arm back through the crack.

When he pulled his phone back and rewound, Thorn found

that he had captured a dimly lit narrow room, water running into the sink, a closed drape, and a naked body lying crumpled on the carpet.

From the position of the woman on the floor, Thorn couldn't identify her as Juliette. His instinct was to bash down the door and charge in to see if he could help her — whoever she was. Thorn fought against his instincts as he and his teammates threw their bags to the floor, pulling out equipment.

Gage lay on the carpet, reaching through the bottom of the door with his gas detector. While they waited for the machine to check the air quality, Thorn pulled a rubber band from his lock pick kit along with a large bandage. He wrapped one of the taped ends around the band to attach it, then looped the band over the chain. "How's it coming? I'd rather just kick it in."

"I'll let you know," Gage said from down at Thorn's feet. "You might as well keep going with that."

Honey had Nutsbe on video chat, so he could monitor the scene.

With practiced fingers, Thorn moved the knot loop of his rubber band up the chain to the point where the catch ball rested in the slide. He put his arm as far as possible around the door, stretching the band up at an angle, then pressed the bandage's other sticky end to the door. "Ready," he said, pulling his arm back out.

"I don't have anything yet," Gage said.

The problem with a downed person with no obvious sign of trauma, especially when they hadn't seen another living, breathing soul in the place, was that there was a reason. If the rescue team rushed in, they could succumb as well. It sucked. But there were solid reasons for this protocol. Though every second tightened Thorn's gut down another notch.

He busied himself, getting his neoprene gloves on, pulling a stethoscope around his neck, and grabbing up his medical response kit.

"Nutsbe here," Thorn heard over the comms. "I have Dr. Jaffrey linked in. He'll be talking you through your medical checks."

"Clear," Gage called as he reached for the doorknob. He pulled the door slowly shut. When he opened it again, the chain dropped from its slot, and the door swung wide.

Thorn treated it as both an emergency and a possible crime scene. He was the only one to go in, not that his teammates would have fit. With his stethoscope in his ears, he held the bell to the woman's back and was rewarded with both a heartbeat and the sound of air filling her lungs.

"Check for bleeds before you turn her," Dr. Jaffrey's said.

Methodically, Thorn ran his hands under the woman, pulling his hands out and checking them for blood. Finding none. He moved to turn her over, making sure that he held her neck and vertebrae straight.

Juliette.

His breath came out in a rush deflating his lungs. Fear coursed through his veins. He did his best to tamp those emotions down. He needed steady hands and a sharp mind. Thorn would think about why this was such a kick in the balls later.

He moved her braid from around her neck. "She's hot as a furnace," he said, reaching for the thermometer wand, pointing it, and getting an instant reading. "105.4 Fahrenheit."

"Any signs of seizure?" Jaffrey asked.

"No vomit. No bruising. No abrasions from the carpet,' he said as his gaze traveled from head to foot, checking her. "She might have rolled around. She's got lint and debris from the carpet stuck to her skin. It looks like she passed out."

"All right. Lift her onto the bed and get her as comfortable as possible. Nutsbe indicates that shy of a true life or death situation, the client will send in medical help."

Thorn didn't like this decision at all. He'd been figuring a way to wrap Juliette in a sheet and run her down to their car and get her to the emergency room. He'd been primed for the dash. He didn't like getting a thumbs down.

From his kneeling position on the other side of Juliette, Thorn reached out and yanked the bedding out of the way. Her pillow fell to the floor by the stool that she'd been using as a night table.

Gage picked it up and lay it at the top of the bed. He pushed the stool outside the room to make a little more space to maneuver. He came up behind Thorn, turning off the water in the sink as he did.

The sudden silence was broken when Honey asked, "Dr. Jaffrey, you don't think she's at high risk? Nutsbe told you about her ongoing health issues?"

"Affirmative," Dr. Jaffrey said. "I need to know if she starts having breathing problems or has a seizure. For now, use tepid water to get her cleaned up, then tuck her in bed."

"There isn't enough room for me to get in there and help you," Gage said.

"I've got her." Thorn had his head down toward Juliette's ear. He wasn't sure she'd be able to hear him. He didn't know if there was a comfortable distance, or pitch, or even language choice that worked better than others. All the same, he said, "My name is Thorn. I'm here to help you. You're lying on the floor, and I'm going to move you to the bed." He shifted so that he was on his left knee, and his right boot was planted on the carpeting. He turned his head to check and make sure that his back was going to clear the rim of the sink so that when he had her curled into his arms, he could simply press up from a one-sided squat.

"This is me pulling your arm around my neck."

She was limp, lifeless, but Thorn felt his words were making their way in. "There you go. I'm going to roll your head against my chest, so it isn't dangling." His tone was as warm and encouraging as he could make it. He didn't want her to become frightened. He didn't want to do anything that would add to her discomfort. "I'm just sliding my hand under your knees." He felt Gage's hand on his shoulder. When Thorn pushed to standing, Gage's hand helped Thorn keep his equilibrium.

Thorn could feel Juliette was on this side of consciousness, and she was trying to help him by tightening her arm muscles around his neck.

He held her there against his chest as Gage spread a towel across the length of the mattress. *Good idea. That'll help keep her sheet dry as I get her bathed.* Thorn stepped forward and slowly lowered Juliette to the bed.

Naked was a non-issue for Iniquus operators. In their line of duty, they'd seen all levels of dressed and undressed. In their medical and tactical training, their subject's level of exposure became a circumstance like a blood pressure reading. But something about Juliette made Thorn want to protect her modesty. He reached out and grabbed a hand towel to drape over her torso.

"Ready for vitals?" Thorn half-hoped they'd be on the cusp of danger just so he could get her transported to a medical facility that could help her. But as he called the numbers out, he knew she was stable enough that Jaffrey wouldn't budge.

Thorn thought it was foolhardy not to have her in a hospital with an IV of fluids at a minimum. High fevers could have serious ramifications on the brain, and Juliette was already living with her brain disabilities. The thought that these decisions –

decisions made by their contractor, which may or may not have Juliette's best interest at heart — might just make Juliette's life even more difficult was untenable.

Dr. Jaffrey signed off on the comms, letting them know that once the med-tech arrived from the contractor, Jaffrey would no longer be in the loop.

Honey held out the phone, so Nutsbe could see the situation. "Nutsbe, I'm not liking this. If you could see her in person, you'd know she's in dire straits. Don't you think you could convince them?"

"Negative," Nutsbe said as Thorn pushed the stopper into the sink and filled it with lukewarm water. "The client had a strategy in place if we found her ill," Nutsbe explained. "They believe a hospital in a foreign country would make security difficult. They would contact the Red Cross and Dr. DuBois, who apparently has power of attorney, to make all legal and medical decisions concerning Juliette."

That didn't rest easy with Thorn. Even if Iniquus had been sitting on Dubois, Thorn had no idea what had happened after that plane landed in DC. DuBois could have headed back to that chichi mansion in center city to call his lawyers and bring on the headaches.

With any luck, Zoe would be getting back in touch soon with some idea about genetics. Of course, Juliette could have been adopted, and they'd be no closer to an answer.

Honey watched the hall.

Gage had moved to the window and had his eye on the front street.

Thorn rolled Juliette into recovery position on her left side. "You're going to feel some soap and water on a washcloth now, ma'am. I think you'll rest more comfortably if you were cleaned up a bit."

Juliette's eyelashes fluttered but didn't open.

Thorn gently lifted her braid out of the way then started at her neck, rubbing the French-styled washing glove over her arm and back. After rinsing the suds from the cloth, he used long, careful strokes to wipe away the soap. He patted that portion dry and moved the hand towel to cover her from breast to thigh, then he turned to her legs. Long and shapely, he was surprised after the talks of her disability that she was this fit.

Thorn consciously shifted away from those thoughts. Except for their tactical use, he wasn't about to contemplate a female as a *woman* when she was vulnerable. That was a moral and ethical line.

When he got to her feet, he stalled. His mouth went dry, and his nostril curled.

Honey stepped forward. "What is it?"

Thorn had to step to the end of the bed to make room for his teammate. They were tightly packed into the tiny space.

"Here are the scars that Lynx was telling us about. Lynx said the caregiver had mentioned burn scars on her feet. Roxanne seemed to believe they were from the accident that killed Juliette's mother. What do they look like to you?"

Honey pulled a flashlight from his pocket to shine onto the silver marks that curled from the pads of her feet, up her ankles, and over the tops.

Honey's face turned to stone.

"Torture?" Thorn asked.

"Yeah," Honey said softly. "I'd say that's right."

To the RN in Northern Virginia, an accident was probably a fine explanation for these scars. But Thorn had seen this too many times to be mistaken. Too many men who fought next to him had survived torture sessions with their feet that looked just like this with methodic burn stripes. But he'd never seen it outside of the Middle East.

Thorn wondered if the amnesia Juliette experienced following her brain surgery wasn't the kindest thing that could have happened. Torture was a hell of a burden to carry through life.

Thorn saw that she had a nightgown hanging on the towel rack. He pulled it down and dressed her in it. He laid a cool cloth over her head and tucked the sheet and blankets up under her chin. It was the most he could do when she was all but passed out.

He needed IVs.

She needed lab work.

She needed a damned hospital.

But here they were, and here they'd stay.

Thorn's gut said this was a big mistake.

28

THORN
Paris, France
Sunday, Eleven Hundred Hours.

"ZOE, HEY, SWEETHEART," Gage said.

The team huddled uncomfortably around the monitor, which rested on the narrow desktop in Juliette's room. There was nowhere for them to sit, even on the floor. Crammed into the tight space, they had tried to angle the monitor so that they could see Zoe, Gage's fiancée, very soon to be wife, talk them through the results of the blood tests she'd conducted. They whispered into their communications systems so as not to disturb Juliette or have her overhear what they were saying.

"Hi, Gage." Zoe offered up her gentle smile. "Hi, Thorn. Hey, Honey." She wiggled her fingers at them. She was sitting at Nutsbe's desk in the Panther Force war room, talking over the encrypted computer connection.

"We really appreciate you doing this for us," Honey said. "I hope it didn't put you in a complicated position with security issues."

"It's fine," she said. Her long black hair was pulled back in a bun, and she wore black-rimmed nerd-girl glasses on a delicately featured face. "I was able to get a quick turn around on my request to let you see what information I pulled up."

"Did you share that with the CIA as well?" Gage asked.

As she turned around to look at Nutsbe, Thorn saw the confusion on her face.

Nutsbe leaned down. "I'm sure that our reports will be shared with the CIA."

Nutsbe had probably come to the same conclusion as their field team, the access to support here in Paris and in Brussels was provided by the CIA. It was very likely that they were also the signatory clients. It was really the only group that made any sense.

"So anyway." Zoe turned and picked up some papers and shuffled them into her lap. "I have the results. As you know, I can't compare two different people's blood samples in my apparatus. But I can send the two separate samples into the BIOMIST system. Once I did that, I tasked the computer to find any individuals that were affiliated with David Dubois, and I got a subset of zero. There was no one else in my system, including Juliette DuBois, that had a familial blood marker match."

"Juliette isn't his biological daughter," Gage said.

"No. Nor are they closely related, genetically speaking."

"Okay, then. That gives us a little more information." Thorn couldn't say why that brought him so much relief. But he had to point out the other obvious explanation. "Of course, he could have adopted her."

Zoe frowned.

The energy in the room sparked.

"You found something, didn't you?" Gage asked.

"The zero subset was for David DuBois. When I ran it the other way around," Zoe said, "Juliette Dubois had a subset of three. Juliette, and two women, Habiba Khouri and Polla Khouri."

"Sisters?" Thorn asked.

"Perhaps," Zoe said. "Or, perhaps, aunts…cousins. Neither is her mother. Habiba is thirty years old, and Polla is thirty-two."

"What else does the file say? What's included in the intake?" Honey asked.

"Oh, well, this was the hearts and minds cover story for the sample collection," Zoe said. "Where the data collectors pretended that medical help was the reason that they were in the region. The techs performed a cursory medical exam on each. The exam results were included. Both women were healthy if underweight. Their vitals were fine. They didn't need any medical attention."

"Does it list where the women went through the check?"

"Yes, let me see." Zoe looked down at her lap. "Polla was in Aleppo at the time and Habiba in Damascus. Their file recorded that they were part of an early wave of asylum seekers, crossing at separate times."

"Syrians?" Gage asked.

"Juliette's Syrian?" Thorn asked at almost the same time.

"Syrian, well, that's not part of the blood marker test. All we can say is that's what Polla and Habiba each listed as their nationality."

Honey turned his head toward Juliette. "She looks like she could be Syrian. The light olive skin, the honey-colored hair, and her blue-green eyes."

"She doesn't look anything like David DuBois, that's for sure," Gage said.

Before they chased this rabbit down a hole, Thorn needed to make sure. "The BIOMIST system has never given a false positive? Could this be a mistake?"

"Good question," Zoe said, and Thorn was relieved that he hadn't insulted her work. "The answer depends on the use. My system was developed to use in the field to tell the officer if a blood sample on site had the same blood biomarkers as the person they wanted to arrest, thereby letting those who didn't conform to the sample go free. This isn't as accurate as DNA. I can't tell you definitively if this is a certain person or not. All it can do is tell if the person is *not* a possibility. For example, if the blood sample came from a woman, and the agent was trying to compare that to a man's, it would come up as a zero subset. If, however, it met all the criteria and the machine gave a green light showing a positive subset, you'd need to get a DNA test *because* that blood sample could be his brother, cousin, or father's. You could be holding one brother responsible for the actions of another."

"But for identifying familial connections..." Nutsbe said.

"Close genetic familial connections, it's extremely accurate. Connections of the heart, like Thorn was saying adoption or marriage." She paused and smiled at Gage. "Well, those don't show up in a blood sample."

"Syrian." Thorn exhaled. *Was that where she was tortured?*

"We have locations on both women in the database for those seeking asylum in Europe. Both women were assimilated into their new countries based on language skills and educational background. They both hold PhDs," Nutsbe was saying.

That would mean that they might be able to get some answers.

"Sciences? Which sciences? Anything to do with neuroweapons or sound technologies?" Thorn asked.

"Uhm…" Zoe flipped through her notes. "Habiba is a geneticist at a university in Geneva, and Polla is a physicist in Munich."

"Honey, you pulled the Geneva straw," Nutsbe said, "and that means Gage, you're heading to Germany. If neither woman can speak English, both list Arabic as their main language, so you won't have trouble. I've uploaded more photographs of Juliette in your files. I would be careful about using the name Juliette DuBois or even Juliette. Juliette is not a typical Syrian girl's name, so it's very likely not the name that these women would know her by."

"Roger," Honey and Gage said together.

Zoe looked around at Nutsbe. "If you're done with me, I need to get back to my lab."

"Thank you very much, Zoe," Nutsbe said. "Your input has been invaluable."

Zoe smiled her cupid bow smile at him, then turned to the computer and waved. "Have fun in Germany, Gage. I'll see you when you get home."

"Thank you," the team all chimed in.

"Hey, Zoe," Thorn said. "Before you go, can I ask you something else?"

She gave him a tip of her head by way of response.

"Just generally, is there anything you can say about David DuBois's work? He has his DARPA lab up at Montrim, doesn't he?"

Zoe was quiet for a long moment, and then she offered up, "I'm sorry, I can't say anything about his work for DARPA. But I can tell you, since it's in the news, that I was at the meeting here at Montrim where the problem with the diplomats from Cuba was addressed. It was all of the scientists on the campus who went to the lecture, not just DARPA scientists."

"This was when?" Thorn asked.

"Oh." Zoe stalled. "Yeah, it was back when the diplomats were first calling in to report physical issues. Montrim asked us if we had any recommendations for avenues of research and who we might know with expertise. There was a guy, George Matthews — a Montrim scientist who worked on a Pentagon contract, who suggested we bring in David DuBois from AU in Beirut. That was the first time I'd heard David's name. And very quickly after that, maybe a couple of months? David was on campus."

"Nutsbe, George Matthews is in the wind, isn't he?" Honey asked. "Did anyone ever track him down?"

"Nope," Nutsbe said from somewhere over Zoe's shoulder. "As far as I know, he still has a nice little bounty on his head. The CIA and FBI would be happy to pay up, too. Matthews is either swimming with the fishes, or he's the fish that got away."

"To China?" Honey asked.

"That would be a good guess." Nutsbe posted his hands on the back of Zoe's chair, leaning down to get his face in the camera frame. "But I wouldn't think so. Something about the China thing seems off. But that's personal opinion."

"The diplomats were having issues there." Thorn pointed out. "What would a sound scientist and a PTSD Traumatic Brain Injury specialist have in common?"

"Explosions," Zoe said. "Well, they'd affect the ear."

"Concussions," Honey added.

"Flashbang." Thorn was thinking back to the team that tried to pull DuBois out of their hands at the safehouse, about the ringing, disorienting tinnitus. "We've all been through it."

"But you know you've been flash banged because of the light, sound, and the smoke," Zoe pointed out. "If they could isolate – well, create – if they could create the air concussion without the explosion."

"That would be an invisible assault." Thorn reached out and adjusted the screen as the light shifted outside, reflecting off the monitor. "A neuroweapon. Hey, Gage, I meant to ask you. Montrim and Senator Billings's name came up along the way. Last year when…" Thorn paused. He didn't want to bring up anything that would cause Zoe harm.

"When Rex Deus was trying to kidnap me?" Zoe asked.

"Yes, sorry," Thorn said. "But as I remember it, you over-heard Senator Billings begging for help bringing down Montrim. They had a doomsday device they were developing?"

"Yeah, something about killing everything in an area that was warm-blooded," Gage said. "Whatever it was wouldn't take out infrastructure. Just kill anything mammal."

"Did you hear the name George Matthews? Anything about sound?" Thorn asked.

"Negative. Nothing like that."

"Why would this guy, Matthews, who is suspected of Chinese espionage–" Gage started.

"I'd say from the evidence it wasn't just suspected," Nutsbe cut in.

"Fine." Gage scratched his forehead. "Split hairs, unindicted conspirator, then."

"Better, thank you," Nutsbe said with a grin.

"Why would he know and suggest Dr. DuBois?"

"I'm going. You guys keep talking," Zoe said as she got up from her chair and walked out. A thoroughly Zoe thing to do.

Thorn smiled. He liked that she was quirky. And he liked that she was a freaking genius and was able to point them to two women who might be able to give them background on Juliette.

"If George Matthews was a good guy, he might want to look

like a team player," Honey was saying. "A bad guy might want to bring in someone who would fudge data."

Juliette, though… Thorn pulled up his memory of the bathroom mirror and his soaped message from Brigitte. The Mossad thought she was the danger. Thorn looked over at her sleeping form. How in the world could Juliette, in her condition and with her disabilities, be dangerous?

29

THORN
Paris, France
Sunday, Twelve Thirty Hours

"CHECKING IN," Thorn said over his comms. He'd just finished eating a meal. Gage and Honey had brought him what supplies Thorn might need if he were holed up there for a few days. Thorn's duffle and computer were stowed next to Juliette's backpack in the armoire. "I've seen hide nor hair of the medic. Do you have an ETA?"

Nutsbe was in his ear. "No, man, how's Juliette holding up?"

"I was digging through her things. She bought some fever reducer. When she was in that café in Orléans, she bought herself a pretty good-sized order of food. I'm thinking she knew she was going to be down for the count. Her temperature hasn't changed. She's just not conscious enough to get anything in — even sips of water. Sponge baths aren't doing the trick." He moved back over to the stool next to Juliette's bed and wiped the damp cloth over her lips. "I need you to let the contractor know that I don't have any idea when she last had fluids. The pinch test tells me she's dehydrated. I'm not going to watch her die because they can't get their damned act together." This last part, Thorn said as a whisper. If she was at all lucid, Thorn wasn't about to plant the seed that she might not make it. "Even if I took her to the hospital and told them I found her in the street, I'm just about willing to do that."

"It shouldn't be long now," Nutsbe tried to reassure him. "Are her vitals still in range?"

"Affirmative." Thorn hated to say that. Even in the time that he'd been hands-on tending Juliette, he felt like she was drifting further and further away. He'd admit it. He was scared for her.

"We have something cooking—"

Nutsbe was interrupted by a tapping at Juliette's door.

"Someone's here," Thorn mouthed. "Could it be a medic?"

"Negative," Nutsbe responded.

"Juliette?" It was a woman's voice. Who would have known she was here? Thorn had found both of her phones, the one from the States and the burner phone. He'd scrambled the room while he opened them up to check whom Juliette had called. And since her "Ciao, I'm headed for Toulouse to visit my grandmother" texts to Roxanne, she'd reached out to no one. The searches on her regular phone stopped in the United States. The searches on her burner phone were to find the movie theater, to check on train schedules to Paris, and to find a cheap hotel that didn't expect an I.D. She'd looked on backpacker and student sites. Smart.

Thorn went to the door to look through the peephole. Someone was covering it. All he could see was black. He loathed not having a weapon on him. What he had was surprise on his side.

The curtains were drawn, the lights were out. He reached up and unscrewed the light bulb.

There was a scrape at the lock.

Thorn had put the ineffectual chain lock in place – just because it was an extra step for someone to take. And in a room this size, with so little in the way of fighting space, every second of warning counted.

He stood right at the door.

The lock tumbled, the knob twisted, the chain held.

"Juliette?" Came a woman's voice. "Can you let me in?" She was speaking in Arabic. Thorn wondered if Lynx happened to ask Roxanne what language she spoke when she was communicating with Juliette. Maybe he'd been speaking to her in English all this time when – no, that wasn't right. She'd texted Roxanne in English. She should understand it just fine if she could hear him.

A hand slipped along the wall until it came to the light switch and pressed the buttons. The woman sighed when the light didn't come on.

Thorn grinned.

It was best if he let this person get the door open on her own. He'd trap her once he could shove her out into the hall. And that was a great idea if she was alone. And not such a great idea if she had back up. He mouthed that part to Nutsbe.

The woman's hand slipped back out.

"Checking satellite footage," Nutsbe said. "Single female parked a car out front and walked in. I haven't seen any other vehicles in the area, and nobody staged in three blocks around."

The hand came back through with a telephone, taking video of the bidet and sink, the closed curtain over the window, and the sleeping Juliette on the bed. It never rounded all the way around to capture him. He noted that mistake and vowed he'd never make it in his future missions. *Always check behind the door.*

Time passed as the woman checked her video.

Thorn could hear the *zip* of tape being pulled from a roll. Her hand came back through the door crack to loop a rubber band on the door chain. Slowly, she worked the loop up to where the ball caught.

Thorn thought how it would freak her out if he were to reach out and assist. It would freak her out even more if he were to grab her hand. Of course, were he to do that, she might not be a law-abiding operator like he was. She might shoot through the door first and ask questions later. He guessed that would depend on what kind of bullets were in her gun and how much she wanted to make sure that Juliette stayed safe from ricochets.

With the rubber band in place, the woman stretched her hand up the door at an angle. Thorn could see that she was a power-lifter and had significant muscle strength. If that was paired with some combat hand-to-hand training, this just might get interesting. Thorn would have to make sure it stayed outside of Juliette's room.

The woman pressed the tape into the door and shut the door.

Thorn ripped the tape away.

The door opened, the chain held.

"Shit," the woman said. She pressed the tape again. She shut the door again.

Again, Thorn pulled the tape down.

She opened the door, and the chain stayed in place.

"For fuck sake," she growled.

Apparently, this woman liked her swear words to be English.

This time when she tore off the tape, it was over a foot long.

Thorn decided that he'd stirred that pot enough. He'd let her get the door open this time. Other than that, she just might get ticked off enough and kick it in.

The door shut.

As the door opened, the chain ran back across its catch slide and released. The chain swung down and banged the door. Thorn listened as she chuckled victory. She had been focused on the chain game and wasn't primed for a confrontation. *Another note to self. Don't do that. Ever.*

The door swung slowly open. "Juliette?"

And before she could put a foot in the room, Thorn swung around the door, caught the woman's wrist, and had her headed for the floor in an armbar. The woman shifted her weight and rolled, untwisting her arm. Forcing him to a crouch to keep hold. Her feet flung up and crossed at the ankles in front of his throat. She squeezed her feet in, right at his carotid, which was the way that he'd made the janitor go to sleep at the airport.

His senses lit up with the danger of the situation.

He had some of his own moves. *Deploying them now would be good,* he thought as the woman suddenly pushed with the hand that he'd trapped and tugged with her feet.

Thorn went sprawling forward. And as he did so, he released her hand and grabbed her boot. He landed and gave her foot a vicious twist that rolled her to her stomach. With his toes tucked under, he pushed out and dove over the top of her, trapping her with his weight.

She reached down and pressed her knuckle into a nerve bundle.

"Brigitte, stop," he hissed. "It's Thorn."

She stilled.

"Thorn?" She twisted around, and he let her up. Brigitte pushed the hat from her head. "How did you know it was me?"

"I recognized your boots from the airport." He stood and reached a hand down to help her up.

She batted it away. "Not bad, that last move."

"Yoga." Thorn shrugged. "It keeps me limber."

Brigitte slid her body up against his and smiled up at him. "You'll have to show it to me again later, when we're alone, and maybe not in the middle of a hotel hallway."

Thorn stepped to the side, so they weren't touching. "What brings you here?" he asked as he followed her into Juliette's room.

"Like you," she whispered, now using English in that warm sexy accent of hers, with her cat and milk smile, "I'm trying to secure Juliette and keep her out of the wrong hands."

"Oh?" Thorn shut the door and slid the chain back in place.

When he turned back, Brigitte was contemplating the lock, then tipped her head to the side and shook her finger. "That wasn't nice."

Thorn whispered, "I didn't know it was you."

She pointed up at the ceiling and lowered her voice, too. "You unscrewed the lightbulb?"

He pressed the light switch off, then reached up and screwed the bulb back in. "When I heard you in the hall, I didn't want you to flash the light on and wake Juliette. You know you really need to work on the clandestine part of your tradecraft. You're kind of like a bull in a china shop."

"Okay, enough of that." Brigitte moved to the end of Juliette's bed where she wouldn't block the faint light coming through a crack in the curtains. "How is our girl?"

Thorn had to check the possessiveness he felt. There was no "our" anything. Especially no "our girl."

"She's sick," Thorn said.

"Really? Is that how you're going to play this? I'm the one

who told you that she was the pink rabbit. I directed you to this bunny trail. You would have gone home with your precious David DuBois and not even known that this was an issue of international importance."

Thorn longed to ask her what the hell she was talking about, but his gut told him not to give her a centimeter. She couldn't think that she had the upper hand. And Thorn couldn't be seen as the lacky or sidekick here. It wasn't ego. It wasn't machismo. It was that Brigitte had started with that game, and it seemed to be the one she felt most comfortable playing.

Not playing that game might put Brigitte on her back foot, and she might slip up. Thorn might just learn something important like Brigitte thought it would be better to talk to Juliette in Arabic. Not French. Not English. Arabic.

Why?

30

THORN
   Paris, France
   Sunday, Twelve Fifty Hours

"BRIGITTE FOUND YOU," Nutsbe said over Thorn's covert comms. "That's fun. Did you check yourself? Maybe she stuck a tracker on you while you two were rolling around the other day. She may not be the best at getting through a door, but you've got to admit, that would be some awesome tradecraft."

Brigitte was watching him, so Thorn didn't respond.

"You're about to have a visitor," Nutsbe said. "Your medic and an assistant are coming up the back stairwell. They're bringing supplies. And along with them, they have a portable X-ray machine. 'Why?' you're asking me, with that mind-meld thing you're trying out. I'm guessing that Brigitte is probably staring right at you. Well–" He chuckled. "Whew! That mind-meld thing is pretty effective, by the way. Just turn down the telepathic volume a bit. You've set it too loud, and it's hurting my head."

Thorn moved over to the window and pushed the dusty sheers to the side.

"'Get on with it,' you're thinking," Nutsbe said.

That was *exactly* what Thorn had been thinking. He popped the closure on the French door and pushed it open, stepping out to check the scene in front.

Nutsbe said, "The medical team wants to take X-rays of Juliette's head. And as to the why, I'm not going to explain because you'll have questions, and you're not alone right now. You have the lovely and talented Brigitte keeping you company. Besides, the team will be knocking in three, two–" Tap, tap, tap sounded at the door. "One," Nutsbe finished.

Brigitte opened her eyes wider and looked over at Thorn, asking him silently who it could be.

Thorn had been waiting until the team was at the door, so he could get Brigitte out on the balcony without her knowing that he had forewarning.

Thorn tipped his head to the French door. She hesitated for a brief moment, then walked out.

Thorn shut and locked the door.

Nutsbe said, "I'll be listening on comms."

After dragging the chain off the hook, Thorn peered through the peephole – just because Brigitte probably had her eye on him, and he didn't want her to know that he had comms up.

Two men stood where Thorn could see their faces through the aperture. He opened the door and moved out of their way.

The front guy's gaze dropped down to Juliette. "Okay, then."

No introductions were made.

Thorn took the case, which he assumed held the portable X-ray machine, from the guy's hand and set it on the desk. It was a lot lighter than he'd expected. Thirty pounds, maybe. He glanced toward the window but didn't see Brigitte peeping through the curtain. Still, he positioned himself to block her view, in case she was recording with video or some other such trick.

Nutsbe's teasing Thorn about Brigitte's planting a tracker on his body niggled in his mind. He'd showered. He'd changed his clothes and equipment. They were coming up with new technology every day. He'd run a wand over himself later. Right now, he'd just assume that Brigitte had followed them in some conventional way, like putting a targeting square on him and programming her computer to track him via satellite. She was Mossad. They were more than capable of doing that.

The men stripped off their coats and scarfs then donned medical masks and neoprene gloves. Between the two of them, they pulled off Juliette's nightgown. They took copious pictures of her face and body. Thorn watched carefully to make sure that everything they did was professionally methodical. These were the kinds of pictures that were taken and put into a computer to try to suss out an identification. When they got to her feet, the men stalled. They conferred under their breaths, but Thorn knew, by the change of atmosphere in the room, that they'd drawn the same conclusions that Honey and he had drawn. Torture.

After taking photographic evidence of the scars, they inserted a catheter and an I.V. "Electrolytes, and some fever reducer," the guy said. They were the first words this guy had spoken out loud to Thorn. Obviously American. From the Bronx would be Thorn's guess.

The urine that started filling the bag was dark brown, and Thorn scowled.

The medic caught Thorn's eye. "We're fixing it, okay?" He lifted his chin toward his tote. "You've got plenty of supplies for the next twenty-four hours. We're going to move her, but there's a border involved, so we need her to get healthy enough to smile pretty at the guards. Yeah?"

"Yeah," Thorn said. He didn't think twenty-four hours would bring about the results these guys wanted.

They maneuvered Juliette on her bed so that they could set up the X-ray.

He wasn't sure what this X-ray was about. He'd told the team stateside that he didn't see any issues from falls or strikes to her head. Maybe this was part of a protocol for her particular disability. He'd be interested to hear what Lynx had to say after these guys got out of here.

Thorn noted their priority list. Photographs number one. Stabilization with the catheter and IV was second. Now, they were on to the X-ray. For Thorn, that was low priority. He'd put blood samples first, so they'd know how to treat her, what antibiotics to introduce.

He had to stand out in the hall when they flashed the X-ray. Hopefully, Brigitte was leaning against the outer wall and not trying to peek through the curtains.

Standing in the hall, looking through the door opening, Thorn watched as they tied a quick band around her upper arm and tapped at her inner elbow to get a vein to come up. She was so dehydrated; their efforts took longer than expected. They must have had an in and out time because they kept checking their watches. Finally, their last vial filled, they gathered their equipment, pointed one last time at the supply bag, and left without a word.

Thorn decided that Brigitte could hang out on the balcony a little longer while he looked through the duffle. IVs, needles, bandages, tubing. Fluid bags, a couple fresh catheters, nothing like an antibiotic. Lynx had said that the fevers had been unexplained...

Thorn zipped the bag and moved it to the armoire and out of view.

Yanking the curtain to the side, he unlocked the French door, and Brigitte stepped back in.

Her focus was on Juliette, dressed in her nightgown again, the sheets tucked professionally up under her arms, the IV dangling from a stand, still completely oblivious to what was going on around her.

"Fluids," Brigitte said. "Good." She turned to Thorn, feet wide, arms folded over her chest. "But more importantly, is there a plan to get her out of France and back on American soil? Because if you don't move her fast, you might not get to move her at all."

31

THORN
> **Paris, France**
> **Sunday, Twenty-one Twenty-two Hours**

THORN TUCKED the wand back in his case. He'd swept himself and then the room for electronics after Brigitte left. He'd sent her out for some supplies. A fresh set of better-quality sheets, better blankets, more clothes. He'd made the list as comprehensive as he could to keep her busy somewhere else. But he expected her back any time.

Hopefully, Lynx would be back from her meeting by now. Thorn wanted to find out about the X-rays.

After another vitals check on Juliette, Thorn put a cool wash glove on her head and smoothed the covers.

Digging his computer out from the duffle, Thorn sat at the desk in the darkened hotel room and pulled up the encrypted account. "What the hell is going on."

"You're unusually testy," Nutsbe said.

"Strange times, man. Brigitte wants to sit on Juliette like a hen who's just laid a Fabergé egg. There's a whole lot of cloak and dagger without a lot of context. I have no real idea of who our allies are, who we work for, who the heck Juliette is, or what's going on. I had a dream about this."

"Yeah? What happened?" Nutsbe shoveled up a bite of chocolate cake.

"Lynx patted me on the shoulder."

"Comforting," Nutsbe dead-panned.

Thorn squinted at the screen. "I thought so. I have meal replacement bars to sustain me, and you're eating dessert. Seems cruel."

"Lynx lost a bet. It's my reward." He shoveled up another bite. "I've never won a bet against Lynx. Let me relish this victory, man. My ass has been in this chair supporting you since the airport. I've barely gotten up but to go use the can."

"Appreciated. Is Lynx there now? Can you update me?

Juliette moaned.

Thorn held up a finger and moved over to the bed to see if she was rousing.

Juliette was mouthing something that Thorn couldn't make out.

"Put your phone at her mouth," Nutsbe suggested. "Let's see what the computer can do with it."

Thorn put his computer on the stool where he could still see Nutsbe. He pulled his phone from his pocket, swept his finger across the screen, and quickly dialed the war room as he heard Nutsbe call out. "Hey, Lynx, I need you here."

"Check." Thorn spoke into the phone and listened for Nutsbe's "Affirmative. I have it connected to the software."

Thorn moved the phone in front of Juliette's mouth.

The computer amplified and compressed the words, making

them comprehendible. Through his ear comms, Thorn heard Juliette saying, "Do you know what's going on? Why are we here?" then the language slipped into something else that Thorn couldn't understand.

She was silent.

Thorn waited.

"Russian," Lynx said. "Hang on, I have a translation on my screen. 'George, for god sake, what did they do to you? Are you all right? It sounded...did they burn you, too?... Whales. Whales...Free I want to be free!... It's science, not magic!'"

"Fevered gibberish," Nutsbe said.

"She said, 'Did they burn you, too?'" Thorn sat down on the bed next to Juliette's leg. "Surely that happened before her accident, right? It happened before her operation?"

Now in English, Juliette mumbled, "Free me. Whales." And as odd as that was to hear, it was a little clearer.

Thorn felt a glimmer of hope that they might be getting some answers.

"This is her subconscious brain," Lynx said. "Per the burns, I suppose that in a delirious state, someone might be able to remember things that were wiped from the conscious brain. My mentor, Spyder McGraw, trained me in hypnotism, and that's exactly the goal, to calm the brain's protective layers so that one can access what's beneath."

"This would be our opportunity, right? To ask some questions and maybe get some answers? Like why is she thinking about whales?"

Juliette was writhing. "I have no choice. Stop...What choice do I have?" That was in English. The words and the agony that came with whatever decision she was making was hard to listen to.

Thorn shifted on the bed. He wanted to soothe her, but he

also wanted to know what was going on. He thought he could lull her back into sleep by stroking her arms. Calming her, though, might shut this window of opportunity. The more their team understood, the better they could protect the outcome. Thorn pulled back from his instinct to gather her in his arms and hold her so she'd feel safe.

Again, he thought about how reactive he was to this woman.

That wasn't a good thing.

Operators had to keep their emotional distance to be coldly calculating. Honey would have been a better choice for this assignment. He had a knack for managing both empathy and calculation. It was a unique trait, and it was why he was so successful at pulling victims away from their kidnappers. Honey could leave them vulnerable, dangling them over the pit of hell, until the means for getting them out safely was cleared. Yeah. That wasn't Thorn's nature. Thorn wanted a bad guy and an opportunity to take that bad guy down. Action. Brute strength. Strategic thought. And a reward on the other side of a job well done.

This time, he'd taken his reward too soon.

He shouldn't have screwed around with Brigitte. The mission wasn't done. She'd called herself a piece of pie; he has known since he was a toddler not to eat dessert before his vegetables.

Of course, if he hadn't, she wouldn't have been able to pass that information. And he wouldn't be here with Juliette now.

Lynx had insisted that he be here. And he bet Lynx had seen in his eyes that this mission felt different to him.

That kind of pissed him off.

It made the situation dangerous. Emotions were *dangerous*.

When Thorn turned his gaze back on the screen, Lynx was hard focused on him. "I'll be happy to debrief in private when you get home. You and me. And you can tell me all about how ticked off you are."

Nutsbe scratched his head. "Our boy is a little moody. I'd say he needed to get laid, but…" He stopped to make a show of looking at his watch. "It's just over the twenty-four-hour mark."

Lynx rolled her eyes.

"Moving on." Thorn mouthed into the comms. "Lynx, I think it should be you who talks to her, a woman's voice."

"What language, though? She's speaking in Russian, and that's not one of my languages."

"If you were here, you could see how agitated and twitchy she is. I don't want to lose this window."

"Nutsbe said that when Brigitte called through the door, she was speaking in Arabic," Lynx said. "If Juliette is Syrian, Arabic might be the most comfortable language for her. I'll try that. Can you hold the computer, so I can read her face as I talk to her?"

Thorn tapped the phone call off and put his cell phone back in his pocket. He angled the computer and checked to make sure that Juliette's face was on the screen.

"I probably need more light." Lynx was still talking into the comms in his ear, and Juliette couldn't hear her yet.

Thorn hesitated but turned on the overhead and was pleased to find it was a low wattage bulb. It didn't rouse Juliette.

"If this is before the accident, she may not be Juliette yet," Thorn said. "Don't use a name."

"Right, okay. Here we go." The next time Lynx spoke, it was a soft encouraging voice in Arabic. Thorn thought her accent was west African, Moroccan maybe.

"I'm looking for you," Lynx said. "Where are you?"

"Snow." Juliette swiveled her head around as if she were looking at a panorama.

"Are you alone?"

"George."

"Is it my friend George? What is George's last name?"

"George Matthews." Louder this time. Desperation. Pain. "I can't…" Tears trickled past the veil of her lashes.

"Is George Matthews hurt?"

Juliette moaned and gripped the sheets.

Lynx changed tacks. "I love whales. Are whales important to you?"

"CHAMP."

Lynx repeated. "Champ."

"CHAMP…stop CHAMP…stop ships…stop pain…" Her agitation increased. She kicked at her sheets and blanket, writhing around.

Thorn was worried that she'd pull out her IV. His phone buzzed. Balancing the computer in one hand, he pulled the cell phone from his pocket. An unknown number had texted. He used his thumb to swipe it open, only vaguely listening to Lynx trying to pry fever-induced words from Juliette. He was looking at dark pictures of a car, trying to make sense of what they showed, wondering who had sent them.

"You're safe here. You're with friends. That's over," Lynx said.

The next picture that popped up on Thorn's phone must have been to show him the street signs. That was one block down. The third picture focused on a car make and license. *Who sent these?* The next pictures turned his blood cold.

Lynx had changed her voice. It was more commanding. "He's not here. He can't hurt you. He won't hurt you anymore. We won't allow it."

But Thorn only vaguely paid attention to her. He was scrolling back through the last photos.

A snapshot of each of the Omega crew from the airport,

wearing black. Tibor Yegorovich was on crutches and looked like he'd be staying with the car.

The next picture was them conferring and pointing.

A picture of the *Petit Coin.*

A picture of five other men rounding the same corner that Thorn had taken before he popped the lock on the front door that morning. They were headed toward the alley.

The next text said: **I give it two – three minutes tops. Get out. Get out now.**

It had to be Brigitte.

32

THORN
   Paris, France
   Sunday, Twenty-one Thirty Hours

THORN SNAPPED THE COMPUTER SHUT.

He was talking through his comms as he explained the situation to Lynx and Nutsbe. "I need back up." He was on his feet and moving. He'd already worked out a plan and staged the room should he have to make a dash with Juliette. He called out, "Give me a two-minute count down."

Lynx's voice began, "One hundred twenty seconds, one nineteen…"

Now, he worked his plan double time. He crammed his laptop into his duffle he'd staged on the bidet should a quick exfil be required. He zipped it shut and pulled the straps over his shoulder. With a *snap, snap*, he clipped the hip and sternum straps into place.

He flung back Juliette's covers. Yanking them free, he

dropped them out of the way. He lifted her head, took the pillow, and tossed it to the side.

"One hundred and twelve, one-eleven…"

Thorn grabbed up the surgical tape that he used to secure Juliette's port sites. Ripping and biting at the tape, he pulled off sections. One hand wrapped her wrist with a thick surgical bandage. With the other, he wrapped the tape around her wrist, staging her for if things turned from bad to worse. After that, he released the IV tubing.

"Ninety seconds. Eighty-nine. Eighty-eight…"

Grabbing the saline bag from its stand, Thorn tossed it toward the window and out of his way. A flick of the hand, he collapsed the stand and folded the feet. He was glad he'd practiced that earlier. He thrust it now − a fat and short configuration, like a closed umbrella − into the side pocket of the duffle. It could function as a weapon if push came to shove.

Thorn opened the door and searched the hallway.

Clear.

"Seventy-six—"

Swinging back toward Juliette, he said, "My name is Thorn. I'm here to help you. I'm moving you to safety." He caught her by the wrist and scooped under her back to lift her torso upright. "I'm going to put you over my shoulders." After she had been riled and fighting in her delirium, Thorn needed her to be still. Passed out would be good here. If she were fighting him, it would slow him down. It might even bring the help of some good Samaritan. And while good Samaritans had their place, this was *not* it.

"Seventy seconds. Sixty-nine…"

Thorn would have preferred to carry Juliette in his arms. It would have been more comfortable for her. But he needed at least one hand available for work. And it was damned hard to run with a weight across the chest. He sucked a breath between his teeth, knowing that he was probably going to hurt her head even more.

Still, nothing good was racing up the back stairs.

Out of this mess was the only goal.

Thorn pulled Juliette across his back in a fireman's hold, reaching through her thighs, using his arm to trap her leg in place on his chest as he grasped her wrist with tight fingers to keep her from slipping off his back.

With his free hand, he pulled the door shut behind him. That might buy him a few seconds.

"Fifty-four, Fifty-three…"

Thorn's phone buzzed. He pulled it from his pocket and swiped as he took off down the hall.

They're in the building. The text read.

Shit, not two minutes out.

"They're in," Thorn called out to his team.

He shoved his phone into his pocket as he raced down the hall toward the far end near the shower rooms. Without breaking stride, he reached out and pulled the fire alarm. Immediately, the bright whirring alarm sounded. Thorn hoped it was connected to the fire station and that within minutes, firefighters would be on scene.

He reached back and felt the side of his pack, grasping for the IV stand. As he reached the window, he turned his back to look up the hall.

People emerged from their rooms, looking confused, and put out.

"Take the stairs," Thorn yelled in French. "Front stairs are down there. Here are the back stairs. Hurry. Hurry. Move!" Then he repeated his commands in English.

His words seemed to do their job. That and the woman passed out on his shoulders.

The complacency of a fire-drill fell off as the people realized they were on the third floor in a possible fire. They pushed at each other, trying to get down the stairs faster. With the stairs clogged and the hall empty, Thorn used the IV stand to smash out the window. He turned and swiped around the edges, clearing the shards as best he could.

He couldn't fit through the opening, with Juliette and his backpack on him.

Leaning out, he swiped the IV stand across the fire escape, quickly clearing the worst of the glass.

He rolled Juliette over the sill.

She lay there on the grill of the fire platform, the wind whipping at her pink nighty. The ground was three stories below.

Her eyes fluttered open.

"I'm Thorn. I'm the good guy." He planted his hands on either side of the window frame and stuck his boot through.

Juliette moved to sit up.

"There's broken glass. Stay still."

She didn't listen. She struggled to sit up.

"Look," Thorn said as he ducked out of the window to crouch on the small landing beside her. "I'm trying to save you. The bad guys are downstairs, and they're on their way up." He'd let her interpret bad guys in any way she wanted to. "If you fight against me, we just don't have a good shot at getting away. They have a team. If they get to you, there's not a lot I can do." Thorn stood up and reached above his head to the ladder that he'd scoped out when his team had first parked in the alley that morning. Even the adrenaline coursing through his veins didn't help as he tugged at the bottom rung. It didn't budge. Thorn got a better grip and leaped in the air to use his weight to help bring it down. But it was stuck just over his head.

"Thorn." Nutsbe's voice was in his ear. "I've got you up on satellite imaging now. You pushed the team outside with the alarm. We're running the photos from your phone. Our count is eight. I'm assuming those texts were from Brigitte. You might not be there all alone. It could be she'll help. You have to assume the Omega crew has eyes on your movements. Don't take the fire escape down."

He'd figured that was the case. The hell he'd crawl down the side of the building to hand Juliette over to Hong fucking Wu. "Roger," Thorn said. "Up it is."

Thorn tried one more time to slide the ladder into place, so that up was an option. It was a no-go.

Thorn rounded on Juliette. She was lying very still, just as he'd asked. As he crouched, Thorn pulled out a police-duty zip tie and fastened it around her bandaged wrist. Things had gone from bad to worse.

Juliette frowned at it.

Yup, this is gonna suck for both of us. It was part of his equation that he'd need to be hands-free. Kneeling, Thorn could feel the glass shards grinding into his knees. He pulled a length of parachute cord from his pocket. "I'm going to put you back across my shoulder now." He didn't stop his movement while he spoke, sticking the cord between his teeth and talking through a clenched jaw. "You're going to keep your eyes tightly shut. And you're going to keep your body as relaxed as you can possibly make it."

He pressed up from his squat with Juliette draped across his shoulders. Though he knew it would hurt, he bounced her up and forward, edging her closer to his neck. "I'm sorry about this." With quick, practiced hands, he fed the cord through her zip tie, wrapped her leg, and pulled a quick knot, securing her much the way he'd used his hand to as they exited. He took an end of the cord and stuck it through the metal survival loop of his tactical belt. "Believe me, this will be as uncomfortable for me as it is for you. We're in this together." He tied a figure eight on a bend knot.

She'd stay in place.

"Everyone's out of the building," Nutsbe said. "I'm seeing jostling—all black clothing. I'm saying that's the Omega crew playing salmons and swimming your way. You've got to get off that X, man."

"Wilco," Thorn muttered as he bent his legs and pulled his arms back. As he swung his hands over his head, he thrust up with his legs, catching the ladder by the second rung. He used the momentum and a flex of his biceps to pop his feet up to either side of the window. Walking his feet up the side of the wall, he let his heels slip until they found the minuscule ridge of mortar between the bricks.

"The only easy day was yesterday," Thorn reminded himself as he pulled up, lifted one hand from the rung, and reached to grab the next one.

Feet sliding, hands slick from sweat, off-balance from the pack and the tethered precious cargo, he pulled up again, scrambled his feet again, moved his hands up to meet the other, pulled and grabbed upwards.

Three stories above ground, a feverish disoriented woman balanced on his shoulders, a daunting ratio of bad guys, and only make-do weapons.

Could be worse, though.

Juliette could be a bad partner, and she could start freaking out.

He moved another rung. Thorn pulled that image back.

People in stressful situations could suck thoughts out of the air, and the last thing he wanted was to plant the freak-out seed. Instead, Thorn said, "You're doing great. You're so damned brave. Keep it up."

"Hey, spidey," Nutsbe was in his ear. "You're going to need to hurry that up."

Thorn exhaled three puffs, grit his teeth, and focused. Now that he had done a couple of swings, he'd figured out the mechanics of the movement and was able to move through each step more fluidly.

The faster he moved, the more things shifted –his pack and Juliette.

She screamed from behind tightly pursed lips, grabbing at his shirt with both hands.

As Juliette slipped the few inches down his back, it yanked the cord on his belt. His pants cut into his balls. That was entice-ment enough to get him moving, to bring the boys some relief.

He hoped it didn't make him puke.

Juliette struggled then went lax, and he appreciated it.

Later, he might consider what it had been like to be in her position, blood rushing to her throbbing, feverish head, zip tie cutting into her wrist, trusting a stranger who appeared in the room, and staring straight down three stories to the pavement below.

He wouldn't have trusted the situation. He'd wonder about why she did later. Right now, he flexed his back muscles and pulled another rung upward. He could hear shouting from the ground. People had spotted him. He heard confusion in their yelling.

Well, hopefully, they'd point the rescue crew this way – that or maybe they were yelling that the bad guys were at his heels.

"They're at your heels," Lynx said.

Of course, they were.

Three rungs, two, one, Thorn was at the top of the ladder. He reached over the lip, clenched his abs, and swung a leg over the edge. The momentum of the shifting weight on his back pulled him over the lip. But he caught himself before he drove Juliette's face into the gravel.

On all fours, he pawed his way to the side and looked over.

Hong was looking straight up at him, pissed as hell.

Thorn grabbed at the ladder and shook it viciously.

Hong lost his grip and fell to the landing outside the window.

A beam of light caught him in its glow.

Hong swiped a bloody arm through the air to signal his guy to cut that shit out. Hong stood and grabbed at the rung. This time when Thorn shook it, it loosened, and Thorn was able to yank it upward out of the reach of even someone as tall as Hong.

He patted Juliette's hand. "Are you hanging in there?"

"Yes." Her voice shook.

"All right, here we go. We're working on an exit strategy." His phone buzzed. This time it was a phone call.

"Brigitte here. I see you made it to the roof."

"Roger." This was as far as his Plan E had taken him. He knew from satellite pictures that he could move from roof to roof the length of the block, but then, so did anyone else with access to Google Earth. He knew he had nothing to the north. His best chance was to move south and hope for inspiration.

"My team is moving into place," Brigitte said.

Thorn's phone was hooked to the Panther Force war room. Anything he heard could be heard by Nutsbe and Lynx, too. "Your team is? Is this the team that was on the motorcycles chasing us out of the airport? The ones with what looked remarkably like explosive devices in their hands?" Thorn jogged along the roof, scanning for options.

"David DuBois and Juliette DuBois are separate missions."

"But you're the common denominator."

"My mission goal for Juliette is to not allow her into the enemies' hands."

"Am I your enemy?" Thorn asked.

"As long as you're keeping her safe, we're playing on the same team."

Thorn turned and sat on the wall separating this building from the next. He lifted his legs and swiveled around, planting his feet and taking off again. "What happens when I get her safe? Are you thinking you'll take custody of her?"

"Save your breath, Thorn. Let's focus on the Omega crew. Hong and his buddy went back through the window. They'll move on to their back up plan. You're heading south. Good choice, actually, your only choice. That fire alarm, by the way, wasn't connected to emergency services. The old dude simply walked the halls and turned it off. Most of the people are out in the alley though with their phones, taping YouTube videos of your superhero antics."

Thorn had made it to the wall separating the next buildings, and he sat, spun, and launched again.

"Thorn," Lynx said, "we have a support team twelve minutes out. We're checking architectural schematics, coming up with a plan."

Thorn whispered, "Yeah, not a lot of options up here, even with the Calvary riding in."

"You're going to need to ditch Juliette and the pack," Brigitte said. "You have guys coming up the fire escape on the building just south of you. It's going to be a fight."

Thorn didn't like the idea of unstrapping and slowing himself down. "Where are you?"

"I'm coming to help, heading up the fire escape further north of you." Brigitte's breath came heavily. Thorn knew she was pushing to get to him.

Still, the idea of pulling Juliette off his shoulder... "How are you seeing all this?" he asked into the phone. His eye searched for a good place to put Juliette down, just in case.

"My guy is blinking a light," Brigitte said.

Thorn was standing between two chimneys, and he could see the SOS blinking from the high rise just west of him on the other side of the alley. With enough rope, he could rig something—

"Ideas?" he called into his comms.

"She's right. Four unsubs visible," Nutsbe said. "They're coming up the two buildings north of your location. You have about forty seconds. Unpack Juliette, *now*."

Thorn pulled his multitool from his pocket, flipping out the penknife. In one motion, he squatted down and took a knee as he sliced through the zip tie and cord that held Juliette in place. "Here you go. I know it's damp up here, But I need you to lie super still, curled up in a ball. I'm going to cover you with my pack. It's black, so you'll be camouflaged here. I need you to *stay* still and curled until I can get back to you."

With chattering teeth and wide eyes, Juliette followed his instructions. Putting her back to the chimney, pulling her knees to her chest, she didn't say a word or make a sound.

Thorn dropped his pack off and leaned it over her. Made with a Kevlar lining, as long as it was in front of her, she had at least a little protection from knives and maybe even from a stray bullet.

All right, four against one.

Brigitte was coming.

Thorn just didn't know how to file that away.

He wished he knew what her mission entailed.

He wished he knew if Brigitte really had his back or if she planned to bury a knife there.

33

JULIETTE
Paris, France
Sunday, After Dark.

JULIETTE *REMEMBERED*.

She remembered!

She remembered that she was in the car with the men who were pointing a gun to her ribs. She was wearing a black pantsuit and a silky blouse. She looked to the side, and George Matthews was there, too. She'd known him from their work together. She'd whispered to him, "We have to escape. The longer we're in captivity, the less likely it is that we'll get free." And George had said, "Be very still. Don't do anything that will call their attention to you. We'll be okay."

She shouldn't have listened to George. It would have been better if she'd been killed.

Juliette clutched at her pink nightgown and realized how

absolutely ridiculous it was as a garment. What had she been thinking?

Tipping her head to see over to where Thorn stood with his back to the chimney, Juliette watched him crouching, his eyes scanning the area. Without standing, he jogged toward the edge of the roof.

Juliette grabbed at his bag and unzipped it. Bags of IV fluids rested at the bottom. She saw her Converses and pulled them out.

She paused when there was a new movement along the edge of the building.

An arm wrapped the wall, and Thorn raced forward.

A man's black balaclava-covered head rose over the edge.

Thorn grabbed the man's wrist, yanked his hand out with a twist to expose the back of the man's arm, and Thorn stomped his elbow.

The man shrieked a high pitched scream that froze other sounds in mid-air.

The sheer violence of the act was stunning.

Juliette dragged her nightgown up to see what had been pulling at her thigh. She found that she was wearing a catheter bag with a tube that ran up to her urethra. She wiped her fingers on some cloth in Thorn's bag, then reached up to pull out the catheter. She tossed it to the ground, then ripped off the tape, holding the apparatus to her thigh. *So there, my veterinarian's assistant training is coming in handy after all.* But with that thought, Juliette knew it was a lie. That wasn't what she did for her work. She was something else. Doctor...the answer niggled at her. It was *right* there. But Juliette pushed those thoughts away. She needed to get herself safe.

She fished around and pulled out one of Thorn's turtlenecks, and there she saw the leggings she'd bought earlier.

Yanking off her nightgown, her eyes caught on a blur as

someone ran from the left, and someone else ran from the right. She froze in her place between the chimneys, as still as a statue.

Angry yelling voices swelled in her head.

It was the sound of fist to flesh that animated Juliette again.

Juliette was shaking so hard that she had trouble functioning. She plopped her naked bottom onto the roof and yanked on the leggings. She did her best to tie the shoes. Picking up the shirt, she lifted to her feet, balanced herself against the chimney, then moved back in the direction she'd come from. She was determined to get away. And if there was no other route to get away, she would go over the edge.

How many times over the last couple of years had she dreamed of doing just that?

Of running and jumping into a great nothing.

Of floating toward the ground, knowing that relief would meet her when her body found the sidewalk below.

As Juliette stumbled forward, she had the hem of the shirt between her hands, and she yanked it over her head, pulling her eyes free just as she came to the wall separating the roofs.

She didn't have the fluid body mechanics that Thorn had. Or the height and strength. Juliette leaned over the wall and, using her hands, wriggled one leg over then the other.

A siren sounded in the distance, and Juliette prayed it would get there and save her. And she also prayed that it would stay away because her head hurt enough as it was.

She stopped for a moment to catch both her breath and her balance on the other side of the wall.

The shirt hung around her neck; her naked breasts chilled by the night air. She pulled out the shirt and stuck her hands into the sleeves.

When she stood, Thorn's shirt came nearly to her knees, the arms dangling far below her fingertips. She looked back, and

Juliette could see that the fight continued. It looked like a lot of people. Too many people to count. The only thing for Juliette to do was to keep going. She crouched back down and shoved the sleeves up past her elbows to free her hands.

This time, she'd put a little more brainpower behind her moves.

Juliette tried to do the squat jog that Thorn had done to keep his head low. But that took a ridiculous amount of energy. And Juliette was weak as a kitten. She decided crawling was going to end up being her best option.

She was on all fours, crawling along the protective lip of the roofline. She'd done this before with bare knees. But people were cheering her on. It was a marathon race; she'd run to the very end and had gotten weirdly disoriented and fell. She had decided she was so close to the end; she'd just crawl the last bit. It was dehydration back then, she remembered. Easily fixed. She remembered! She was remembering! She'd been an athlete.

In *this* marathon for survival, Juliette's goal was to get back to the ladder she'd come up. It was the ladder she knew and the building she knew. Her passport and her money were back in her room. If she was going to escape, she needed those things.

Down, in, grab, go.

That was her plan.

Her other plan, the one that she'd do if anyone grabbed at her, was to go over the building and maybe take them with her.

Death was the ultimate escape.

She pushed against the memories that crawled from their hidden places. She tried to slam them back, at least for the time being. But from the memories that snaked their way out, Juliette knew that she'd never let them take her again.

Never.

34

THORN
Paris, France
Sunday, Twenty-two Ten Hours

HANDS ON HIS KNEES, Thorn dragged big gulps of air back into his lungs.

Brigitte was on all fours catching her breath, too.

He staggered past with a pat on her shoulder. Her team had backed them up. They had four goons zip-tied and lying on their stomachs. He'd broken one guy's arm before he'd even rounded into the fight. The three he really wanted to chat with, the Omega crew from the airport, were in the wind. Hong had been in the fight. He'd clearly seen Hong doing his famous roundhouse on some poor guy. But he and Norman Colburn must have slipped the noose.

Thorn had snapped pictures of their captives' faces and ears, rolled their fingerprints onto his app, and sent them on to Iniquus for identification.

He'd hoped that amongst their prisoners, he'd find the two men who had kidnapped Juliette in the first place. There was no guarantee that the kidnappers and Omega were on the same team. There could, very easily, be four sets of players – Iniquus, Omega, Mossad, and the kidnappers – going after Juliette now that she wasn't safely tucked away in America.

Thinking that, with each step, Thorn found new energy. He raced over the rooftops, trying to get back to where he'd hidden Juliette.

When he arrived between the chimneys, his bag was there, open. Juliette's pink gown and her medical equipment were strewn about.

His eyes scanned, but he didn't see her.

"Where is she?" he panted into his comms.

"She headed north. She went over the first wall, and then she was lost in the shadows. It's been twelve and a half minutes since we saw her."

Thorn turned back toward Brigitte. She was on her feet now and moving his way.

She was one hell of a hand to hand fighter. In that instance, Thorn was glad she was on his side. Glad she did her wicked thing, taking down those Omega crew. Yeah, she was the real deal when it came to soldiering.

Thorn jogged north. When he got over the first wall, he could see shifting debris under his penlight. Juliette left funny side-sliding tracks for a few steps, then it looked like she'd fallen and started to crawl.

That must be why the eyes in the sky didn't pick her up.

With his penlight switched to a green light that would preserve his night vision, Thorn tracked her over two more walls, then she rounded east, crawling toward the skylight, propped open in the middle of the roof.

Thorn hoped like hell she hadn't tried to go through that skylight. These buildings had twenty-foot ceilings. It would be a trip to the emergency room, spine and brain injuries, leg fractures…Thorn was preparing a list of possibilities and how he'd handle the situation if he found any of that to be true.

Thorn had come to the same conclusion that their contractor had; a hospital was a no-go for Juliette. It was just too dangerous.

Brigitte's hand laid on his shoulder two seconds after Nutsbe warned Thorn of her approach. "You okay?" she asked.

He looked her way. Then pointed his flashlight to the ground and the crawl pattern in the debris.

They stalked forward.

Brigitte put her hands on the edge of the skylight and looked down.

Thorn rounded the side.

Juliette lay crumpled along the far edge.

"What were you doing?" he asked as he dropped to his knees. He knew, of course. She'd dressed the best she could and escaped the best she could. It was what he would have done. He couldn't believe she'd gotten this far. He touched her head, and her fever was raging. He mouthed his findings back to Nutsbe.

"What's the plan here?" he asked Nutsbe.

Brigitte was crouching just to the side, the light from the skylight illuminating her form. She must have chosen to let herself be seen.

"We've reached out to the Mossad and asked them to coordinate with us. They've denied any actions in Paris, denied any knowledge of Juliette DuBois or David DuBois or interest in them, and any knowledge of an active operator or a team deployed."

"So she's rogue, or black ops," Thorn mouthed, pulling off his duffle.

"Or the Mossad is disavowing," Nutsbe countered.

Thorn opened the pocket with his medical kit. "Get Jaffrey on the line." He checked her temperature. "Hell of an infrastructure for rogue. Juliette's temperature is a hundred and five, still."

"Agreed. You asked for a plan. Once the two crews clashed, your back up backed off. I'm guessing they thought their intervention might end them up on the front page of the newspaper, so they'd go after Juliette only if the bad guys won. They'd assumed it was you against seven guys, so not a problem." He chuckled.

Thorn ran his hand over his bruised face. He was glad that he'd decided to leave his beard alone. It helped to glide the fists along his jaw and let the punches slide off ineffectually.

"Our client is disavowing, too. FYI. They aren't thrilled that a video of you is going viral on social media," Nutsbe said.

"Is this the video from Brigitte and me at the hotel or me and Juliette on the ladder?"

"Hard to keep track of all the ways you're viral, brother. But in this case, it was your superhero antics. All you lacked was the cape and maybe a sexy little unitard. Dr. Jaffrey is getting on an encrypted line. Give him a minute."

Thorn could hear Brigitte on her phone speaking in Hebrew. He didn't know enough words to understand what they were saying. But Nutsbe was taping ambient noise, so he'd figure it out. "You getting the background here?"

"Brigitte? Yeah, the computer says she's arranging for an exfil team to get Juliette to a private clinic just outside of Paris. I have Honey and Gage deplaning soon. You'll have them with you tonight."

"My team got the information we needed?" Thorn's hand rested on Juliette's shoulder, and he stroked his thumb back and forth, comforting her.

"I'll catch you up when your danger level isn't on red."

Thorn looked down at Juliette's silhouette. "Are you ordering me to take Juliette to the clinic with Brigitte?"

"Titus says he doesn't see another way off that roof. He thinks that if you stop cooperating, they'll just grab Juliette and take her themselves. You're outnumbered. At least they can get her off the roof safely. We'll figure it out as we go along. Play nice with your new friend. If this shit show hits the fan, it's spraying back on Iniquus. We still have background intel support from our client, but no more white vans are going to pull up and snatch you out of the streets."

"That's the plan then, go with Brigitte and hope for the best. Where is *Jaffrey*?"

"Patience. He's coming. Look, if Juliette were conscious, we might have been able to make a play for a one on one escort over the border to the 86th airlift at *Chièvres* Air Base in Belgium. As it stands, you need to hold hands with Brigitte and hope Gage and Honey get there before this mission goes from bad to worse. We're tracking you via your phone and computer. Good luck."

35

JULIETTE
Paris, France
Sometime

"WHAT IS your team doing with the men you captured?" His voice was a rich bass. Strong. Steady. It was *that* man, Thorn. He'd been with her. Fought for her. He was the one with the gentle, competent hands. He'd found her, again. The thought of him sparked a small flame of hope. Something about him made her feel like she needed to survive. That she had to fight a little harder. A little longer. And stay at least a step away from the precipice that called her to fly free.

"We're going to leave their fighters tied in place. They'll sort themselves after we're gone." That was a woman's voice that Juliette didn't recognize. "We don't have a way to handle them. And they look like the muscle, the brains took off."

"Ma'am." Thorn's hand rested on Juliette's shoulder. "I'm

going to roll you to your side. We have a stretcher here that we're going to use to get you off the roof."

Juliette wanted to open her eyes and look at him, but she was so tired. She'd rest just a moment more…

JULIETTE CURLED her fingers into her sheet and blanket. Something was wrong with the sensation. With her eyes still shut, she licked at her lips. Where was she? Her mind went back to the flight to France, her trip to talk to her grandmother. The fire from the apartment that had destroyed all her childhood pictures surely wouldn't have destroyed the pictures her grandmother had of her. Juliette just wanted to see what she'd looked like as a baby.

And for the first time, her brain stuttered over a simple fact. There were no pictures.

When she'd asked her father, he'd talked to her about her childhood memorabilia, but that was only half the story, wasn't it? Juliette thought back to the interactions. He'd pointed to the burn on her inner thigh, a pink mark that wrapped her like a garter belt. He'd said that she'd been burned in the fire, and her mother had saved her. Her mother was her hero — she'd risked life and limb to save Juliette.

But now, lying here in no man's land of consciousness, that story didn't hold up. She had lived beyond her youth, beyond the fire, beyond her time in France. Why were there no new pictures? Even if they were a family culture that didn't take a lot of photos, it was improbable that there wasn't even one.

Her head was noisy.

It was a clash of tinnitus, heat, and thoughts.

Memories were exploding through her mind, and she gripped at her bedclothes and hung on for dear life.

Where was she?

She thought of the Russian men. They were scientists, and she'd seen them before. They'd kidnapped her before. George had been there, tied up beside her, looking terrified. But she'd escaped from them here in France. Had she escaped them before?

When she tried to think about it, her body shook with terror.

A gentle hand ran down her arm and rested on her clenched hand. "You're safe." It was *his* voice.

Juliette worked to blink her heavy eyelids open. She found herself in a dark room. The only light came in from a street lamp shining through a crack in the drapes not far away. The dark shadow of a giant of a man was beside her.

Where was she?

Her mind raced. She'd driven a car. She'd bought a phone. She'd found a ride. Paris. She was in Paris. She'd found a small hotel room, and the fever had been a slash of red across her vision. She vaguely remembered falling and the rough feel of carpeting beneath her cheek. That was all she could remember. Was she still in that room?

The sheets clasped in her fingers were soft, and they had been rough and cheap before…

The man was talking to her, but Juliette's mind was so busy that it was just waves of sound that her ear recognized but didn't register.

The man stopped touching her. He stood, his body looming over her. Her muscles contracted, bracing, making herself smaller as she cowered on the bed.

There was a click, and a soft light came from behind her. Her eyes scanned the room as she turned her head. It looked like a hospital room. Her gaze settled on his face.

Wracking her brain, she was fairly sure she'd never met him before. He moved slowly and showed her his hands. Juliette thought it was to help her feel safe. And oddly, she did. Something about this man felt solid and kind. She wanted to see his eyes, to look into their depths and see if she could trust him, or if he was just playing one of those roles, like had happened when she was held prisoner – good cop, bad cop.

Juliette stopped breathing.

Had they caught her again? Was she going back? A sound crawled up her throat and pushed past her lips. She sounded like a wounded animal as she tried to huddle farther away.

The man sat down on a chair.

He showed her the flats of his hands, again, and then he used sign language as he said, "Hello. My name is Thorn. I was sent by the United States government to protect you."

Juliette longed to believe him. But she'd been duped before. George had duped her. George had played her for a fool, and then…her body quaked. She couldn't put a reason behind those thoughts or feelings.

Thorn slid a warm hand from her shoulder to her wrist. Then he tapped where it felt stiff and painful. He let go to say and sign, "This is an IV. You're in a clinic now. In Paris. I found you ill on the floor."

Juliette reached up with the hand that didn't have the IV and fingered the hospital gown at her neck. "Who else is here?" she whispered.

He stopped and smiled at her. "It's nice to finally hear your voice. You and I are the only ones in the room. Can you hear me?" He signed.

He must have been told about her hearing disability. He had a wonderful low rumbly voice. She could hear him past the ring-ing. "Yes. I hear you."

"We're the only two people in the room," he continued. "I came here to help you. From America. From DC. I want to get you home again, safe and sound."

"Washington?" Juliette whimpered. She turned herself into her pillow and started to cry. The move was wholly a body response, and it had surprised Juliette. The analytical part of her brain seemed to stand off to the side. It didn't try to comfort her. It simply tried to understand. Something about the government and Washington DC equaled pain. "Are you here about the whales?" Juliette asked, past her sobs.

Thorn had sat perfectly still as she was reacting to her thoughts. He didn't try to shush her or tell her to stop. He simply sat with one warm hand resting on her arm. It felt like a safety line. Even if he was frightening her.

"I have nothing to do with whales. Is there something I should know about that?"

Good question. What was upsetting her about the whales? All she could conjure was the vision of men in white military uniforms. And so that was what she blubbered out.

And her analyzer brain said, no, they had been her foe, but they weren't her enemy.

She must have said that out loud, too, because Thorn said, "I need to know who your enemy is, so I can protect you."

Juliette focused on that question. *Who are my enemies?* The voices that she heard in her head were speaking in Russian and then the pain. Her feet jerked up toward her stomach as she pulled into the fetal position.

"Who hurt your feet? Who burned you?"

Russian was the language, but who were the people? She had

no idea. Yes, she did. It was the men who had tried to kidnap her in Toulouse. "They were scientists."

Wait.

Juliette froze – mid-thought, mid-breath, mid-beat of her heart – froze. These were memories. Again, the fact that she could remember was startling.

"Say it out loud. I need to know how to protect you."

"I remember," Juliette whispered. "I'm experiencing a memory from before the accident." Her hand moved up to her scalp to touch the scar, but the move made the tape of her IV pull, moving the plastic insertion uncomfortably, so she went back to gripping the sheet. "I had an accident."

Thorn nodded.

"I've formed memories since the accident, but I had amnesia from what happened before the operation." Her words weren't even whispers. Her lungs had stiffened and felt solid in her chest. She couldn't deflate them to push air past her vocal cords. "I had a few memories of my childhood, but they weren't like a film. They were like stagnant pictures like I was turning pages in a photo album. I...I'm remembering something. I'm remembering something that happened before."

Thorn lifted his hand in a fist and coughed but left his hand up, covering his mouth. From the shift in his jawline, Juliette thought that he was mouthing something. She'd seen a movie where the secret service talked into their cuffs, but Thorn was wearing a turtleneck that was made out of sports material and was tight to his body. There was nowhere for him to hide a communications device.

Juliette's gaze traveled up his arm to the sheer strength of his shoulders and chest. He looked like he was capable of heroism. But Juliette wasn't sure it would be enough.

Wow, that was a thought.

How did she come to be in such a predicament? What about her made her unique enough that someone would hunt and try to capture her? More pictures of the men kidnapping her from her grandmother's street, crawling under the leaves through the ditch, changing her appearance in the bathroom.

How did this Thorn guy find her to protect her? And why would she be worth protecting?

"That's a rabbit hole," Thorn said.

Juliette cut her eyes to him.

"Or a tsunami. Hard to tell what's going through your mind. But I can see the thoughts whirring. How about I help you calm them a bit?" He waited for her to nod before he spoke again. "Take a moment and think about the word 'serenity.' Where would you go – anywhere in the world – to feel peace and quiet."

Juliette thought that she didn't have a lot of experience with places where one could find peace. "Peace isn't quiet," Juliette said.

Thorn put his forearms on his thighs, leaning slightly forward. "Tell me about quiet not being peaceful. I'd like to learn."

That was an odd turn of phrase. She ran her sentence through her head again as a question. *Why isn't quiet peaceful?*

Juliette decided to open her mouth and see what came out. "I was thinking the word silent when you said quiet, and they're really not the same at all."

"Interesting," Thorn said. "What's the difference?" He reached out, and his hand came back with a cloth that he used to wipe over Juliette's mouth and forehead.

It was soothing.

"Okay, silence, the human brain is not well equipped to deal with silence. There are places that are built for exactly that purpose — rooms that absorb sound waves — they're called anechoic chambers. There's a lab in the Midwest in America that has a noise decibel level below zero. It's supposed to be the quietest place in the world."

Thorn nodded.

"It's a terrible place. I was in there once…" Juliette stalled. Did she read it? Did she watch a documentary? No. This seemed like a memory. Her body reacted with agitation. Her legs flutter kicked, and her hands clasped and kneaded the blanket.

"It's safe for you to tell me the story," Thorn said. "We're nowhere near there. You won't go again unless you want to."

But Juliette's agitation wasn't about the place, but that this information came from before the accident. She pushed on to see if she'd didn't have some kind of revelation, forcing herself to be brave and stand in front of what felt like a tidal wave. "Yes, there was a penetrating, horrible silence. And then it was crazy sounds that I could hear. I mean, like spiders crawling over your skin, horrific. I could hear my lips rubbing across my teeth when I moved my mouth. Swallowing was so loud that it hurt. I could hear my pulse throb. It was…gross. Awful. Torturous."

And when she said torture, she gasped in horror. She was back in a room, tied down so she couldn't move. They showed her a candle, then they said they planned to melt her skin. The pain of it. The horrific, world-collapsing pain of it. She had to promise her cooperation. And if she didn't, they had her sisters. Whatever torture happened to her, they'd perform the same on her sisters. "Comply or suffer," he had said in a thick Russian accent. Juliette didn't speak Russian yet. Now she could. After years under the men's power, she could.

As those thoughts bubbled to the surface, Juliette's stomach rumbled and burbled. She threw herself to the edge of the bed.

Thorn, in one swift move, swung a wastebasket under her mouth with one hand and lifted her hair away with the other.

Her body heaved, and she couldn't get anything out.

Long minutes of cramping and hacking and no relief.

Thorn had tucked her hair and had his hand on her back. He was crouched by the side of the bed. "Say what you just remembered out loud. Get it out."

She did as he said, word for word. And amazingly, as the last words came out, "Comply or suffer," her stomach stopped its violent attack. She collapsed, panting. Her sweat-covered body started trembling.

Thorn touched her hospital gown, then got up and opened a cabinet. He came back with a fresh one folded in his hand. He shook it out, then showed it to her before he helped her get changed.

Modest by nature, Juliette realized she didn't have an ounce of embarrassment around Thorn.

She remembered the last time she was in the hospital and her dad was introducing himself to her. "I'm your father. David DuBois."

"What was that thought?" Thorn asked, adjusting her sheet and blanket around her hips. "Better out than in right now."

"I have scars on my leg and feet. My father told me that I got the burn mark on my thigh when I was a little girl, and my mother had saved me from a fire. And that later, in the accident when she died, I got the burn scars on my feet. But I had a flash of memory. That's not how I got any of those scars."

Thorn's face was a study in calm. But since Juliette had lost a lot of her hearing, she'd learned to watch and read faces. The muscles around his eyes and at the corners of his lips tightened. There was a fierceness — a protective fierceness — that swelled his chest. Thorn said he was here to protect her, and in this moment, Juliette felt right down to the marrow of her bones that this man would throw himself in front of anything coming her way. She was safe with him. It was such a painfully, surprisingly, crazy thought that she gasped.

Thorn stilled and focused his gaze on her eyes, then bent around to snap the back of the gown.

"Thank you," she said.

"You'll feel better now that you're not damp." He got up and tossed the old gown in a receptacle. "Go on with your story about being in the anechoic chamber. You hated being in perfect silence because your body made its own creepy noises. What kind of sound makes you feel peaceful? Do you have a happy sound memory?"

36

Thorn
Paris, France
Monday, Zero Dark Thirty

"She's asleep?" Lynx asked

"She's not responding to me. It doesn't look like sleep. It looks like a cage fight." Thorn's computer was open and resting on the counter. He spun the monitor, so Lynx could see.

Blankets had been duck taped to the safety bars of Juliette's bed, and the blankets and top sheet removed as she fought against whatever demons were chasing her.

It was hard to watch.

He spun the computer back to talk to his support team.

"We're in a better place than we were just a few hours ago." Lynx's voice was pitched to soothe. "We have a better handle on what's going on."

Thorn wasn't really in the mood to be mollified. He wanted

to know what was happening to Juliette's body. With all this thrashing, they'd even taken the IV away.

When Thorn had asked about something to help her rest, the doctor said that if she was in detox, adding something to her system might just be the worst thing he could do. He said to let her ride it out.

"Ride it out" sounded like balancing a surfboard on a beautiful wave.

What he saw, she was riding a bucking bronco, ready to be thrown.

One of his buddies from back in his SEAL days got on pain meds after an explosion took part of his foot. For the sake of his brand-new baby girl, his buddy decided he had to get away from the pills. He'd become addicted. His fellow operators went deep out into the middle of nowhere, hid the keys to the truck, and watched him go through hell. Tremors, sweating, nausea, delirium, and depression. A deep, dark void of depression. They kept him there for three weeks.

It was one thing to watch a SEAL fight his demons. It was a whole other ballgame to watch Juliette face this down alone.

Thorn rubbed a hand over his face. "Good. Let's do this fast. This case seems to be dynamic. I have no idea how long I'll have a lull." If he could call this a lull. He remembered back to the dream where he'd been doing the fancy footwork to stay upright on the quickly rotating Earth. And he couldn't say that had been far off. "Start with the X-rays and blood work."

Nutsbe did a split-screen. Now, Lynx took up the right-hand side, and Nutsbe's image was talking from the left, though both of his teammates were sitting in the Panther Force war room back at Iniquus Headquarters. "Gage and Thorn met with Polla and Habiba. They both said they had a sister with whom they'd had no contact in years," Nutsbe said.

Thorn's gut tightened. "Name?"

"Arya Khouri." Lynx typed it onto the screen, so he could see the spelling. "Dr. Arya Khouri."

"Her specialty was audiology?" Thorn asked.

"In a way," Lynx said. "Arya was studying subsonic vibrations to understand large mammal communications."

"So elephants and whales?" Thorn leaned his hips into the wall.

"Exactly. So the why of the X-ray – the pictures that Polla and Habiba had of their sister don't match Juliette's photographs. The computer analysis gives us only a moderate chance that these are the same women. Juliette has the same coloring as Arya. We speculated that perhaps she'd changed her appearance with plastic surgery."

"Perhaps with the accident, she needed facial reconstruction," Thorn speculated.

"That had been exactly my thought," Lynx said. "This woman's nose is different than Arya's – straighter and more slender, her cheekbones are more prominent, her teeth shaped differently. We gave the X-rays to a plastic surgeon to evaluate for us. He said that the work was not indicative of a trauma event or reconstructive in nature, but that these were voluntary procedures."

Thorn walked over and looked down at Juliette's face. "Do you think Juliette wanted to change her looks for aesthetics' sake, or do you think she was trying to disguise her identity?"

Lynx's voice was behind him. "Again, I don't know enough right now to answer that. I can also tell you that the scar on her head is just that – a scar on her head. The plastic surgeon said that it looks like it was created on purpose, as if cut with a scalpel then sewn up again. There is no skeletal damage to her skull. She didn't have brain surgery."

"So who's lying here?" Thorn turned and walked back to his place against the wall. "She could well be Arya," Thorn said, "but we're not sure?"

"Not a hundred percent," Nutsbe confirmed. "Now, Honey telephoned his wife. Since she works with animal migration in the Ngorongoro region, he thought that she might know something about another female scientist interested in elephants."

"Yeah." Thorn crossed his arms over his chest and leaned his hips back against the wall. "I'd imagine that was a close-knit group of scientists. Did Meg know Arya?"

"Yes," Nutsbe said. "They'd been quite friendly. But Meg hasn't heard from Arya in years."

"Because?"

"Meg is frequently out in the bush, so she's not always in contact," Lynx said. "Meg speculated that probably Arya had lost funding, so she had to stop her field research and was teaching at a university somewhere. More interestingly, Meg said that the last she heard about Arya Khouri was when she was supposed to go to court to testify against the U.S. Navy. She remembered enough of the details that I was able to find it on the docket. Arya Khouri's documents were admitted into court. She was slated as an expert witness, but she was never called to the stand. It's on my list for tomorrow to get in touch with the lawyers and find out why."

Thorn nodded. "White military uniforms, she had said. Okay. What was that case about?"

"Whales." Lynx smiled. "I'll give you the highlights, but I'll stick this in your cloud file in case you want to read deeper. I honestly don't see that you'll have time. We have a lot to cover."

"Roger," Thorn said.

Juliette lay panting in her stupor, and Thorn was anxious to get to the information about her blood draw.

"Okay, this was out in California, and it had to do with low-frequency active (LFA) sonar that naval ships were using for training. The Navy was hauled into court because it was violating the Marine Mammal Protection Act. From what I culled from Dr. Khouri's documentation, the LFA was having a negative impact on the animals like walruses, whales, and dolphins that are dependent on sound for navigation. It's messing up migration and reproduction. It separated mothers from their calves and stressed the animals out. Well, the sounds basically torture the animals. These sounds can travel hundreds of miles and can be found in seventy percent of the oceans."

"This trial was a while ago?"

"Years ago. Yes. The courts are trying to balance needs. The Navy is developing a plan to use the LFA more carefully. It's in study."

"And Dr. Khouri's written testimony was there, but she wasn't on the witness list. Did you take a look at that list?"

"I did," Lynx said, "and guess whose name was there, in defense of the Navy?"

Thorn didn't need to guess; he knew in his gut. "George Matthews."

"Bingo." Nutsbe looked at his watch. "I need to run to a meeting. Lynx is going to finish your briefing."

"Roger that." Thorn plunged on. "All right, George Matthews and Arya Khouri are on opposite sides of a major military trial. He goes, she does not."

"I need you to put that to the side." Lynx tapped at her keyboard, and Thorn watched as her focus scanned over the information she'd brought up. "The possibility that Juliette is Arya Khouri is one part of the puzzle. We know she's genetically tight with the other two, Dr. Khouris. We know that her physical appearance has been changed. We know that she seems to have disappeared from research before the naval trial. I'm working on timelines of Arya Khouri, George Matthews, and David DuBois and finding locations and intersections. Here's an important piece of information. Arya Khouri was born in Syria. Her father was a professor of medicine, and he spent time with his family in both France and America. Arya Khouri spoke Arabic, French, and English fluently, as does Juliette. Arya Khouri returned to the United States for her university studies, eventually getting her Ph.D. in zoology. Her dissertation was on subsonic communications in large mammals. She became a United States citizen. She's an American now."

Thorn stalled. "And Brigitte knows that. Brigitte must know Juliette's true identity."

"How do you come to that conclusion?" she asked.

"When Brigitte and I were in the hotel room when I first met her, I asked, 'Do you know where they took Juliette? Would you help us get her back? She's an American citizen. We won't let that go.' And Brigitte's response struck me as really odd. She said, 'You either know that is the truth or you're trying to play me.'"

"Interesting. Yeah, I'd interpret that the way you did. Brigitte knows Juliette's true identity, *and* that includes her American citizenship." Lynx looked down, tapping at her keyboard. "Another tick in the box saying Juliette is Arya." She brought her gaze back up. "Now, I need to shift gears and talk about her blood samples."

Thorn sucked in a lung full of air and braced himself. Fear – just raw primal fear raced beneath his skin.

Lynx stopped to look at him. "We're doing our best to get her home. I promise you, Thorn. Everything that I can think of is happening. Okay?"

"Lynx, I..." The sensations running through him were so

intense that they threw him completely off balance, just like in his dream.

"Right. I get that." She nodded. Her smile was sad. Her eyes worried. "I've seen this a time or two before. Honey when he met Meg. Gage when he met Zoe. I think it's a thing with people who have their lives constantly in danger. They don't have time for personal drama or games. I haven't quite worked out a theory in my mind of why this is how things play out, but go down the list Brian and Sophia, Deep and Lacey, Jack knew with Suz, Gator and Christen. Across your team, across my team, the operators are humming along, and then its−"

"A kick in the balls."

"It can feel that way. Love isn't the same thing as joy."

"Love? No. This happened before I met her. It's a mind game. Not anything real. It started when I saw−"

"Her photo," Lynx said. "Haven't you heard that same story from Honey? Randy showed Honey a picture of Meg, and it was a done deal. His heart didn't belong to him alone anymore."

Thorn nodded. "It seemed more believable when it happened to Honey. He was more−"

"Deserving of happiness? Is that what you were going to say?"

Thorn rubbed his hands over his face and shifted on the wall. "It's just not my style," he said. "I don't do relationships, and I certainly don't do falling in love. What I do is I complete missions and enjoy what the moment brings. And that's not even diving into the whole it takes two to tango thing. Back to the mission. You were about to give me a medical update on the precious cargo." Thorn glanced over to Juliette to make sure she hadn't heard any of that.

She lay in a ball at the bottom of the bed, mouth slack, eyes in REM.

"Well, since we aren't sure of her name, 'precious cargo' will work. And I won't even pause to tell you that you can run, but you can't hide. Giving her an operator's term to keep things from becoming personal is too little, too late. Now, as to her blood – we got the test results back. Everything seems to be normal as to her health – her white counts were elevated, but we'd expect that with her temperature so high. Two substances of interest were flagged. First, there are traces of a sedative that might have been used in this instance for chemically restraining Juliette. This drug is a very effective rapid tranquilizer used in emergency departments for psychiatrically agitated patients. By its half-life, we believe she was tranquilized in the last twenty-four hours. Not knowing the original dosage, it's impossible for us to tell."

Thorn shook his head. "What she's going through right now doesn't seem like anything to do with her being sedated when she was kidnapped."

"Right. So the second substance that was found is a bit of a puzzle. We called in a professor of pharmacology to take a look at our results and give us her best guess as to what we were dealing with. This class of drugs, as it pertains to our case, hang on…" Lynx typed at her computer. "Yes, here. Remember when you asked me why DuBois was facing ethical charges? It was because of a drug that was similar to Propranolol. A bit of background, Propranolol is legally prescribed. This does not have to do with its FDA approved usage. A Propranolol look-alike was being studied in its use for wiping out memories associated with post-traumatic distress. There were lots of medical ethics issues that came up around wiping out memories."

"DuBois was using a look-alike medicine?"

"Yes, on various human subjects, including the studies where he was working with the US sailors. His study not only included wiping memories but applying his sea snail experiments in trying to replace the memories with alternatives. I'm referring you back to that article I sent you to read on your way down to Toulouse."

"Wait. DuBois wiped out old memories and put new ones from someone else in the old memories place? That's a sci-fi horror plot."

"Exactly." Lynx nodded emphatically. "The subjects said that they recalled the memories as static pictures that made no sense to them until Dr. DuBois gave them context. For example, a picture of a dog was implanted, and he'd tell them, "That was your childhood dog." They remembered that picture as a memory of their dog. He did places this way as well. He'd put a picture of a building and tell the subject, "This is where you lived as a child." And that picture would supplant other memories. This held only in the instance that medications were also used, and they wore off with time."

"That's nuts," was all Thorn could think to say.

"Can you imagine a world where not only was that possible, but it was in active use?" Lynx asked. "You'd have no grasp on reality, what really was, and what was just a manipulation of memory. Bottom line here, the drug in Juliette's system is similar to Propranolol but is something new. The pharmaceutical professor doesn't know what it is or what effects it has on the mind or body."

"Crap." Thorn watched as Juliette tried to scratch up the sheet underneath her. "It's in her system."

"If the drug is not recognized by the computer software, it means it hasn't passed through the FDA and isn't even in medical trial. It's rogue as far as the United States goes. I'll make a note for Nutsbe." Lynx turned her head and scratched a pen across a pad of paper. "It's a stretch, but I'll have him check and see if the search engine checked worldwide databases. Perhaps it's used and approved in another country. Hard to imagine, but let's cross the Ts and dot the Is just to be sure.

Thorn swallowed. He'd spend some time later trying to calculate the ramifications of being a human guinea pig for an unethical pig like DuBois.

Lynx turned back to him. "Let's talk about memories. We don't actually know what they are. There's a lot of debate in the scientific community. Zoe, for example, got involved in her research in blood biomarkers and the BIOMIST system to try to help the Innocence Project. They've found that many of the people who are imprisoned, by eye-witness accounts alone, are often innocent. The witness swears it's the person who perpetrated the crime because they completely believe − have certitude in their conviction − that their memory and recognition can be depended on. I'll give you an example. In 1984, there was a college student, smart woman, twenty-two years old, 4.0 GPA, asleep in her bed. A man broke into her house, and with a knife to her throat, he raped her. She spent the time of her rape memorizing everything about him so she could identify him later. Hairline, tattoos, scars, she was searching for him specifically to find identifiers."

"Brave and very smart. But there's a *yeah* here, isn't there?"

"She found out that when identified by DNA, not only was this guy *not* the guy who raped her, but the guy who actually raped her and admitted it to the police was brought to her. 'Do you recognize this man?' 'I've never seen him before, no.' The innocent man spent eleven years in prison."

Thorn let out a low whistle and scrubbed his hand over his head.

"Memory does not faithfully record events and store them away in the brain. Research shows that memory is neither persistent, nor is it unchanging. As a matter of fact, every time someone recalls an event, it's altered in the memory. The thing we think we know about memory is that it creates a change in the brain. New synaptic connections form between brain neurons. So…" She turned her head to read from another monitor. "Scientists have been working to understand memory and its effects on anxiety. They've been trying to find a drug that leaves the memories intact but takes out the emotional charge."

"Someone who saw his buddy blown up in front of him remembers the instance but has no emotion? That sounds like a psychopath," Thorn said.

"They weren't working on that. They were working with people who are afraid of snakes," Lynx countered. "The scientists exposed people who had a snake phobia to the snakes, and then they gave them a shot of their drug. After that, the subjects showed no sign of fear as they handled the pile of snakes."

"I'm still saying that sounds dangerous as hell. Is this being used now? You said it was used on people, so it's in human trial?"

"I don't have that. I could look it up for you, but this is a different drug that they found in Juliette's blood. I was just giving you that information as background to help you understand what might be happening in Juliette's mind. The drug given to Juliette is mostly a mystery. We won't know how long it can stay active in her system or what the long-term effects could be. If this is the reason why she doesn't remember before the accident, then it might be caused by the drug. Another possibility is that she's purposefully using the drug to deal with the ongoing anxiety of not knowing anything about herself."

"But the plastic surgeon says there was no accident."

"No," Lynx corrected. "He said that facial reconstruction was not done to correct for trauma. And that the incision on her head was clean as if cut on purpose by a scalpel with no underlying cranial damage. There could still have been some kind of accident."

"Got it," Thorn said. "I have a question about the Propranolol look-alike when it was used for PTSD. Was the memory loss permanent?"

"The results were varied," Lynx said.

Thorn took a few breaths and let the information sift through various outcomes, so he could get strategies together. "I need to get a couple things accomplished here. Mainly, I need to get her under some competent care. If her memory is being held hostage – probably not the right word."

"I was thinking about it similarly," Lynx said. "In the car, they used a chemical restraint to stop her physically. They could also be using a chemical restraint on her mentally. They may just be holding her in a state of disorientation until they need her to remember again. If she is who we think she is, and she's tied to George Matthews, then they might have been forcing her to help him succeed with his project – the apocalyptic neuroweapon."

"And this may just be putting her on hold for some reason." Thorn had never heard or contemplated the possibility of this kind of pharmacological warfare. "As the drug leaves her system, that could have its own ramifications. If her memories start to return, it might be one thing if they come in at a trickle. It might be a whole other thing if they come in like a flashflood. We have no idea what she's seen or heard or been through." He shook his head, his eyes fixed on Juliette. "I'm not equipped for that. I don't know what that might look like. But if she's not willingly playing on the bad-guy team, I think we owe it to her to have the softest landing possible."

37

THORN
Paris, France
Monday, Zero One Fifteen Hours

BRIGITTE STOOD IN THE DOORWAY, watching him take a piss.

He sent her a raised eyebrow.

"Where I come from, it's a matter of decorum to shut the door when using the bathroom."

"Yeah? They do that in Israel?" He shook himself off and fastened his pants.

"You don't feel safe here? You can't take your eyes off Juliette even for a few seconds?"

"My mission is to keep my eyes on her, not worry about my manners." He soaped up and rinsed his hands under the hot water.

"Get rid of Brigitte. We have information to pass," Nutsbe said in his ear.

"Hey Brigitte," Thorn said, drying his hands then moving to

her side. "I'm wondering if you could do me a favor. I'm about to starve. I've been running on meal replacement bars, and I could sure use something more substantial."

"Sure, I'll keep an eye on Juliette for you. Take your time."

He ran a hand down her arm and entwined his fingers with hers. "Actually, I've been ordered not to leave her side. The bathroom with the door open was as far as I'm allowed to move." He pulled her hand to his lips for a kiss. "It's a big ask, but would you mind getting something for me?"

"Raw steak and lots of vegetables?"

"Would be amazing. It's late. Maybe there's an all-night grocery somewhere with some sandwich fixings," Thorn said.

Brigitte looked over at Juliette.

As Juliette seemed to fall into a deeper, more restful sleep, Thorn had lifted her back to the top of the bed and straightened her out on her side, with a pillow under her head and a sheet and blanket over her body. He'd combed out the tangled mess of her hair and braided it again. He thought that might make her feel more restful.

When Brigitte turned back to Thorn, she squinted her eyes and tipped her head. "Are you up to something?"

Thorn shrugged. "Duty, ma'am. I'm just keeping my job."

"Ma'am?" Brigitte asked, swiveling to line her body up with his and paint a hand down to cup his balls, giving them a playful squeeze. "I can work with that. I don't mind a little dom play."

Thorn sent her a slow smile and a wink.

"Red meat it is." Brigitte grinned and left the room.

The second he heard the door in the corridor snick metallically shut, Thorn touched the side of his communicator as he whispered into the mic. "Go. You have new intel?"

"Yeah, you could say that." Nutsbe's voice sounded tired.

"I'm posting a blow-up of the janitor's picture on your computer."

"I didn't kill him, did I?" Thorn asked, swiping his monitor and leaning in for a retinal scan. After a few taps to his keyboard, up came the photograph.

"As far as we could tell, he roused himself and walked back to his window washing. Hung out there while he inspected the area, then left. He was either fine or a Zombie, but nothing about brains being eaten on the news."

The image shifted. Thorn was looking at the left wrist, partially hidden by a watch, but the watch had been shoved down closer to his wrist bone, and half a Rex Deus tat was visible.

"Shit." The word hissed out from between Thorn's teeth.

"Yeah, that pretty much sums it up."

"Wait. Margot said that Brigitte was Mossad. The Rex Deus we've run into were all Israeli special forces who were KIA in the records. This guy's playing on the same team as the Mossad? How in the hell does that make any sense?"

"Funny that," Nutsbe said.

"Shit," Thorn repeated. "Let me guess."

"Yup, Margot's BFF was Mossad, KIA, in a building explosion. So...You were making sweet love to the devil, my man. You may want to get to a doctor and get your gonads checked."

"I wrapped them up, Mom, but thanks for your concern."

"Did you see a tat on her while you were rolling around?" Nutsbe asked.

"Nope. But she could have covered it with theater makeup. She was wearing a watch. Truth be told, my focus wasn't on her left wrist – but live and learn. It's going on all my checklists from now on."

Panther Force had come up against the Rex Deus a few times now. They were formidable opponents. So far, they'd all been males who had taken a pledge of brotherhood. That was how they described it to the FBI. They claimed their tattoos had no implications beyond that.

The tattoos were always placed on the left wrist where it could be hidden behind the large face of a wristwatch. The design was a series of circles and lines constructing the Sephirot, the tree of life. In esoteric Judaism, it was the central mystical symbol that originated in the Kabbalah. Different spheres represented a different aspect of enlightenment.

Back in Washington D.C., Panther Force had taken down a dozen men with this same tattoo on their wrists. Iniquus had learned nothing about the tattoo in the interrogations. The CIA, if they had anything, wasn't sharing. But his commander, Titus Kane, had brought a scholar in to teach them the basics. They'd nicknamed the group the "Rex Deus." Panther Force didn't know what they really called themselves. What they did learn from the scholars was that in myth, the Rex Deus, sometimes called "Star families," was supposed to be the stuff of conspiracy theories and imagination.

The group of twelve Rex Deus who went down in the US had illuminated the first triangle in the design. That highlighted aspect symbolized wisdom, understanding, and knowledge. That group had tried to kidnap Zoe when she was building a micro-robotics WASP prototype.

Another man with the tattoo had shown up on their radar even more recently. Panther Force was protecting two archaeologists who were helping to safeguard Syrian artwork. Unlike the other tattoos they had seen, this one had the sixth sphere illuminated, *Tiferet*. Their resource said this one had to do with beauty, balance, and harmony.

In Africa, Honey and Meg had been with another man with the tattoo. He died of his wounds when their group of scientists were taken hostage. The sphere that this man had illuminated was *Gevurah* – an instrument God used to judge humans and punish the wicked.

"Did you ID the janitor? Was he Mossad too? Some special ops guy that got himself 'blown up'?"

"That's a delicate subject between the US and Israeli governments. But we're working the channels."

"I'm not happy sitting here, Bro."

"Roger that. FYI, when she left, Brigitte headed to her car, fanning her face."

"Act of duty. I was letting her play. She thinks she's got me by the boys, and I want her to believe that."

Thorn examined the janitor's wrist tattoo. It looked like yet another sphere was illuminated.

"Which sephira is highlighted on the janitor's wrist? What are we dealing with here?" Thorn asked.

"That's *Netzach*. It stands firm with no regrets, no fear of death. Words associated would include victory and endurance."

"Victory maybe not so much. But I can tell you, his endurance was over the top. When I was trying to take him down in the bathroom, he was formidable. Having fought next to Brigitte, I'm saying she'd fit that pattern. What does all that mean?"

"I checked our file," Nutsbe said. "It seems that those would be the Kamikazes of the Star Families. They're willing to die for their cause."

"Perfect. Kamikaze Rex Deus. Have you noticed that the *only* place we've ever picked up signs of Rex Deus in action has to do with science? It seems to me, from the pattern Panther Force has faced, that if there's a dangerous weapon, like this apocalyptic neuroweapon, or an energy system, or even like Zoe's work in blood pattern recognition and micro-robotics –

that they are out there trying to get that technology for themselves. Is it for development for their own use or suppression?"

"Keep running out that line of thought," Nutsbe said.

"It's important to know – if Juliette is their target, is it so they can learn from her and keep on the trajectory? Or do they want to know what's out there, and then they make sure she's no longer a threat by neutralizing her?" The muscles around Thorn's jaw tightened. "I'm not going to let it happen either way. She's an American citizen."

"We think."

"Fine. Whatever," Thorn said through gritted teeth. "Get us the hell out of here."

38

JULIETTE
Paris, France
Night

JULIETTE RESTED on the razor edge of consciousness. She could hear the low rumble of male voices. They seemed distant, from the other side of the room. It was a nice sound. Calm.

She'd picked out the names Honey and Gage along with the one she already knew, Thorn.

Her hand was comfortably warm, and there was a slight pressure. She was holding hands, she realized. And the hand she held was a tether, a grounding cord, an anchor. She rolled her hand and intertwined her fingers, feeling happy. Her lips slid into the ghost of a smile.

She liked it there in this neverland between wake and sleep.

This was peaceful.

The tinnitus was still a high-pitched hum, but it didn't stab into her brain. She could almost ignore it. Maybe the male voices were a counterbalance.

"Hey, Brigitte, how about you, me, and Honey go and get an exfil plan together? Somewhere quiet where we won't disturb her."

Silence followed.

"We'll leave Thorn where he is and fill him in once we have a course of action."

Another stretch of silence. She didn't want to wake up. If she opened her eyes, then she'd pull herself away from this moment of contentment. It had been so long since she'd felt this level of peace. She actually couldn't remember, no, wait, yes, when she was in Tanzania with that amazing herd of elephants. The sun setting, the herd climbing from the water. That had been bliss. It seemed like a lifetime ago. Someone else's mind and body.

A deeper voice chuckled. "Are you afraid Thorn's going to scoop her up and run? His orders are to keep eyes on until the exfil, and, that barring a sudden emergency, there should be no exfil without the doctor signing off on her stabilization."

"Thorn, you aren't going to go rogue on us, are you?" the other guy asked. "You're planning on following orders?"

Thorn didn't answer. She had to assume he'd given them some sign.

A door opened, there were sounds of steps and movement, and then the door snicked shut.

Good. Now there was quiet, and she could float.

"Arya?" The fingers tightened a little on hers. A hand smoothed back her hair then rested on her head. A thumb swiped smoothly across her forehead. "Arya, can you wake up?" the man asked in Arabic.

Maybe she had just been dreaming – a terrible nightmare and then a peaceful dream.

"Arya, I'm sorry to have to do this. But I really need you to wake up now."

Arya knew that on the other side of wakefulness would be truth. And truth would hurt. Her smile fell off, and she squeezed her eyelids a little tighter together. But far from helping her grip into that space in between, it bobbled her to the surface of consciousness.

"That's right, you're doing great. Listen to my voice and wake up. I need you."

Arya blinked her eyes open. The thumb soothing her forehead stilled. She was staring into deep brown eyes filled with affection and concern.

"I'm Thorn," he reminded her. "Can you hear me?"

"Yes," she spoke to him in Arabic. Her head turned, and her eyes slid around the room.

"You're in a clinic. You got sick in your room in Paris. I brought you to the clinic."

"You skipped over the bad people that you beat up to save me."

Thorn didn't answer that.

"You're calling me Arya now and not Juliette like last time."

"Is that your name?" he asked.

She stilled. "I *think* it is. I *think* that my name is Arya Khouri and not Juliette DuBois. Why would I have two names?" she asked.

"That's what we're trying to figure out. My job–" he stopped and gave a little shake of his head. "I want to protect you, and I need to know who it is that wants to hurt you. We're here in the clinic, but we want to take you back to the United States." He was watching her. He seemed to be absorbing every nuance of her reactions.

She could tell he was trying to say the right thing in the right way for her sake. Arya squeezed his hand to encourage him to just speak.

"My team needs the information, so we know how to keep you safe, but you've had some medicine that's made you forget things. It's possible that you might remember the answers now." He leaned a little farther forward, resting his elbows on his knees, bringing his face down more in line with hers. "I wanted to ask you while we were here in the clinic, so there was a doctor here if you needed help."

"Thank you." Arya tried to work up a smile to ease him a bit. But it felt wrong on her face. She wanted to be honest with Thorn, and that meant even a silly lie, like a fake smile, would be a break in trust. She felt like trust between them was profoundly important. "I'm ready. I'll answer my best. Would it be okay if we spoke in English? It's been a long time since I spoke in Arabic."

"Of course," he said, switching languages. "Whatever makes you feel more comfortable." Without releasing her hand, he swung around and gathered a laptop, bringing it closer to where Arya could see that someone was on a video call.

"Hello," said the young woman with a gentle smile and long blond hair. "My name is Lynx. Can you hear me all right?" she asked.

Arya let her gaze drift to catch Thorn's. He smiled at her encouragingly. "She's a colleague who works for my company, Iniquus. She's helping me get you home."

Arya nodded.

"She wanted to talk to you about how you're feeling and some things we've learned about why you're feeling so sick."

Arya's eyes widened, and she stopped blinking or breathing.

Thorn rubbed his thumb over the back of her hand. "I'm here. We'll do this together, okay?"

Arya nodded.

"Thorn asked me to speak to you," Lynx said. "He thought that my talking to you over the Internet would give you some distance from the situation." Her face broke into a grin. "And to be honest, he was afraid that his speaking to you might feel intimidating. He *is* kind of intimidating." The tone of her voice made it sound like the two women were best friends sharing a good joke. "It's his job to strike fear into the hearts of our enemies. And he does that very well."

It was working; Arya's face began to relax. Her shoulders weren't all the way up to her ears.

"*You* are not the enemy. And Thorn, along with our whole team, is dedicated to keeping you safe." She paused and waited for Arya to nod. "Is there anything you need right now? Anything that might make you feel more comfortable? You've had a rough seventy-two or so hours, now. You've been very ill, and at the same time, you've been heroic in saving yourself."

"Thank you," Arya said, her voice rough and rasping.

"As time has passed since you haven't felt well, I'm wondering if it's possible that you might be remembering things that go back in your past? Maybe remembering things that happened before you had an operation?" Lynx asked.

"Yes." Arya exhaled.

"Let me give you a bit of information that might help make sense of at least some of it. Is that something you would like to know? Or maybe it's something you'd prefer to wait until later, once you're home—"

"No, now," Arya interrupted her. "Please," she tagged at the end, more quietly. She reached over to where Thorn was holding her hand and wrapped her other hand there too, hanging on as if for dear life.

"All right, but I need you to stop me if this becomes over-whelming."

Overwhelming? Everything right now was too much—bursts of sound and color, thoughts and names, faces and theories. Everything swirled and dipped, then soared overhead. Facts might just be the place where Arya could rest.

"We have some information for you about your memory. The blood sample that was drawn by the medics showed that you had a drug in your system that is unrecognized in pharmacological literature. I want you to stop me if I say anything that you don't understand or that you'd like me to repeat. We can put voice-to-text on the screen if it would be helpful."

"Yes." She sighed. "Yes, thank you. It takes a lot of energy to try to focus and hear everything."

There was a pause, and when Lynx said, "Testing, testing, testing." It came up on the bottom of the screen.

"This is working," Arya said.

"We brought in a professor of pharmacology and had her look at the results of your blood test. She said that the medicine in your body was similar to another drug that had been tested for people with severe PTSD. The one in your bloodstream had some differences. She believes, as this drug leaves your body, you would develop a fever and have an experience very much like a heroin addict coming off of that drug."

"Is it addictive, the PTSD medicine?"

"No. She thinks that the initial detox will be the only issue. Though, it could be that you might crave it for psychological relief. But we can get you help with that and get you on some better medications if you need them." Lynx tipped her head. "My understanding, from talking to Roxanne, is that you had intermittent fevers that were not predictable in terms of the length between them. Is that right?"

They had gone to talk to her caregiver? "Yes, sometimes a few days, sometimes many weeks…"

"And Dr. DuBois took you to his Montrim lab and gave you a bag of IV fluid?"

She cleared her throat, wondering just what was in those IV drips. She'd always felt so sick – she'd just trusted. "Yes, it always helped."

Lynx nodded with a gentle smile that felt friendly and concerned. "Did you ever burn through the fever to see how you felt without the IV fluids?"

She squeezed Thorn's hand. "Never."

"It's probable that he was administering the drug, and when it started to leave your system, he would give you another dose."

"But how would a dose last that long? I remember distinctly that once I was up to my twenty-second day. I was giddy, thinking that I might not have that fevered reaction again. How could the drug stay stable in my body that long?"

"The professor said with encapsulation. But, to be clear, our expert didn't study the drug. She was making some educated guesses."

Arya's gaze traveled along the far wall of the small clinic room. "I thought a new fever was starting just as I got on the plane. I almost turned around. By the time I got to Toulouse, I was feeling pretty bad. The next morning, twenty-four hours into feeling ill, things started to feel off in my brain with my memories when I went to my childhood apartment. The pictures that I called 'memories' flashed up as – I'm looking for the word – all I can think about is phantom pain from an amputation. It was disorienting. As I went to visit the places from my memory, pictures in person – what was described as a childhood apartment and then my grandmother's house – it seemed odd to me how nothing had changed from those pictures to twenty years later."

"That fits, doesn't it, Lynx?" Thorn asked.

"With what the sailors said in their description of their experience?" Lynx asked. "Yes, I just got hold of an unredacted file from back in 2000 on that, and Arya's experience sounds parallel."

Fit? Obviously, there was data available. Later, when her head was quieter, Arya thought she'd ask to read it.

Lynx turned her focus back to Arya. "Others were part of a PTSD experiment that was conducted in 2000. The men reported the same sensations and confusions. It can be extremely disorienting – all of this can. I'd like to take a break from the information and check how you're doing."

"Science helps. Facts…" Arya took a few deep breaths. "The longer I felt feverish, the more things shifted for me. It was like a veil was being pulled back. When I saw the men, the Russian scientists, who pointed their guns at me and forced me into their car in Toulouse, I recognized them. There are other memories now. They're coming back to me. Not – well, it's like a tide, isn't it? The water laps out, then a wave brings it in. Each time, the water is just a bit higher on the shore."

"When we get you back to the United States, you will be given all the support you need. The professor hypothesizes, based on lookalike drugs that all of your memories will return, good and bad. But you won't be alone as you integrate them."

Arya looked up until her gaze met Thorn's.

"You have Thorn there with you," Lynx said. "You can trust him. You can lean on him. He's there for you."

"Yes," she said, and in that moment, she fully believed it. But she'd trusted others, and they had betrayed her.

39

ARYA
Paris, France
Nighttime

"**H**ANGING IN THERE, A**RYA**?" Thorn asked. "We can take a break."

"No, we can't," she replied. "You need to understand what's going on, right?"

"Yes," Lynx said. "So, we can make plans on how best to protect you. The better our picture, the better our plan."

"Out of self-preservation, breaks aren't a good idea." She looked straight at Thorn. She really had become, since her hearing was damaged, very good at reading expressions. Thorn was conflicted.

"I think this is a balancing act," he said. "We need the information, and we don't want to push you too fast or too far."

"No way to tell, though, is there?" She pulled her gaze away from Thorn's to ask that of Lynx.

"Unfortunately, that's correct."

Arya turned back to him. "Better out than in, right Thorn?"

He shook his head. "In this instance, I don't know. I think you're going to have to be the one who sets the pace."

"Okay. I'll keep that in mind. I'm not...there's a lot. It's not organized in my head. It's kind of like a kaleidoscope." Stress pulled at her forehead. A headache lurked in the wings, ready to fill her head with a gonging cacophony. She thought her time for being helpful was probably short-lived.

"I'm going to ask you about your relationship with a series of men. I don't know all of their names. I have their photos. When I show them to you, if it causes you too much distress, you'll tell me. Will you promise to do that?" Lynx asked.

Arya licked her lips and nodded. She tightened her grip on Thorn. She wasn't willing to let go of this anchor. He seemed to understand because he said, "I'm here. I've got you."

"Can I sit up a little?" she asked. She put her free hand to her forehead and was surprised that her brow was cool.

Thorn pressed a button to raise her head, then spun around to sit next to her. They were shoulder to shoulder, hip to hip, thigh to thigh. He left one foot on the ground. The other dangled off the edge of the bed, keeping things fresh and clean.

He never let go of her hand.

"Okay, the first two pictures. Do you know these men?" Lynx posted pictures of the men who kidnapped her.

"Dr. Petrov is the balding man. Dr. Sokolov is the other one. The blond."

"When did you first meet them?" Thorn asked.

Arya swallowed. "Well, I was at a conference. I was meant to give a talk about whale communication, but these two kidnapped me before I was able to speak."

"This was the Zoology and Animal Behaviors Conference in

Sacramento, California?" she asked.

"Yes." Arya paused. "That sounds right. Sacramento is right. I met George Matthews at the conference. He was taken by gunpoint at the same time I was."

"This George Matthews?" Lynx put up another picture.

Arya stared at that one for a long time. Her brain stuttered. "This could be him. He was younger looking, the George Matthews I remember."

"Do you know why they took you away?" Thorn asked.

"Then? No. Later, I learned that they needed help developing CHAMP."

Lynx said, "I'd like to understand more about champ."

"Explain it? Do you have a scientific background?"

Thorn focused on her with a steady gaze. "I have a fighting background. I worked for the Navy as a SEAL. Does this have to do with the Navy? Did they put you in danger?"

Arya scowled. "Why would you think that?"

He swept his thumb over the worry lines on her forehead. "Relax. Breathe." He seemed to wait until he was satisfied that she had calmed the flood of anxiety a bit before he said, "You were going to testify in court about your whale studies and how the Navy affected marine mammals with their sound waves."

"That's right, I was. But George and I were kidnapped before that happened. We were both supposed to report about our find-ings of how the naval soundings harmed the ocean mammals."

"You were both kidnapped before the trial. And you were held. And George was not?" Lynx asked.

"He was a prisoner. We were there for a very long time. Years, it seems. But my time perspective is warped. We escaped together." She tilted her head to the side. Something about that wasn't quite right. "We were forced to work together on their projects."

"Champ?" Thorn reminded her.

"CHAMP is Counter-electronic High-powered microwave Advanced Missile Project. But that's not where we started."

"Do you want to tell me what happened when you started?" Lynx asked. "What happened after they took you from the conference?"

"We were blindfolded and moved. There was a flight, I know that. We were taken to a place that was cold and very lonely. There were no other people or houses. It snowed all the time. They told me I was in Siberia, but I have no idea if that was right or not. I have no idea where I was." Arya could feel hot tears dripping down her face. But she ignored them. "They wanted me to use my science to help them build a weapons system." She laughed, and it tasted bitter next to the salt of her tears. "I'm not really a weapons kind of person. You might say that is rather opposite of where my heart lies. But they...hurt me very badly. And they had captured my sisters in Syria. They were holding them prisoner. If I misbehaved, they would not just punish me, but they would punish my sisters in kind." Her chin wobbled. "They're probably dead now. I wasn't able to do what was asked of me." Arya set her focus on a small stain on the wall. "Yes," she whispered, "probably dead."

"Can you tell me your sisters' names?" Lynx's voice pulled her back with a jolt.

"Polla was my older sister, and Habiba was the middle sister. They had been scientists, too. They were very bright, very lovely women."

Lynx put up two pictures of women in hijabs.

Arya reached out to grab the screen and stared wide-eyed at the pictures there, drinking them in.

"The woman on the left is Dr. Polla Khouri. She is working

in Munich as a physicist. She sought asylum from Aleppo at the beginning of the war. This picture was taken last night."

Arya gasped and started shaking.

Thorn reached his free arm around her and pulled her tight against him.

"And the woman on the right is Dr. Habiba Khouri Schmid. She is working as a geneticist in Geneva, Switzerland. She lives there with her husband and two children. Another child is on the way. That picture was also taken yesterday. Neither woman was captured at any point. And neither woman was ever hurt in retaliation for anything you did or did not do."

Arya couldn't believe it. Could not wrap her thoughts around the relief of this. "I have nieces and nephews?" she was able to gasp out.

"Just nieces." Lynx smiled. "I'm sorry we don't have their pictures for you." Lynx gave Arya a moment to assimilate that information.

A moment wouldn't do it. A lifetime might not be enough to do it. To let go of the fear and guilt. To let go of the pain and anguish. They had been fine all along, despite the recording that had been played for her. And now that Arya thought about it, she knew that sound waves could be altered. Her captors had tortured her physically, but probably worse, they had tortured her mentally.

"Ready?" Lynx asked.

Arya nodded. She felt weirdly out of her body, disconnected.

"The two Russian scientists used the idea of your sisters being hurt to get you to work for them. CHAMP was later. But can you explain to me what it was?"

"Yes, they wanted to develop a weapon that was supposed to be used instead of traditional firepower. It was supposed to be as effective as a nuclear weapon without hurting buildings."

"Just taking out all of the warm-blooded animals?" Thorn asked with a nod toward Lynx.

Arya just stared at him wide-eyed. In her mind, she was too horrified to contemplate a sound weapon that would take out all warm-blooded creatures in a space. That would be apocalyptic, and to stop such a thing, she would have allowed them to torture her and her family to death. What were the options? To take out whole swaths of populations? Horror coursed along her nervous system.

"Breathe," Thorn reminded her, and she took in a great gulp of air, held it, and thrust it out with as much power as she could muster. She did it again. And again. And again, until her brain started to function.

"The first thing they wanted me to develop was a shield. This shield was to be carried by the riot police. It was to make it so that the protestors would not be beaten or shot, but simply that the sound it emitted was painful enough that it forced them to leave the area."

Lynx change the screen. "This?"

There was an article written in Russian. It said the pension riots in Russia were getting out of hand, and the Russian government was deploying new weapons to contain the rioters. One of the items was a sonic riot shield that immitted sound waves that were physically torturous and would drive back the crowds. People with unprotected ears could be permanently damaged by the effects of the subsonic sound waves.

"That was a theory. A prototype," Arya said. "They must have started to manufacture them." Her gaze scanned down the article. "Developed by Dr. Petrov and Dr. Sokolov, who were given medals of valor by the Russian government."

"That article came out recently," Lynx pointed out. "But they must have been in production for a while for the police to get a supply in place and train their forces."

"These are very dangerous weapons, and they could hurt friend or foe alike. I'm sure the training was extensive," Thorn said.

"Time is a nebulous concept to me right now," Arya whispered. "I can't put my research on the calendar for you. I'm sorry."

"You're doing just fine," Lynx encouraged her. "What happened after you had the sonic shield prototype ready?"

"Next, they wanted George and me to work on another riot weapon, one where you could shoot the sound at a pinpointed opponent."

"And you were able to do that?" Thorn asked.

"Not the way they wished. Sound waves radiate out. So it's not like shooting a bullet – getting the gun on target, pulling a trigger, shooting a round, and having it hit someone specific. I wasn't able to figure that out, and I discovered that kind of weapon did the same kinds of physical damage on all the people, in say, a space as big as an office-sized building."

"Let's move away from that for a moment. I don't think knowing your exact research will help us right now. Let's talk about George. He was held prisoner with you?"

"Yes."

"You saw him daily?" Lynx asked.

"No. I saw him sometimes. Every couple of weeks. I was told he was in a different facility, and he'd be brought in so we could compare out research notes."

"He was tortured the way you were?"

Arya stared at her lap. Was he? "I assumed he was...I don't know. I never saw anything. We were watched carefully when we were together, so we were cautious about speaking only scientifically. I do know that when he didn't comply…when he failed… when he tried to make mistakes to slow down the work, they would come in and beat me. They had a video camera. They wanted George to see that his behavior hurt me very badly. And…well, I tried very hard to comply so neither George nor my sisters were hurt."

"Do you know what happened to your hearing, Arya?"

"Yes, it was an accident. I was explaining the issues with pinpointing the weapon. I went into the soundproof room to adjust the experiment, and someone set off the subsonic sounds. I heard an odd noise. And then everything changed. My ability to hear. The tinnitus. The confusion. Short term memory loss. Uhm…disequilibrium."

"And what happened next?"

"I was in my bed one night. George was able to get my door unlocked. He said he was going to escape and asked me if I wanted to come with him. Of course, I did. I was willing to risk anything at that point – my life, my sisters' lives. *Anything*. They had told me more about the weapons they wanted me to develop after CHAMP, a low-frequency infrasound that would explode blood cells–" Her eyes stretched wide. "Wait! Is that the apocalyptic weapon you mentioned, Thorn? Taking out mammals and leaving infrastructure? I didn't line those up. It was – I didn't." She shook her head, vehemently. "I didn't even want them to have CHAMP–"

Lynx interrupted, "Arya, George asked you to escape. Were you successful?"

"He drove us through the night to a small field. There was an airplane, and we stopped to eat and have something to drink, waiting for the morning light. I fell asleep. When I woke up, I was in the hospital, and DuBois was there with George. That's Dr. David DuBois, who is absolutely *not* my father."

40

Thorn
    Paris, France
    Monday, Zero Three Twenty Hours

"Other than those sketchy details, I don't remember the escape right now. Maybe it will come back to me later," Arya said.

"I'd like to know who was there at the hospital," Lynx said. "I'm trying to get an understanding of the relationships."

"George was helping me at the hospital. He spoke to the doctors on my behalf. They were speaking a language I didn't know."

Lynx seemed to brighten. "Portuguese, maybe?"

"It sounded like a romance language. When they gave me paperwork to sign, I could guess at some of the words. It was too complicated for me to figure out, so I just signed it. I needed surgery." Her fingers came up and traced along the scar on her head. "And when I woke up, David Dubois and George were in the room with me. I needed time to recover. I was there for weeks, I think."

"Close your eyes. Go back to your recovery time," Lynx said in a smooth low voice. "Let a picture come up for you. Tell me what you see."

"My head and face were bandaged. George told me they'd had to shave off my hair."

"George was still with you." Lynx's voice was hypnotic. "Anyone else?"

Thorn had to trust Lynx knew what she was doing. He watched Arya's face slacken.

"He introduced me to David DuBois. He was famous for his neuro-biological studies in PTSD and brain trauma. He said he couldn't fix my ears, but he might be able to help me with interventions that could make my injuries less disabling."

Arya's eyes slid back and forth behind her closed lids.

"You're remembering a scene." Lynx's voice soothed. "Tell me what you see."

"I woke up and pushed my call button, but the nurse didn't come. I got myself out of bed. I needed to use the toilet. When I opened the bathroom door, I found David and George having sex in my bathroom. I was horribly embarrassed."

"Isn't Matthews married to a woman?" Thorn mouthed into his covert mic.

"That doesn't mean anything," Lynx said back in his ear.

True…

Arya opened her eyes. "I'm so sorry. I think I need to lie down and close my eyes. The vertigo is making me nauseated. My head is pounding."

"You gave me everything I needed. Thank you, Arya. You rest, and we'll keep moving forward with our plan."

Thorn shifted to get off her bed, but Arya wasn't letting go of his hand. He closed the laptop lid and stretched out to place it on the hospital table. Reaching across his chest, he pushed the button to lower the head of the bed back, then turned on his side so she could burrow up next to him, their fingers still entwined.

He stroked her hair, and soon, her breathing changed.

But he didn't want to move.

He wanted to stay right there in that place, tangled up with Arya. He'd kick his own ass later. He was breaking all kinds of rules, personal and professional.

"Can you hear me, Thorn?" Lynx said in his ear.

"Roger," Thorn mouthed back.

"She doing okay?"

"I think she's sleeping. I hope so."

"What times she identified and the timeline I've been developing line up neatly. It looks like DuBois and Matthews met while they were trying to identify a cause for the twenty-one military personnel who had just gone into theater with no previous head injuries, suddenly showing up with symptoms of traumatic brain injury. You have that article in your cloud file."

"Copy."

"Both George Matthews and Arya were speaking at the zoological conference I was asking her about. I tracked down the organizers and asked about Arya's program. She never showed up for her talk. Later that day, Arya sent word that there was a family emergency. No one that I could find saw her from that point on. Her financial obligations were closed out, and she disappeared."

"But not Matthews," Thorn said.

"No, he had already given his talk. And it doesn't seem that there were any breaks in his appearances or his employment. Arya didn't show up to testify at the Navy hearing, but George did. Interestingly, colleagues at Montrim told us that George often traveled out of Washington D.C. He flew to a private laboratory in North Dakota. That's where he conducted some of his sound experiments. His colleagues said that George Matthews went there fairly frequently, if not once a week then every ten days. That was true, on my timeline, until several months before the first sounds were noticed by the American diplomatic corps in Cuba."

"Arya believed that Matthews was held prisoner all that time. But obviously, they were duping her into working with him." Thorn swallowed down the bile the sat on the back of his tongue. "Why did you ask about Portuguese when you were asking her questions?"

"There was another intersection when Matthews went over to lecture at the American University in Beirut. From his visa papers, he listed DuBois's home address. I believe that Matthews was there recruiting DuBois to his project.

"Because?"

"A week later, DuBois had a new influx of money in his American bank account, and he flew to Brazil on the same flight as Matthews. When DuBois traveled back to his home in Beirut, he had a daughter with him, traveling on a French passport."

"Arya was injured in a sound experiment gone awry, thinks she's escaped and is getting medical help, falls prey to this scheme to what end?"

"I *think* I have that answer. Remember, I was brought in to a Montrim case. Montrim thought they had a mole feeding information to a foreign power about an ongoing Pentagon research project. Since I was read into that program, I have access to the files. I did a search and discovered that our surveillance of Matthews shows that he was frequently speaking with DuBois during the whole time period when I believe that Arya was held captive."

"Arya said Matthews and DuBois were having sex in her hospital bathroom. They were lovers, were their communications romantic in nature?"

"Nothing in there about the content of their communications. I think we had a warrant to monitor incoming and outgoing numbers, not content. But our contractor was able to get me the DARPA files on DuBois, so I could figure out when and why he was hired by DARPA. It seems that Matthews was trying to convince DARPA to bring DuBois to the US to work as the counter for his work with sound weaponry – what he broke, DuBois could fix, should the enemy be working on similar neuroweaponry."

Thorn extrapolated that thought. "And Matthews very well might have broken Arya for the purpose of giving DuBois a guinea pig to experiment on."

"My thoughts," Lynx agreed. "And the whole charade of wiping her memory would make sense for several reasons. One, Dubois was experimenting with his new drug. Two, if he wiped her memory, he could do human experiments on memory trans-ference. You heard how Arya had weird pictures in her head that were labeled for her, and she believed them to be true. Three, he could monitor the long-term effect of the weapon that I believe, in some form or other, was directed at our embassies. I think that the CHAMP is a thing. Maybe not the thing it was first envi-sioned for."

"By Russia."

"Russian scientists, in cahoots with Matthews, might very well have been selling to the highest bidder. It looks like Russia won the bid when it came to the riot shields."

"Makes sense. And that works out with the details you've run down?" he asked. It was both complicated and simplistic. If Mathews and the two other scientists wanted to make money on the international weapons' stage, they needed the goods. Arya's unique expertise in studying how sounds injured marine mammals could be incorporated into the research Matthews had been conducting for the Pentagon while at Montrim. If Matthews already owned the property for experiments, why couldn't they just snatch Arya up and fabricate this ruse? Those were three shitheads that needed to be caught and brought to justice.

"It needs further investigation, and our client is taking that on."

"Then our contractor can't be the CIA." Another theory blown.

"Nope, not if they're doing a domestic criminal investigation. I'm guessing it's a Pentagon contract, maybe FBI," Lynx responded. "They could certainly dial-up their spook friends and give us a leg up. That is until you started playing Spidey, crawling up the side of the building."

"Don't," he growled.

"Touchy. All right. To my eyes, this all lays out as a neatly executed plan. The players wait for DuBois to stabilize Arya in her new persona. When DuBois has a firm hand on her, he then puts out a series of academic papers on TBI and PTSD. A PR campaign is waged to increase his limelight, media paints DuBois as the world authority. I remember him being in the paper about this because of Striker's buddy Reaper Hamilton's medical issues. I was hoping to see some important strides being made."

"In retrospect, it's good that Reaper dodged the DuBois bullet," Thorn said.

"Amen. So, in this possible scenario, while DuBois's "I'm the best of the best" PR campaign is going on, the sounds and symptoms start showing up in our diplomats. DARPA already has his name. Montrim now has it from George Matthews, as well.

"They didn't think that a nod from Matthews was disqualifying? He was being watched for sharing weapons secrets with the enemy."

"Matthews's surveillance wasn't known to DARPA, Montrim hired Iniquus to protect their Pentagon contract. DARPA might never have made that connection. *Probably* never made that connection. They just wanted the best of the best when it came to this issue. They needed to understand what happened if they were to develop systems to protect our people."

"Roger."

"In this scenario, then, DuBois is aligned with and possibly being paid by Matthews and his buddies," Lynx said. "I can speculate that they needed him for a variety of reasons — possibly to enter false data, possibly to give poor remediation, possibly to report back on the health findings."

"When Arya flew to France, they realize that she's endangering the entire scheme. If she starts looking into her citizenship, she will find that her papers are falsified. When she tried to talk to her grandmother, all the false memories that DuBois planted would be exposed. They needed to capture her. DuBois realized this too. Once he knew that the two Russians had grabbed Arya, he didn't stop to talk to his mom. He headed straight out of town. DuBois couldn't let the French pick him up for questioning since he's listed as her father on her green card."

"Agreed," Lynx said. "He had to get out of the EU stat."

"If we're working the hypothesis that DuBois called in the Russian scientists, how do the Rex Deus and Omega goons get involved?"

Brigitte rounded into the room. "Okay, lover boy, stop whispering sweet nothings into Juliette's ear. We've got incoming."

41

Thorn
    Paris, France
    Monday, Zero Three Forty-one Hours

"Thorn," Lynx said quietly in his ear. "Deep is doing logistics while Nutsbe's at the meeting. He's indicating that there's a series of cars driving in tandem up the highway, moving in fast. If you go now, you can get out of their way."

"What are you seeing?" Thorn asked as Gage and Honey spun into the room, grabbing up the computer, his duffle, and the supplies that were easily at hand.

"Seven cars racing our way at this rather shitty time of night," Brigitte said. "I think we need to head to the border."

"Why not the American Embassy in Paris?" Honey asked. "It's closer and puts us on American soil."

"*Because,* that's why," Brigitte said.

Thorn had roused Arya. "We need to move you again."

Her eyes were held wide as her gaze swept the room full of

people. "Those guys are Honey and Gage. They're on my team. That's Brigitte." Thorn didn't know what team she was on. He'd been trying to get a good look at her left wrist, but so far, he hadn't been able to see if she wore the Rex Deus tattoo.

Arya held still as Thorn unfastening her IV line, then reached out shaking hands to pull on the clothes Thorn held out to her. If they were headed to the border, Arya's being in a hospital gown would make things delicate. The air force base in Belgium would have everything they needed. It was a better place to be. But the closest harbor might be the best thing. They could argue about it once they were underway.

"Ready?" Thorn bent to pull her arm around his neck. With one arm supporting her back and another hand scooped under her knees, he rolled her in until she rested against his chest. He stood, and everyone in the little clinic room peeled out into the hall and jogged up the corridor.

"Five minutes." Nutsbe was back in his ear. That was good. Deep was a pro at his job, but Nutsbe was his teammate. It was just a more comfortable dynamic.

Bursting through the doors, the Panther Force found that a row of cars was lined up, drivers behind each wheel, doors opened and ready. Lights extinguished.

The Panthers came to a screeching halt.

"What's going on here," Honey said. "That's our car there in the middle. I drive."

"We don't have time," Brigitte said. "My team is trained to work together to lose a tail — even if they have eyes in the sky. Get the fuck in the car."

Honey nodded toward Thorn. Thorn bent to get Arya in the car, moving her over and climbing in beside her.

Before Honey could climb in the front, Brigitte, gun in hand, moved to the front seat and pulled on her safety belt. "Buckle up," she told Thorn. She turned toward Honey and Gage, who looked unsure of how to proceed.

"One in front. One in back," Brigitte ordered. "We're the filling in this sandwich."

Honey and Gage took off together to the car that was behind them.

"They don't really listen, do they?" Brigitte asked.

The door slammed. The engines revved. Their driver pulled night vision goggles from his lap and strapped them on his head.

They proceeded on without lights.

The drivers moved in a tight formation at a fast clip through the black of night. Training. And tons of it.

As impressive as that was, it actually set off Thorn's warning system.

He didn't like being separated from his team.

Arya was trembling beside him. He wanted to reach out and comfort her, but his attention needed to be outward. He needed his head to be disengaged from emotion. It was time to be coldly calculating, and, by all measurements, this scenario was off.

"How do you know Brigitte?" Arya whispered. "She's on your team? Why don't you want this man to be driving?"

"It's a control thing," Brigitte answered. "Thorn doesn't like it much when someone else is at the helm. Do you, darling?"

"Funny," Thorn said, but he knew that Arya would be searching for clues on who to trust and who not to. Brigitte was playing games. That endearment would have an effect on Arya. He needed Arya to trust him, even if he was a stranger. And there was Brigitte casting her seeds of doubt.

Arya cleared her throat. Looking toward Brigitte, she said, "I really need to understand what's happening here. I recognize your voice. You were on the roof after the fight."

"That's right." Brigitte's voice came from the front seat. Her silhouette just visible from the gauge lights.

"You're American?" Ayra asked.

"I'm Israeli," she answered. "Only Honey, Gage, and Thorn are American. You are, right now, in the custody of Israel."

"Custody," Arya whispered.

"And Thorn is my boyfriend," she tossed out. "He handed you over to me."

Thorn could feel Arya shifting beside him. "I'm no such thing, Arya. It's a lot to take in, but there are four groups that I know of who are involved here. There's Iniquus, which is my team. We were sent by the United States government to find you, protect you, and bring you home safely. There are the two scientists that kidnapped you, and they are associated with both George Matthews and David DuBois. There is another set of operators – very much like Iniquus in training and expertise – who are somehow linked to David DuBois. They're called Omega. And then there's Brigitte."

"But why?" She gasped.

"I'm guessing it has to do with CHAMP and the possibilities of the other neuroweaponry systems."

"Oh." She breathed out. "Then, as long as I know what I know, people will be chasing me down."

"They'll stop chasing you now," Brigitte said. "It's not going to be a problem anymore."

"Why should I trust you?" Arya asked. "You lied about Thorn. I…he's not…he's…"

"Oh, sweetheart, you are so naïve, aren't you?" Brigitte tsked. "I knew it when I watched you two on the roof and in the clinic. You think that this big handsome soldier boy swooped in as your hero and that he would be your new pet. You've convinced your little heart that you love him."

"I…" Arya's voice wavered off.

Brigitte was laughing. "Oh, I know, you thought that Thorn felt the same. And he does. Which is equally laughable."

"Tracking. We put out a May Day. The French police are gathering a team," Nutsbe said. "So far, Gage and Honey are still in the car behind you."

"But Thorn is a dessert-loving man," Brigitte was saying. "Aren't you Thorn? You just love to get a piece of pie. You don't even care about the flavor. Just pie. Yum."

Thorn heard a click to his left. He slid his hand over and felt Arya's seat belt, and she'd unfastened herself.

"Here," Brigitte said. "I'll show you." She was quiet for a moment, and Thorn knew exactly what she was doing.

He filtered various ideas for handling this through his head, and all he could think was that he was the wrong man for this mission. It should have been Honey all along. He was emotionally compromised. He couldn't think straight. He had to put this to the side and be calculating. He could worry about Arya's heart when he was sure he'd kept the rest of her safe.

Brigitte held up her phone. "Check the date and time stamp." And there he was, screwing around with Brigitte.

"Shit, is that what I think it is?" Nutsbe said as the moaning and sighing filled the car.

"This is FUBAR." Thorn mouthed. "That's enough," he said to Brigitte. Though he couldn't see Arya, he turned her way. "If you saw the time stamp, you'll see that I was with Brigitte before I was assigned to this mission."

"You love her? You're a couple?" Arya asked.

"No." It was as simple as that. He didn't have any other way to talk about this – bad timing, bad company, really bad choices. "Lights," he called.

"That's not from the team that was heading to the clinic," the driver said.

"What do you mean?" Brigitte asked.

"That group is heading up behind us. Those lights are on the crossroads. Two cars."

"I have the incoming team that Deep warned you about behind you," Nutsbe said. "I have those two cars coming in from the south. I don't know who they are. They aren't support."

"Just so you're aware," Thorn told the driver. "Those cars aren't associated with Iniquus."

Brigitte and the driver switched to Hebrew.

Their car slowed as it popped over a metal plate. There was a whir beneath them. They must be going over a bridge of some kind.

The driver yelled, "Stop!" then braked the car hard.

Thorn twisted and grabbed at Arya to protect her since she was no longer buckled in.

The car behind them with Gage and Honey slammed into them and pushed them forward. They hit something in front as well. Thorn's night vision glasses were back in his duffle. He couldn't tell what was going on.

Arya's door popped open, and she was clambering out, shaking off his grip.

As Thorn slid along the seat to follow her, he grabbed the shoulder harness of the driver and, with a quick yank, pulled it to full length, wrapped it around the back of the headrest, looping it around the guy's neck and let it snap, locking it in place. It might buy him a minute. Thorn snatched the goggles from the guy's head and jumped from the car.

Quickly he realized that move was wasted. Car headlights beamed out.

Now, he could see that they were on a single lane bridge with grating as a surface. He could hear water racing beneath their feet. The end of the bridge had been barricaded, and the first car had hit the barrier. That car was crushed.

Honey and Gage were rounding out of their car, clambering over the roof, trying to get to Thorn's side.

Thorn's eye took all of this in, but what it didn't take in was Arya.

Where had she gone?

His eye scanned the length of the bridge. He saw Brigitte standing by the guard rail looking up. Thorn's eye tracked the trajectory.

There was Arya climbing up the arch.

"Good girl, Juliette. Keep climbing," Brigitte yelled as she walked down the bridge to get under Arya. "Keep climbing. You know what you need to do. This is the time. The higher up you go, the better your chances of succeeding."

Succeeding?

Lynx was in her ear. "Thorn, she's going to jump. Talk her down. You're the *only* one who can."

Thorn thought back to his buddy coming off his detox. He had been suicidal. They had to post two men on active guard around the clock. He remembered his friend had just kept repeating, "I can't handle the pain. I just want it to stop."

"Stop, Arya," Thorn called.

"Climb!" Brigitte countered.

"Arya, this isn't the answer you're looking for. I'm going to get you out of this. You'll see your sisters again. Don't give up on them. Your sisters need you. Your nieces need you. The freaking whales in the oceans need you. *I* need you. I *need* you, Arya. Let me help you with the pain."

Arya had stopped and was listening to him.

Brigitte took out her phone and turned on the video of their screwing to its loudest setting. The sounds filled the night.

Arya climbed higher.

And he knew what was going through her head. She'd trusted too many people. Trusted George Matthews. Trusted DuBois. Had even trusted her captors, who lied and manipulated her. Trusted that they'd told her the truth about her sisters. There was no reason for her to trust anyone right now. Not even him.

He could bare his soul to her tell her that he'd been fighting his emotions but to no avail. She was written in his heart. That he wanted her to come down and be safe because he couldn't lose her.

But all of that was selfish and self-centered on his part and probably meaningless to her.

Thorn did the only thing he could think of, he stopped talking. He jogged down to the other end of the arch and started his own climb.

"Keep going, Juliette. At the top, you can just let go and fly fr—" Brigitte's words were cut off.

Thorn could see Gage's fist following through on a right hook as Brigitte slipped to the ground.

42

Paris, France

Monday, Zero Four Hundred Hours

THORN CLIMBED WITHOUT A WORD.

He watched Arya swaying. Gripping. Moving one hesitant foot, then the other.

Fear washed through his system, cold waves tingling over his skin. His heart crushing under the weight of his terror. He couldn't push past it. He depended on training to move him up the side of the arch. Up. Up.

Once he crawled across the top, he stilled.

Lynx wasn't in his ear, giving sage advice.

His team was on the ground. Everyone, friend and enemy alike, stood, hands on hips, heads back, watching Arya on her climb.

She had to make the climb.

He understood that at some primal level.

As sure as Thorn knew he hated everything about what was happening, he knew this was her journey. He straddled the arch, then lay on his stomach.

He looked through the metal bars. Arya turned her face up and caught his eye.

"I understand." He choked on the emotions that clogged his throat. With an iron grip, he took hold of his own fears and thrust them aside. He cleared the debris. His conviction flowed freely. *This* was about Arya. He was there to support *her*. Solid. Strong. Unwavering. He hoped she could read *that* in his eyes. "We'll do this together."

"What?" she called out.

But he didn't answer her.

After a moment, she climbed. Thorn was laser-focused on her. He watched as her fingers unclasped and reached rung after rung. There was nothing he could do right now but wait. His mind raced around, trying to find ways to solve this problem. To win the game. To pull out a victory. But there was *nothing* that he could do. He had to wait for Arya to get to the top.

In his head, the tactical crap bounced around. The fact that she had vertigo. She hadn't eaten in days. She was coming out of detox on a drug that they didn't understand. Her mind was flooded with new and horrific memories. That she was able to get her body to climb that arch meant that she had a goal in mind.

It was his buddy all over again, only that had been his brother in arms.

And Arya was an undefinable part of his cell structure. She was part of him.

Her head rose over the side, and he could see her eyes. "You did it. I'm here."

She looked at him, then she looked down.

Thorn's body froze. He forced himself into combat breaths. Pushed his focus to the left and the right, trying to break the hold of the freeze that could be so deadly. He'd never experienced terror like this. It washed through him, and he let it flow out again until he was solid. Unwavering in his support.

"Keep coming up," Thorn said. He was surprised that his voice sounded warm and welcoming. He hoped she could hear that. Hoped that his sound waves were stronger than the wind and that her tinnitus wasn't too loud. "I'm here. We'll do this together, okay?" He put his hand out, and miraculously, she reached out and took it.

"Do what together?"

"Why did you climb up here, Arya?"

She looked down at the water far below them. It threw her weight off balance, and she had to grip his hand harder not to fall. Thorn wrapped his feet into the girding to hold them in place.

Arya turned her gaze onto Thorn. "I'll never go back. I'll never be a prisoner again. I'll never do anyone's bidding."

"That's right. That will never happen again." Solid. Unwavering.

Her face pulled into tight lines of confusion. "You have to let go of my hand now."

"No. I made you a vow. And I would never lie to you or hurt you. I will not compromise that vow."

"Give me my hand back, Thorn." Her words were louder, angrier this time. "I want this pain to end. I can't *do* this anymore."

"That's right," Thorn said. "I'm here. We'll do this together."

"You...what? Do you not understand the situation? I'm going to jump." She closed her eyes. "I'll just let go and lean back. And my body will fly. I'll keep my eyes closed and feel the wind. And then, suddenly, I'll feel nothing anymore. It will all be gone."

"All right, that's the plan then. Shall you come up to me? Or shall I climb down to you?"

"Neither. I…what are you saying?"

"I'm saying that I'm here. We'll do this together."

"But then…"

Thorn stopped. This was it.

"But…" She looked down, and he felt such longing in her body.

He had so many friends who had died by suicide. They just wanted release. So many men and women he'd fought beside. Men and women who just *couldn't*. They came back to the civilian world where they should be safe, and they found no peace.

"*Thorn.*" Despair painted his name.

"Whatever you decide. I'm here. Whatever you decide, we'll do it together."

"Gage has got the rappelling gear," Nutsbe whispered. "He's out of sight, behind you. Tell us when you want us to proceed."

The sky stilled as if taking one last inhale of night. And with an exhale, dawn broke, unveiling the indigo that had hidden beneath the blackened sky. The birds roused from their nests, calling to each other.

Thorn and Arya poised there, grasping hands.

Arya rested her head against the metal.

It took long minutes. Thorn's heart hadn't stopped racing. He felt like this was the hardest marathon he'd ever run. Letting go of control was not his nature. But if he tackled and wrestled Arya back down, she'd just look for another opportunity. She had to choose to face the pain. He'd never experienced what she did, and he couldn't even imagine it.

Finally, she looked up, and their eyes locked.

He swallowed hard. And forced himself to stay still and silent.

"When I first saw you, I felt such an affinity for you, as if we belonged together," she said. "That felt hopeful, like maybe there was a slice of happiness in this world for me, too."

"Thank you for finding the right words." He smiled. "I've been looking for a way to explain my feelings to you. That's about right." The smile slid away. "And it feels like my chance to have hope and have that belonging is hanging by a thread." And he stopped himself from adding anything else, like *please, for my sake, don't jump.* Because this wasn't about him. This was about her. She had to *want* life.

43

THORN
Paris, France
Monday, Zero Six Thirty Hours.

"THORN," she whispered.

"I'm here."

"I want to go down now."

He froze. What did *down* mean to her?

"I think I need your help. I'm…really tired and shaky. And I can't think of what to do. All those people are down there, and they'll take me away from you."

"I won't let it happen." Thorn called out, "Gage, come up." He never let his focus waver. "My friend is bringing you a climbing harness, so you'll be safe."

"But down…"

"We've been up here for a while. And you were focused on your choices. You probably didn't see that the other teams pulled out as the French police arrived. We're going to get you down and take you right to the airport. Take you straight back to the United States and take you to the hospital to get you the help you need. You've done great."

Thorn felt pressure on his thigh, then a pat at his hip. Gage worked a harness around Thorn to keep him safe.

"Gage is going to go under the arch and swing up behind you. You're not going to pay any attention. You're just going to focus on me and hold my hand like we've been doing. Gage is going to put a harness on you. Then we'll all go down together."

"WHAT ARE YOU THINKING?" Thorn asked.

They were sitting side by side on the plane. Iniquus had booked out the whole first class. Honey was up ahead of them and Gage behind. They'd loaded last, coming through a private door from the airport, and would unload first down a mobile staircase before the airplane came flush to the gangway.

They were almost home. And suddenly, Arya had started shaking. Thorn didn't know if that was mental or physical. He tightened his arm around her as she lay her cheek on his chest.

"They're out there," she whispered. "They weren't arrested."

"You'll be in the United States soon. They can't cross the borders and be here legally. The CIA and FBI are tracking them. The Israeli government has been put on alert and are cooperating. Your hospital is secure."

"But I won't stay there forever," she whispered.

Thorn took her chin between his fingers and tilted her head up so he could read her eyes. He lay a soft kiss on her lips. "The plan in place is that you will stabilize in the hospital, then my team will move you to one of our support houses. Roxanne was vetted. Did you know she'd been an Army nurse?" He rubbed his thumb over her cheek, then brushed her hair back from her face.

"Yes, I've seen her pictures."

"She's been cleared by the FBI, and if it's okay with you, she'll be coming to live with you at the house. Her salary is being covered. And you will be getting a stipend. You aren't to worry about finances." He pulled out his phone and pulled up a picture of the Victorian-style house with the ancient oak in the front yard. "It's right across from a clinic that specializes in military rehabilitation. I have a friend from the Strike Force team named Randy who's there. They have a world-renowned trauma-psychology department. We'll get you the best support available."

"DuBois," she whispered.

"Is in custody with the FBI. DuBois was considered a charlatan by the medical teams at this clinic. The FBI, DARPA, and the Pentagon have a lot of questions, so they'll be part of your life, okay?"

She nodded.

"Until things are stable, Iniquus will be providing your security. I'll be living in the carriage house out back." He scrolled to a picture of the back yard and a two-story carriage house.

She nodded. "Those were the things I was the most worried about. What my next steps looked like. How I'd survive without funds. How I could help get these criminals out of society." She stared at the picture on Thorn's phone. "It looks peaceful and quiet." She shifted out of his arms, so she could look Thorn in the eye. "You asked me about peace and quiet, and I told you about the anechoic chamber where I could hear my pulse. But when I was on the bridge, and the birds started to sing, I remembered something else. Out in the middle of the Hoh Rainforest in Olympic National Park, there is a small red stone. It was part of a sound pollution project to find a single square inch on the planet Earth that was not obscured by human sound. No traffic, no planes, just pure nature." She turned to look out the little oval window. "I was studying noise pollution in the oceans, and for curiosities sake, I wanted to go there, to see the red stone and experience natural acoustic purity." Arya turned back to Thorn. "Finding peace was *really* loud, teeming with life." A tired smile tweaked at the corners of her lips. "It was *amazing*. Hiking back, there was a spiritual quest. I remember that when I came out of that glade, I had to sit on a log and sob. Such a miraculous experience. Sound doesn't have to be painful."

Thorn nodded.

"It's interesting, with that one square inch project, airlines started changing their routes to try to lessen the noise pollution. I wanted that for the oceans. It was my life's work. I was fighting for sound peace for the ocean's mammals." She looked down at her lap and swallowed hard. "The whales need me to stop being selfish and get back in the fight for them."

"They do. You will. We'll do this together." He leaned down, resting his forehead against hers. Then he sat up and reached into his pocket and pulled out the little red stone. "It's kind of funny to hear your story about the rainforest." He placed the cool smooth surface in her hand. "I found this on the day we met. Just as I was heading from Toulouse to Paris trying to find you."

"Red jade. It's beautiful."

"I picked it up and put it in my pocket for no reason at all." He pressed a kiss into her hair, then laced his fingers into hers. "At that point, there was a lot going on, confusion about you and your case, people coming and going. There was a lot of noise, but in my brain, at that moment, everything stilled as I reached for the stone. When you were sharing about your experience in the rainforest, I thought yes, that was exactly right − life can be really loud, and crazy, and confusing, but in the chaos, peace can be found."

The end

This is *not* THE END of Thorn and Arya's story
Join them and the other valorous men and women of the Iniquus
World
as they fight for a better tomorrow.

Keep reading for sneak peek of *Cold Red (FBI Joint Task Force Series Book 2)*

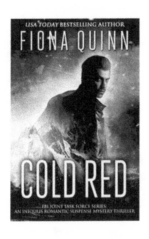

But first, Suicidal ideation (thinking about suicide) is not uncommon. If you read this book, and it has triggered you, or you feel you need support, please talk with someone. A number to call is:

1-800-273-TALK
1-888-628-9454 (Spanish)
Crisischat.org

My very best wishes go out to you.

Fiona

Readers, I hope you enjoyed getting to know Thorn and Arya. If you had fun reading THORN, I'd appreciate it if you'd help others enjoy it too.

Recommend it: Just a few words to your friends, your book groups, and your social networks would be wonderful.

Review it: Please tell your fellow readers what you liked about my book by reviewing THORN on Amazon and Goodreads. If you do write a review, please send me a note at hello@fionaquinnbooks.com. I'd like to thank you with a personal e-mail. Or stop by my website, FionaQuinnBooks.com, to keep up with my news and chat through my contact form.

Please Turn the page for chapter one of Cold Red!

COLD RED

**They might survive the madmen trailing their every move…
if the elements don't kill them first…**

Getting arrested was *not* part of Anna's mission. Neither was the crash that left her stranded on a mountain road with an injured FBI agent. Now, Anna will have to rely on her special forces training to survive the terrorists who want them dead *and* the unforgiving winter storm—all while maintaining her cover and trying not to fall for the man she's honor-bound to protect. The man who has *no* idea who she really is…

It was supposed to be a simple prisoner transport. Steve *never* thought he'd end up having to trust an enemy with his life. But… here he is. And the truly scary part? Anna doesn't *feel* like his enemy. She feels like his redemption. His forever. He can only hope he'll live long enough to claim her.

With a brutal storm looming and enemies closing in, Anna and Steve will have to figure out how to trust each other and work together. Otherwise, they won't stand a chance of making it out with their heads (and hearts) intact...

Cold Red is an intense, enemies-to-lovers, action adventure military romance suspense filled with spies, conspiracies, and international terror.

Join the fight for survival.

Grab your copy and lets go.

1

ANNA

WHEN THE FLASHBANG blasted in the hallway, Anna dropped to her knees. Her cheek crushed into the dirty carpet where she sipped at a pocket of air not yet filled with acrid smoke. Her head seemed to swell and expand with the high-pitched whistle that followed the explosive's concussion.

The FBI SWAT team swarmed simultaneously through the front and back doors. Dressed head to foot in black protective gear, these guys weren't playing games. While the ringing in Anna's ears muffled their directives, Anna knew if she did anything other than lay very still, they'd shoot her without a single question asked.

So, there she lay with her legs wide, fingers laced behind her head. She lay there and waited for her body to regain equilibrium, for the hard hands of the SWAT force to find her through the gray cloud of smoke.

The FBI was here doing their duty, cleaning up the riff-raff, scrubbing the world of conspirators, and home-grown terrorists, then they'd head back to the banality of their homes, a dinner of meatloaf and mashed potatoes in front of the TV. *They're just everyday guys doing their job*, she told herself, trying to shift her brain toward rational thought and away from her survival instincts.

A boot stomped down in front of Anna's face. A knee pressed into her back. The weight of the rather sizable man pinned her, pressing the breath out of her body, leaving her oxygen-deprived.

He has to do it this way. He doesn't know I won't fight.

Anna was spending a considerable amount of energy on not fighting.

The man clapped his handcuffs around her left wrist before he swung her arm to bring it down to the small of Anna's back. He twisted her right thumb and brought that hand down to match them. Click-zip went the metal encircling Anna's wrist. It was cold against her heated system. She had to work to make her body compliant when everything in her screamed that she should fight for her life.

Anna had known all along that she could be caught up in a law enforcement raid.

She just didn't expect it to be today.

But here it was.

The SWAT guy ran thorough hands over her body, searching for weapons. He pulled her phone from the cargo pocket on her pants and confiscated it. He snatched her knife from her waistband. Anna was hefted to her feet and walked out to the street in front of the horrified neighbors. When they reached a nondescript SUV, he turned her around and compared her face to the photo he pulled from under his chest plate. "Zelda Fitzgerald?" the guy asked, using Anna's undercover name.

Anna nodded.

He read her her Miranda rights as he leaned down to clamp shackles around her ankles, then left her propped beside the open door.

Her guard probably held her there in case she needed to vomit - a frequent side effect of being in a room with flashbang and having your limbic system lit up like the grand finale on the Fourth of July.

Anna watched as they wrestled Johnathan out of the house. It looked like he'd been in the shower. Suds still clung to his hair and beard. A towel draped over his shoulders. His gym shorts rode low on his hips as he stumbled forward, wearing two different colored flip flops.

It was twenty degrees out here.

Things could be worse.

She could be Johnathan.

As a SWAT guy moved Johnathan toward the car, her view was blocked by a man wearing tactical pants and boots. His midnight-blue jacket was emblazoned with FBI in bold yellow letters. A set of car keys in his hand, Anna bet this was her driver. He stared hard at her face. A hair shorter than six feet with broad shoulders and a slender waist, this man was fit. Strong. And had a battle hardness to him.

Anna had been instructed by her militia commander at the Southern Iron Cross that if this day came, she was to escape and evade. Her real-world commander at the United States' Asymmetric Warfare Group had signed off on that. She needed to stay in the game if she was to gather the intel the Pentagon needed – the odd connection of Slovakians to a West Virginia militia.

Looking at this special agent from the FBI, though, Anna couldn't see herself being successful at escaping without incapacitating him.

Nope. She couldn't imagine that going well for either of them.

Anna wished the FBI had sent someone else. In imagining this scenario, she had expected someone older – less sharp-edged. A guy with too many doughnuts around his middle, too many scotches belted back after long days and longer years of service. Someone who was tired. How the heck had she pulled the short straw and gotten *this* guy?

One of us is going to end up dead before this is over. That thought burrowed into her mind before she could grab it and throw it off to the side. Now, it was in there, scratching and scrambling around as it nested into her subconscious.

"Are you Special Agent Steve Finley?" a suit called over. Finley broke eye contact and moved to talk to the man.

Steve Finley. That name niggled at the back of her mind, something from last year, a story that somehow connected to her investigation. Something she'd learned from the CIA back in Slovakia.

Hearing that name, again, seemed like an odd coincidence.

A second SWAT guy moved to the other side of the car, where he tied a white blanket from off the dog's bed around Johnathan's neck. It had a static coating of black Marmaduke hair.

Well, at least it's warm, Anna thought.

Johnathan stood there, sobbing like a little kid in a make-believe superman cape.

Anna bet Johnathan had never considered that he would be arrested. Laws simply didn't apply to people of his ilk. Raised by a set of ladder-climbing parents who pushed their baby boy into financial and social circles where he couldn't compete, Johnathan became stupid-hungry for power – political, financial, anything he could get, really.

The desire for influence and respect drove Johnathan from his Connecticut country-club lifestyle over to Slovakia to see if he couldn't hook his future to a Russian star. He had connections. He could schmooze with the best of them – maybe even better than the rest of them since he'd had to fine-tune that skillset to stay relevant in his youth. The Zoric family recognized him for what he was, a sycophant, though not in an oily way. And they'd sent him here to West Virginia to do *something*. And Anna had been sent by the Zoric family to monitor him.

Anna did as she was told.

Anna scrutinized Johnathan in this new light of captured criminal and decided that Johnathan's rather effeminate face and mannerisms meant that once he got to the pokey, he was going to have a rough ride, indeed.

Shoot. Anna huffed out a puff of air. She realized that when she escaped from the FBI, she was going to have to save Johnathan, too. The Zoric family would expect her to get Johnathan free or make sure he was silenced. No man could be left to tell tales about the family. After all, they'd sent her to handle him.

That upped the stakes.

Anna sent Johnathan an anger-filled glare. He couldn't run fast on a normal day but in flip-flops and a blanket cape?

This scenario was ridiculous.

Johnathan's guard popped the backdoor open, folded Johnathan into the seat, then belted him in place. As the guy slammed the door shut, Johnathan's sniveling escalated.

Anna's lip curled with derision.

She felt no compassion for him. He was just a pawn, easily pushed around the playing board, part of a strategy, but cheap and disposable. She wondered what Cal would think if he could see this scene playing out.

Huh.

That was a problem.

Cal.

The leader of Southern Iron Cross here in West Virginia was

Cal Tucker. Cal did his manipulating from behind the scenes. He kept his fingers clean.

He'd probably slip through a keyhole and keep on keeping on.

Keep the movement growing.

Follow the directives of the person in real power – Yes, someone was handing strategies to Cal. They had to be.

Cal was raised with backwoods' smarts.

He was prepared for doomsday.

His gut was packed tight with the kind of anger at life that seethed and leeched out, poisoning his system. Anxiety powered his every thought. It salted his actions. But despite all the bile that Cal consumed and spewed, his ideas had been small. His impact had been localized.

That was true until Johnathan, and his international reach was introduced into the fold.

And that reach was necessary for the Southern Iron Cross to grow and prosper.

It was an odd marriage of minds, Johnathan and Cal.

An arranged marriage.

A marriage of convenience. That was a thought that had looped through Anna's brain since she'd followed Johnathan from the fine dining and nightlife of Bratislava Slovakia to Middle of Nowhere, West Virginia: How did these two men with diametrically different world views end up joining hands?

Anna listened as Johnathan's crying hit a crescendo.

Why the hell was she suddenly under arrest with Johnathan?

Something had happened.

Cal? Anna wondered. Had he fed them to the FBI?

No. Johnathan knew too much about the organization. And Johnathan knew why *the family* sent him from Slovakia to West Virginia.

Johnathan was the wallet.

Their gravy train.

The SIC meal ticket.

You don't bite the hand that feeds you.

But—and this was the great big but—Cal was smart; he'd know that if and when Johnathan was caught, Johnathan would flip on everyone. And there lay the danger. If Johnathan's testimony and information were deemed worthy, Johnathan could walk away as a free man, and Cal— with all his careful detachment—could be the one facing prison. Knowing that, Anna also knew that Cal would find some way to stop Johnathan from cooperating and probably stop her, too. After all, they'd come into the organization as a matched set of outsiders.

An animal control truck pulled up on the other side of the FBI perimeter. Anna watched the guy pop open one of his cages – no way in this world could Johnathan's Great Dane Marmaduke fold himself into that space. He'd probably end up on the front seat, riding shotgun back to the pound.

Anna turned her head, absorbing as much information as she could, trying to get a better grasp on everything going on.

Behind their car, the journos were showing up. Anna shook her head until her hair covered her face. The last thing she needed was to be publicly recognizable; that could be career-ending.

From behind her long blond strands, Anna shot a look of disgust at Johnathan, who had gathered himself, as much as he could, given his restraints, into the fetal position, nigh on hysterical. It was hard to believe that Johnathan could hold Cal's feet to the fire when no one else could. Even Anna couldn't do that, though she'd tried to get the information. She was missing a critical piece to the puzzle.

But now it looked like it was too late for her to learn what was really important – the how and why of the Slovakian Zoric family—with their connections to the Russian spy agency FSB—getting involved with a militia group conceived in the forests of West Virginia.

Mission fail.

From around the back of the house, pranced Marmaduke on a leash held by a SWAT guy. Marmaduke was the sweetest, most gentle dog Anna had ever met. He was a hundred-and-fifty-pound baby who liked to sit on her lap and give her long, rough tongue baths. The big old dog looked excited about a new adventure. Marmaduke must have been out back when the FBI burst in the door, or he would have been shot by the SWAT team as he tried to race up to hug and lick them. "Good for you, Marmaduke. It was nice knowing you, buddy. Have a great life." Anna whispered under her breath

The cold sting of icy wind burned across her face.

The storm was coming in. The sooner they got underway, the sooner they'd get to their destination. She wondered if the FBI realized how dangerous it was going to be to move from Point A to Point B, what with the weather moving in and Cal and the Sons of the Iron Cross out there.

She'd have to get herself freed up as soon as she could. She pictured the cuff key she'd taped to the inside of her belt.

As if reading her mind, the SWAT guard reached down, unbuckled her leather belt, and pulled it from the loops. "Looky here," he said, seeing the duct tape. He pulled it free to show the handcuff key. "Expecting us, huh?" He pushed her into the car, so she was sitting next to Johnathan on the faux-leather seat. The guard reached down to unlace her boots then yanked them off. "Got a shiv hidden in these?"

He spun her into her seat, strapped on her safety belt, and

said, "enjoy the next six hours," before he slammed the door shut.

Six hours? She glanced at the windshield and saw the Washington DC tags. Well, this is going to be miserable, Anna thought as she focused over on Finley.

Washington? Something felt off.

Something didn't add up.

If only the ringing in her head from the flashbang would stop, then she could hear herself think.

Grab your copy of COLD RED and follow the adventure!

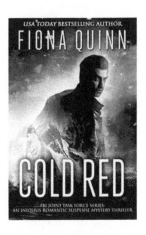

THE WORLD of INIQUUS

Chronological Order

Ubicumque, Quoties. Quidquid

Weakest Lynx (Lynx Series)

Missing Lynx (Lynx Series)

Chain Lynx (Lynx Series)

Cuff Lynx (Lynx Series)

WASP (Uncommon Enemies)

In Too DEEP (Strike Force)

Relic (Uncommon Enemies)

Mine (Kate Hamilton Mystery)

Jack Be Quick (Strike Force

Deadlock (Uncommon Enemies)

Instigator (Strike Force)

Yours (Kate Hamilton Mystery)

Gulf Lynx (Lynx Series)

Open Secret (FBI Joint Task Force)

Thorn (Uncommon Enemies)
Ours (Kate Hamilton Mysteries
Cold Red (FBI Joint Task Force)
Even Odds (FBI Joint Task Force)
Survival Instinct - Cerberus Tactical K9
Protective Instinct - Cerberus Tactical K9
Defender's Instinct - Cerberus Tactical K9
Danger Signs - Delta Force Echo
Hyper Lynx - Lynx Series
Danger Zone - Delta Force Echo
Danger Close - Delta Force Echo
Cerberus Tactical K9 Team Bravo
Marriage Lynx - Lynx Series

FOR MORE INFORMATION VISIT
WWW.FIONAQUINNBOOKS.COM

ACKNOWLEDGMENTS

My great appreciation ~
 To my editor, Kathleen Payne
 To my publicist, Margaret Daly
 To my cover artist, Melody Simmons

For the love and support I've always received from Scott Silverii and Liliana Hart and from SilverHart Publishing, who began Uncommon Enemy's journey.

To my Beta Force, who are always honest and kind at the same time.

To my Street Force, who support me and my writing with such enthusiasm. If you're interested in joining this group, please send me an email. **Hello@FionaQuinnBooks.com**

Thank you to the real-world military and CIA who serve to protect us.

To all of the wonderful professionals whom I called on to get the details right, especially: B. Boswell, my search and rescue team, Chesterfield EMS, VCU LifeEvac, and the NYC FBI. Please note: this is a work of fiction, and while I always try my best to get all of the details correct, there are times when it serves the story to go slightly to the left or right of perfection. Please understand that any mistakes or discrepancies are my authorial decision making alone and sit squarely on my shoulders.

Thank you to my family.

I send my love to my husband, and my great appreciation. T, you are my happily ever after. You are my encouragement and my adventure. Thank you.

And of course, thank *YOU* for reading my stories. I'm smiling joyfully as I type this. I so appreciate you!

ABOUT THE AUTHOR

Fiona Quinn is a six-time USA Today bestselling author, a Kindle Scout winner, and an Amazon All-Star.

Quinn writes action-adventure in her Iniquus World of books, including Lynx, Strike Force, Uncommon Enemies, Kate Hamilton Mysteries, FBI Joint Task Force, Cerberus Tactical K9, and Delta Force Echo series.

She writes urban fantasy as Fiona Angelica Quinn for her Elemental Witches Series.

And, just for fun, she writes the Badge Bunny Booze Mystery Collection with her dear friend, Tina Glasneck.

Quinn is rooted in the Old Dominion, where she lives with her husband. There, she pops chocolates, devours books, and taps continuously on her laptop.

Visit www.FionaQuinnBooks.com

COPYRIGHT

Printed in the USA
CPSIA information can be obtained
at www.ICGtesting.com
LVHW050301200923
758631LV00046B/495